Praise for *The Quiet Roar of a Hummingbird*

"I fell in love with Hummingbird, a generous, willful teenage narrator on a futile mission to rescue her grandmother from the ravages of Alzheimer's. I read this debut novel avidly; I learned a lot about dementia; and I was greatly moved. Gentile writes exquisitely."
                            - Monica Wood, author of *We Were the Kennedys*

The Quiet Roar of a Hummingbird is as compassionate as it is courageous. If we are what we remember, imagine that self in the throes of forgetting all that was. This is the story told by Catherine Gentile, though what compels isn't so much its subject matter, but how she tells it with such grace and hope and conviction.
                            - Jack Driscoll, author of *The World a Few Minutes Ago*

"The Quiet Roar of the Hummingbird captures you on page one with a charmingly edgy protagonist: a young woman on the cusp of adulthood who is both gifted and needy. With intelligence and compassion, she challenges the rules in the memory care unit where her grandmother lives, its assumptions and strategies. Within the loving frame of relationship, the reader sees that world though two sets of eyes: one losing its hold on reality, the other approaching it with the freshness and intuitive skill of a loving grandchild. Hummingbird's transformation is not the only one, for the story will teach you, make you question, and open your heart to a view of Alzheimer's care that is grounded in compassionate listening; even when the only voice is silence."
                            - Mary E. Plouffe Ph.D.

"I read this story with great interest because I am a Neuropsychiatrist and have been caring for many years for patients with Alzheimer's disease. In addition, for almost 10 years I have watched my father's slow decline at the hands of this terrible disease.

Hummingbird reminds us that Alzheimer's disease is not simply a condition that affects individuals; it affects the entire family. Throughout this story, Hummingbird remains steadfast in her efforts to maintain her grandmother's dignity in the nursing home. She reminds us to always strive to understand the meaning that underlies the behaviors of the Alzheimer's patient. This is a story that will appeal to many readers and it is certainly a must read for anyone whose family has been visited by the unwanted guest Hummingbird refers to as "Arlene Alzheimer.""

- Dr. John Campbell, Maine Medical Center

"Catherine Gentile grabbed me on the dedication page of *The Quiet Roar of Hummingbird* and never let me go. Her thoughtfulness in showing the frustrations of those living with Alzheimer's and their inability to have others listen to their new way of communicating will touch anyone who has cared for loved ones during their end of life struggles. Drawing parallels between Hummingbird's being bullied and her grandmother's descent into Alzheimer's, the author connects two generations to create a bond that helps each find a voice that will be heard. It is a caring portrayal of love, loss, holding on and letting go."

- Lesley MacVane, Community Television Network

For: Sue
— a gift from Darrel Rosander —

THE QUIET ROAR OF A HUMMINGBIRD

A Novel

Catherine Gentile

In hopes this quiet roar inspires humane treatment of those suffering from bullying and the ravages of Alzheimer's disease.

Catherine Gentile

December 17, 2013

Published by IGCSA Publications, Yarmouth, Maine.

Library of Congress Control Number: 2013915581

ISBN 978-1-62646-413-1

Printed in the United States of America.

First Edition

Dedication

For Mom, who followed her heart
while dancing with
Alzheimer's

Chapter 1:

When I was at Granville High, where I'm supposed to be a senior, I got involved with a group of bad actors, fashionistas my age who called themselves "Blingers." At first, when they named me as their pet project, I went out of my way to get them to like me. I aced a series of initiation stunts that tested my loyalty and as my father, Jake, later observed, my intelligence. He didn't understand that I was intent on showing the Blingers how much they needed me. Truth was, I needed them and would have done backflips to get them to help me. Eventually, they reciprocated by doing important, lifesaving favors for me, which was exactly what I wanted. Problem was, if they did me a favor, I owed them one. That's where I went wrong. Get-into-trouble-with-the-police-wrong, which is why I had to stop going to Granville High. For a while at least. That's the story I tell myself as I roll onto my tiptoes and pull the overhead buzzer on a public bus in a Maine town I hardly know.

The bus lurches past Bellesport's morning traffic, flattening my feet to the riveted steel floor, forcing me to grab the seat handles to either side of the aisle. Thanks to my gymnastics training, my shoulders are thick and wide, and my hips, well, they don't exist. Despite leaving me with a little girl's physique, gymnastics taught me how to regain my balance after botching a routine and come out looking like a ballerina. As the bus driver pulls to the curb, I jam my arms through the straps of my backpack and wish those endless hours in the gym had taught me to stick a perfect landing whenever kids my age throw me off balance.

I bolster myself with hopes that the next eight weeks will be an adventure and pretend the taste in my mouth is sweet.

"Goodbye old life," I whisper, jumping from the last step of the bus to the hard ground. The chill wind skirting along the river whips a funnel of leaves around my ankles. I open my arms to embrace my new life. "I proclaim this, the second Monday in October, my official new birthday. Today, the Blingers of Granville High morph into a memory, a bad dream I'll soon forget."

The bus doors close with a groan as I silently review my birthday wishes: First, to prove to Jake and his new wife that though I got myself in a pile of really stupid trouble, I'm not about to become a repeat juvenile offender. And second, to find a real friend, someone who isn't put off by a short seventeen-year-old girl who is brighter and more flat chested than most.

Suddenly, I feel something is missing. My hand shoots to my shoulder, where the strap to my waterproof camera bag, the black Wal-Mart's special dubbed "freak wear" by the kids at school, usually rests. I panic. I've been so focused on getting off at the right stop that I left the digital camera my grandmother gave me on the bus.

"Wait! St-o-p!" I shout and wave and jump up and down, but the blue bus shoots into the lane farthest from me. Traffic spills from the nearby intersection, filling the space between the bus and me, drowning my voice and any possibility the driver will notice me trying to get his attention.

I imagine bolting into traffic, dodging cars and slapping hoods to alert texting drivers that I'm standing in the road. By the time the bus driver hears the commotion, startled commuters are rushing out of their cars toward a small heap. Eighty-five pounds of lifelessness. The high-pitched whine of the ambulance adds to the chaos … *Get a grip,* a tough voice from inside me scolds, *it's only a camera.*

I scramble backwards toward a bench and leap onto it as though it was my old balance beam, stand on my tip-toes and crane to see the bus. My heart clutches, not from exertion, but from the feeling that I've lost my camera for good. I yank a notebook out from my jacket pocket and scribble the bus's license plate: *Maine. 701,* then add *Route 31,* the number below the red NO PARKING BUS STOP ONLY sign.

From alongside the rhododendron garden arching protectively by the bench, a low rolling movement catches my eye. "Lucky for you your eyesight is so good," a deep voice says.

I'm not inclined to chat it up with a stranger of the male variety, but I'm so upset I'd talk to the bench if I thought it would help. "I forgot my camera on that bus..." I pause to catch my breath. "I can't believe this. I'm usually super-organized, unless something's on my mind. Then, my thinking floats driftier than the Straw Man's before he's awarded his degree from the Wizard of Oz." The minute I mention the wizard, I roll my eyes; when will I stop pretending that my life is one giddy fantasy, complete with a happy Auntie Em ending?

Slouched in a wheelchair, is a kid my age, his black Hell's Angels jacket zipped against the wind, his shaved head sporting a tattoo, unlit cigarette, and a pained expression. "Wizard of Oz? You're kidding, right? Unless the wizard lent you his magic wand, I'd call the bus company, pronto. If you move fast enough, you'll get your camera back. I guarantee it."

"And who are you—the biker boy who's going to save me, is that your deal?" I imitate his cynical tone, then feel like a cretin for mocking him and his clothing, a super cheap move.

It's unlike the "new" me to have an in-your-face conversation with a guy. I've stayed clear of the species since last spring when one of their kind landed me in a heap of trouble. I even refused to let my brother's best friend take me to my junior prom. No, thank you very much, I don't want to have anything to do with any male under the age of thirty-five, the age at which I might start to date again. Still, I'm happy this kid isn't intimidated by me and my recent vow not to dress, think, or act like others, especially the Blingers. If there's one thing I'll never do again, it's let myself morph into someone else's "ditto."

He slugs down a mouthful of his whale-sized Coolatta, then digs inside his jacket pocket. "Here, call this number." He waves the card upward but can't reach me, standing on the bench, nervously anchoring my unruly hair behind my ear with a rhinestone-studded hair comb. "This would be a lot easier if you came down to earth. A minute or two won't kill you."

"Sorry," I mumble as I step down and take his laminated card with the bus schedule for Route 31 and an easy-access phone number. "Do you always carry this? You must use the bus a lot."

"Not until I get my degree from the wizard in there," he nods back toward the three-story brick building with Highfield Health Center in tarnished letters above the entrance, "then I'm gonna ride what's left of my sorry bones all over Bellesport."

I glance at his limp sweatpants, folded and pinned at the base of two stumps that protrude from the edge of his wheelchair. Not wanting him to think I'm staring, I cut to his eyes. Deep blue, they shine with the defiant honesty that once stared back at me when I studied my face in the mirror. There's more to this guy than a leather jacket and a wheelchair, and I'm surprised to find I'm curious about him. "You look like you'll be boarding that bus before you know it." I consider how to say what I want to say next without offending him. "You've got problems, that's for sure. But my grandmother would grab yours over hers in a worm's wink."

"Worm's wink? Wizard of Oz? Where do you get that stuff?"

I point to the top floor. "From my grandmother and the magic she once wove into her language. It's my way of hanging on to what I know of her before...." My chest tightens as I look up at the Highfield building. "Do you think she can see me from up there?"

He wheels his chair around and squints into the sun. "Third floor, huh?" I nod. "I get it. Nothing's worse than Alzheimer's."

I let out a mournful little yip. I hate lumping my grandmother, Sukie, and that label into the same sentence. If circumstances hadn't forced me to explain to my probation officer that because my grandmother and others with Alzheimer's deserved good doctors, I was more determined than ever to become a geriatric physician, I may not have edged across that balance beam. I didn't have much of a relationship with my probation officer back then, so I censored the tidbits I offered about Sukie. Like I'm doing now.

I turn my notebook over and flip my cell phone open. Biker boy scrunches his eyes as he takes in my slim spiral notebook, attached with two-sided carpet tape to my billfold-like phone. "If you're going to tell me I can buy a Smart Phone, don't. That's old news. I don't have time to chase gadgets." Scary as he looks, I sound scarier, and he pulls back against his chair. I can hardly blame him for commenting on my rig; the few kids who hung around with me before I hooked up with the Blingers did, too. "My turn to apologize. I didn't mean to snap. It's just that I was supposed to visit my grandmother an hour ago and now I'm late. All because I'm stupid."

A thoughtful expression comes over the boy's face. "You're definitely out of sync, but I don't think you're stupid. Far from it."

Everything that has happened on my first full day in Bellesport has flustered me. This morning turned to a mad rush after my alarm didn't go off. Trying to do too many things at once, I spilled orange juice on my stepmother's expensive new skirt. Then, after leaving my camera on the bus, I meet a strange kid who hits me with the most sincere compliment I've ever received. "Thanks," I murmur, jabbing the bus company's number on my cell as seagulls screech overhead.

Leaves skitter across the sidewalk as I press star for an English-speaking human, then explain my situation to the woman who answers. "No, I don't have insurance. Yes, it's an expensive camera." I gulp a mouthful of crisp air. "It was the last gift my grandmother bought for me before she…" I pause while the woman expresses her condolences. My grandmother hasn't died, but the woman gets the idea. Loss is loss. "Thanks for understanding. Sure, you can reach me at this number."

The boy whirls his wheelchair aside. "Don't let me keep you. I'm all for visiting grandmothers; wish I had one of my own. By the way, I'm Elliot. Until the wizard grants me a pair of my own legs, I live one floor down from your grandmother."

I stick out my hand. "Abby Windsor, but call me Hummingbird, everyone does." I wait for a sarcastic remark about my name. But he doesn't make one.

Chapter 2:

Cargo-sized double doors at Highfield Health Center automatically open, urging me along. I enter the glassed-in foyer that protects patients and staff in the reception area from the elements. EMTs wheel a gurney topped with a shriveled woman wrapped papoose-like in a pink blanket. An elderly man whose eyeglasses are snuggled into his disheveled white hair sits on the sofa, leafing though a magazine. The hall display brightens the waiting area by the elevator. Artificial pumpkins, gourds, bunches of silky orange and yellow leaves aside a trio of grinning scarecrows have the same homey feel as the panorama in my old fourth-grade classroom and are just as childlike.

In the elevator, I press 3 for the Anne Fitzgerald Unit for the Memory Impaired, and seconds later, step out. No thoughtful display here. Only drab steel fire doors that open into the unit and outside them, a keypad. I key in the numbers I committed to memory: 953-148. A whistle sounds and the lock on the door releases with a piercing noise that makes seagulls' screeching sound like a lullaby. I follow the directions on the sign: *Help Keep Our Patients Safe - Be Sure to Close the Door* and wait until the door reconnects. The lock click-clicking into place sends a shiver through me.

I'm desperate to see my grandmother, but afraid of what I'll find. My parents were divorced when I was eight. Shortly after, my mother enrolled in graduate school and I spent every day from 2:30 on with Sukie, who lived on the saltwater farm across the street from my grade school. Once I entered Demming Middle School on the other side of Granville, I saw less and less of my grandmother. Gymnastics occupied my time along with photography club and tons of projects for my gifted and talented classes. When I finally finished my first-quarter exams, I made time to visit Sukie. Instead of asking for the latest news about my brothers and sister as she usually did, she kept asking what I loved best about school. *Was she trying to make me feel guilty for not having seen her in so long?* I dismissed this possibility—Sukie's not like that. Flustered and more than a little frightened, I answered the same question over and over with, "I'm like you—math and science are my favorites."

Soon Sukie, a devoted shopper, gave up her favorite pastime: going to the stores to buy surprises for me—the next book in the Harry Potter series, sunshine-bright cotton tops, or small notebooks like the one in which she copied a poem that started with *When I get old...* over and over on every page.

I venture down the hallway; on either side, large cookie-cutter bedrooms with lighting as gray as the meat locker in Benny's Maine Market. Twin hospital beds are disguised with oak headboards, matching nightstands, and tall shoebox shaped armoires. Nothing like my grandmother's room at home with her comfortable four-poster double bed and her and Pop-Pop's bureau dotted with family photos, Pop-Pop's keys, and the lustrous pearl earrings Sukie would fasten onto my ears so I could see how beautiful I'd look when I grew up.

I pad along the tweedy carpeting. Eyes lost in pale faces, those of wives, mothers, grandmothers, and the occasional grandfather follow me, a sturdy young novelty.

Dressed in practical wash-and-wear-style clothing that you see at Wal-Mart, the gray-haired residents look sadly alike: women in elastic-waist slacks and tops bleached of sparkle; the men favor rumpled khakis and t-shirts with the faded lettering, *L.L. Bean*, over their hearts. Occasionally, the collar of a button-down long-sleeved shirt peeks from the top of a cardigan or two.

Some folks shuffle along the outer edges of the hallway, their shaky hands fondling banisters that run waist-high along the walls. Others dodder within the safety of adult strollers—large versions of the one I waddled in before my legs grew strong enough to hold me. The third and sickest group sags into the contours of molded wheelchairs. Members of the smallest clique stand on their own, their proud faces distinguishing them as geriatric eagles among broken sparrows.

My grandmother stands by the nurses' station, wearing an oversized plaid bathrobe she wouldn't buy if it were the last robe on the planet. Had my stepmother, Solange, been here, she'd have scurried to Sukie's room to find her a change of clothing. Two weeks earlier, instead of accompanying Sukie to the admitting unit himself, Jake had talked Solange and Aunt Elizabeth into bringing Sukie to her "new home." The smiley Admissions Director greeted Sukie, then bustled her off to meet some ladies—a lie that still makes me furious. Meanwhile, Solange and Aunt Elizabeth hurried to the car before Sukie, thrilled at the possibility of making new friends, thought to ask where they'd disappeared.

Seeing Sukie being hustled off was as gut wrenching as watching Jake drive away late Christmas Eve ten years ago, never to return. Aunt Elizabeth, who'd been caring for Sukie after Pop-Pop died, said stepping inside the locked doors of the Anne Fitzgerald Unit was the same as being sentenced to life in prison. I'll never break the law again.

Thank goodness the Juvenile Community Corrections Officer and my school counselor agreed I wasn't your run-of-the-mill punk juvenile offender. Last April, after putting me through a battery of tests, the officer said I was basically a good kid who'd made a desperately wrong decision, and therefore wasn't a risk. My parents and I met with the officer.

Together we decided that I should bundle the Senior Service Learning Project required by Granville High and the restitution work I agreed to do at Highfield Health Center. To make up for the classes I'd miss, I enrolled in summer school, where I aced my English, Trigonometry, and American History courses. To make up for the class time I'm missing this semester, I agreed to complete extra assignments so I could graduate with my class. Of these, a project log with an accompanying report is the most important.

I started that log with a prediction of what this, my first visit since Sukie's admission, would be like, describing it from nerve-wracking to a flood of weepy accusations to a hugfest reunion. I imagined Sukie in her usual skirt, sweater, and pearl earrings with her white hair combed into the short "good looking" style she loved, one large wave across her broad, smooth-skinned forehead. In short, my grandmother would be as beautiful as ever.

If not for her dazed smile, I would think she's fascinated by all the activity behind the nurses' station. Between the man's bathrobe, those fuzzy slippers, and the crumpled handkerchief she dabs her nose with, she looks as though she'd shopped at the local thrift store. The possibility that she's no longer interested in her appearance makes me worry that she's changing for the worse. That she's becoming like the others on this unit. A weight like a lead apron wraps itself around my heart. *Alzheimer's steals you, one piece at a time, until - No!* My insides rumble. *Sukie isn't sick like the others.* I tell myself that she's stronger than they are. That this isn't the beginning of losing the one person in this world who really loves me.

"You must be Abigail," a voice from behind me says. I turn toward a woman with the nametag *Corki Goodale, Social Worker* pinned to her way too low-cut blouse. Her big henna hair corkscrews around her large square features, blue eyes, and bubbly cheerleader's enthusiasm.

Relieved to hear my name, I return her white-bright smile. "Hummingbird, call me Hummingbird—that's my grandmother's nickname for me."

"I can see why. Your grandmother's been asking for you," she burbles without taking a breath.

"I knew she would." I gobble this satisfying morsel, thrilled and proud that this part of Sukie's memory hasn't changed. "I should have come sooner."

"If it makes you feel any better, she's been asking for Solange, too. And she's here at least once a week."

Happy that Solange visits regularly, my shoulders sag with disappointment over yet another example of Sukie's declining memory. But Corki is nonchalant, as though a failing memory is standard news, and gently leads me toward my grandmother.

"Someone's here to see you," she says in her chirpy voice. "Do you know this young lady?"

"I can see, it's my granddaughter," she says, as though Corki's reminder is completely uncalled for. Sukie opens her arms for the hug she has always given me; the one I've been longing for.

"Your grandmother has been complaining of a runny nose. She has a history of allergies, so the nurse gave her a Claritin about fifteen minutes ago along with her afternoon dosage of Depakote. As soon as it kicks in she'll feel less congested," Corki says confidently, seating herself behind the half-wall of the nurses' station.

"My grandmother's allergies always act up in the fall. Claritin is what she took at home." I'm not sure what "Depakote" is and I forget to ask.

I slip my arm in Sukie's and we stroll down the hallway toward her room, number 311. "And how is my Hummingbird?"

"I'm glad to see you. How's my Sukie?"

She studies a cart packed with cups, syringes, hygienic alcohol swabs, and medication charts. "I never thought I'd land in a place like this. But here I am. It'll be good, you wait and see. It's like I tell you, you've got to make the best of today—"

"—because it's the only one you'll have." We giggle and as we do, my shoulders relax.

"So you remember," says Sukie. Her gray eyes soften.

"Well, sometimes I forget things…" *my camera bag for one*, " …but I remember most everything you've told me."

Sukie taps the frame of her glasses, as she always does when she's trying to shake her memory free. "Something awful must have happened to me, or I wouldn't be here," she says. She stops in front of room 311, doesn't recognize it as hers.

From down the hall, someone shrieks once, twice, again. Expecting one of the nurses to run from the station to see who is hurt, I watch. No one comes. Sukie's perplexed expression disappears. In its place, the all-knowing look that comforted me whenever I'd scraped my knees. She takes my hand in her firmest, most "in-charge" grasp and marches toward the noise.

A boy without legs, old people without expressions, an overly cheery social worker, shrieking from the corner room— Sukie and I have landed in a B-rated horror movie. The bizarre sound coming from down the hallway reminds me of the audio version of *The Cask of Amontillado* and it scares me. "What *is* that?" I ask, straining to filter the distress from my voice.

But Sukie is unperturbed, her face calm. Her eyes brighten with intention just as they had when she owned All

Occasion Custom Dress Designs. "Come with me, Hummingbird. I want you to meet someone."

Before I know it, Sukie slips away and disappears into the corner room. I hurry after her. By the time I enter, the screeching has stopped.

A crocheted bedspread lies in a heap on the floor between twin beds. A woman with the kind of hacked haircut I once gave my sister's Barbie doll stands on the spread, holding Sukie's hands. The woman's jaw hangs open as she gazes into Sukie's gentle face.

Sukie catches sight of me, her face brightening as though this were the first time she'd seen me today. "Oh, hello, Hummingbird, I'm so glad you're here. I want you to meet my friend."

The toothless woman faces me. I gasp. I've never seen anything quite like her. Her thread of a body supports a baggy jersey and slacks that leave her looking like a scarecrow.

"Hazel, this is my granddaughter. Isn't she beautiful?" Unaware of the hideousness of the picture she and Hazel cast in the grimy light, Sukie beams.

I understand. She wants me to see she has a friend and for a wild moment I long for someone with exactly the kind of acceptance they share. Someone who doesn't roll her eyes when I make a weird, know-it-all kind of comment. Someone who will look beyond my geekiness and like me for who I am. This is what Sukie craved during the months after Pop-Pop died but could never find the words to tell us.

The setting sun adds an unwelcome chill to Sukie, nestling into Alzheimer's "now," and Hazel, fading into Alzheimer's "later." They form a living time line like the ones in my history book, except this is real time in a surreal place. Blue-black shadows inch their way up the wall and close in.

The poorly lit corridors feel like tunnels inside a cage that keep getting smaller and smaller. Warm brown smells like those in the school cafeteria waft from the steel meal cart being rolled toward the dining room. Sukie and Hazel will probably have meatloaf and gravy, mashed potatoes and overcooked string beans, a wilted salad, tea (decaf, please) and apple crisp. The smells nauseate me but don't seem to bother my grandmother or Hazel.

Sukie chatters in delighted girlish tones, telling me that Hazel can't talk. "She makes sounds like a crow. Hear her? Do you? She has no one, no friends, no family. We have to take care of her, Hummingbird. Promise?" She is talking non-stop just as she did when she lived with Pop-Pop. "Sundowning" was what her geriatric psychiatrist called it. A late afternoon phenomenon. Fear of not knowing what will happen next. I know how my grandmother feels.

Beneath my fear, a mounting anger, one that appears each time I talk myself into believing Jake will do what he says. Last night—the first I spent with him since he and Mom had divorced—he promised to call the supervisor and remind her to have alarm mats placed on both sides of Sukie's bed. Today as I stood outside her room, I checked, a quick peek: not a mat in sight. What's the matter with him anyway? I reminded him about Great Aunt Patty's accident. Between her stroke, the unfamiliar surroundings of the rehab unit, too much medication, and an urge to use the toilet, she got out of her bed and fell. Broke both her wrists.

How could he forget? Just last night, after we talked about Aunt Patty, I overheard him on the phone with Aunt Elizabeth. "Mother's safety is at the top of my to-do list." He doesn't get that Sukie's safety begins with him taking the time to make sure she gets what she needs. Same goes for me. He didn't get how much I needed him when I was younger.

"You're going to the dining room to have dinner now," I tell Sukie, pointing to the sign for the dining room, hoping this prediction will ease her worries and slow her chatter. Holding hands with my grandmother, who holds hands with Hazel, we pad down the corridor to the nurses' station. No one is there. Not a staff person or patient in sight. No one had come to get Sukie or Hazel for dinner. What would have happened if I hadn't been here? I look at the clock; it's late, if I don't hurry, I'll miss my bus. But I can't leave them here alone. I feel as nervous as the night I pressed my nose against cold-numbing glass to watch Dad's taillights dim. Christmas Eve, the night he left my mother for good. The night of a very significant birthday. Also mine.

Sukie tugs my hand. "Hazel and I are hungry. When are we going to eat?"

Glancing at the clock, I kiss her cheek. "We're on our way to the dining room. You'll have your dinner in a few minutes."

"Will you take a picture of Hazel and me together?"

I blink in surprise. *Sukie knows?* "I'm afraid I don't have my camera with me."

We round the corner into the dining room and, thankfully, Sukie forgets. The eagles, who are feeding themselves, distract her. Others eat while aides open their milk cartons or sweeten their tea. The sparrows sit beneath huge white bibs, opening their wrinkled little mouths to spoonfuls of pureed food. Suddenly, Sukie drops my hand, leads Hazel to a seat, then seats herself. As soon as the aide places Sukie's tray in front of her, she starts eating. I wave from the doorway. She doesn't look up.

Chapter 3:

Jake's house sits on the highest point in Bellesport on Madison Hill Road, overshadowing normal-sized homes, Cape Cod houses snuggled like worn Monopoly pieces on small square lots below. Yesterday, when my mother dropped me off alongside the oversized brick home she'd been telling me about, I was blown away. Head tilted back, I gaped; the house was just like Jake: imposing and unaware of the effect it had on surrounding homes. As my mother's Saab roared off, Jake joined me in the dusky light. He didn't ask about my mother, or me, for that matter, although as we stood on the back patio, my laptop and duffel bags at our feet, he gave me a stingy hug.

He pointed to the house, as if this was what I came to see, and launched into a lecture about the craftsmanship of the masons "who fashioned this remarkable piece of early twentieth century architecture, soon to be featured in *Architectural Digest*." I oohed and aahed, as my mother had coached, listening politely while twisting a paper clip into knots. Jake went on about the exacting calibrations required for the arches, the carved precision of the lintels, the mathematical artistry of the tiled ballroom-sized porch gracing the front entry, and the copper-covered turret, now undergoing restoration. Amazing. So like him. I marveled at his ability to wax eloquent about the standards necessary to create his caliber of excellence. Never did he blush with embarrassment—the man could have been describing the child-rearing philosophy he'd practiced on my sister and brothers and me.

"Standards. Without them, buildings and people crumble," he said, looking down over his glasses at me, referring more to his theory of why I landed in trouble than to his house. I got the message but refused to say as much.

We hadn't seen one another since he and my mother and I appeared before the Juvenile Community Corrections Officer, and first thing out of the starting gate, he laid this on me. Unfortunately, Jake's standards are as two-faced as the masonry he so admires. And though his carotid artery didn't pulse furiously, as it did when we were with the officer, he was still plenty angry—my arrest made it clear that the mortar holding his stony standards in place was more watered down than he cared to admit.

As I walk along the side of the house, a gust of wind startles me. It reminds me of Jake, who, when we lived under the same roof like a real family—two parents, five kids, a cat, two dogs, and a hamster—snapped at my sister and brothers and me whenever we failed to meet his precious standards. I yank my hand from the cold brick and jump, but not as far as I'd jumped from Jake when he broke up my wonderful squabbling family.

Ordinarily, my mother kept her opinions regarding Jake to herself, but when she learned that he'd bought the old MacMullen place she made her displeasure known. Claiming she didn't understand why he'd lashed himself to a house in need of repair, she glanced forlornly at her extra-large sweatpants. "He left me when I started to need restoration," she said, "claimed he needed his freedom. But tell me, since when is being saddled with old real estate freeing?" The bitterness in her voice told me I'd failed big-time. The youngest of five kids, I was the baby who was supposed to rekindle the spark that had brought my parents together in the first place. Instead, I drove them to divorce.

"Fight back," I suggested to my mother. "Get out of this dumpy sub-division and buy something neat. Show him you don't want his leftovers."

My mother disagreed. "Your father always wanted to build a contemporary. What's come over him?"

Solange came over him, that's what. Fifteen years younger and beauty-pageant-queen pretty. I teasingly quoted my English teacher to my mother: "…subtexts are the charged undercurrents crackling beneath the story's surface." My mother insisted she was referring to the old house in Bellesport, but the electricity in her voice crackled like subtext through and through.

My thoughts vibrate with my own subtexts, those having to do with Sukie's alarm mats. Later this evening, I plan to ask Jake what had happened to insuring Sukie's safety. If it really was "no big deal, eminently doable" as he claimed, then why hadn't he called Highfield? If Sukie had been his client, he would have scrutinized the most obscure details. Unfortunately, she was family and when it came to family, details were a nuisance.

If my experience as the youngest kid who could count on not receiving a birthday card from him rang true, then Sukie, the oldest member of our family, was up to her pearl earrings in trouble. Undemanding bookends of the Windsor clan, Sukie and I were easy to ignore. Until we both got into trouble.

I cross the patio and let myself into the mudroom. His and her rain slickers, matching olive green Wellingtons, and a case of empty wine bottles line the back wall. No catchers' mitts, sweaty baseball caps, flat bicycle tires, muddy sneakers, coffee cans filled with worms for tomorrow's fishing trip; this is strictly an adult zone. I unlock the door to the kitchen and flick the light switch on. Instinctively, I feel my shoulder for my camera bag—it's the first thing I remove when I get home from school—and remember this morning's bus ride. The woman at the bus company hadn't called back. The image of Sukie and the friend she'd adopted flash in my brain, a photo from hell. It had been a terrible day. My mother was right—coming here was a mistake.

Just then Solange bursts though the kitchen door, taps it shut with her heel, and practically plows into me. She's pulled her hair, tinted a take-me-serious shade of walnut, back from her angular face into a sophisticated knot that makes her look harsh. I'm learning she is all but. She has a sense of humor about her professional appearance, and giggles when she describes it as "a tad scary." I understand. Kind of.

"Sorry, hon. Did I hurt you? Are you okay?" She pops a kiss on my forehead as I shake my head, no, then yes. "Remind me to tell Jake that Sarah Burns called. She and Bill can't make it tonight for drinks, which means the three of us will have the evening to ourselves."

I was about to have myself a good cry, but I'll have to save it for later. I blow my nose loudly into one of Sukie's embroidered handkerchiefs.

"I have a surprise for Jake." She plops a brown paper bag on the countertop, starts to open it, then stops. "I nearly forgot—how was your day? Have you been home long?" Solange studies my now filmy eyes. "You're not catching a cold are you? Everyone's sick—something nasty is going around."

"Allergies," I fib. "There are tons of allergens in the air at this time of year."

"Allergens? Where'd you learn about them, young lady?" I'm about to explain that a plump vocab is the legacy of being the baby in a family of adult over-achievers when she says, "I'm so happy that you're going ahead with your plan to apply for early acceptance in the pre-med program at Tufts. Jake says you're the smartest of his kids."

As if on cue, Jake enters with a wide swing of the door and an upbeat, "Hey, babe." For a hopeful second during which I remember him coming home from work and saying that to me, I assume he's talking to me. I glow with pleasure, lean toward him for his kiss, then pull back as Solange presses herself into his arms. Whew! That was close.

"Either you missed me something fierce or..." he eases her to arm's length. "No, something else has happened. Tell me."

If Solange had been a puppy, she'd wag her tail a thousand beats per minute. "After drowning the docs on Market Street in drug samples," she says, "they finally decided Healthbens, Inc. is *the* up-and-coming pharmaceutical company." Solange draws her smile into her dimpled cheeks. "So they handed me an enormous order. One that jumps me into the top sales position for my district." She disengages from his arms and spins around in front of him. Kinda like I used to.

I frown. Solange has hijacked the little girl routine I imagined returning to once Jake and I lived under the same roof again. Surprising as it is, *I* want to be in his arms, telling him all about *my* day, about how upsetting it was to see Sukie locked behind steel doors.

But something else niggles at me. A few years back, Jake won a wrongful death suit against one of the big pharmaceuticals. I'd watched him on television as he led the call for tighter federal regulation of drug companies. Years later, after collecting his share of what the *Granville Daily Reporter* referred to as "an obscene contingency fee," he married one of big pharma's top sellers. How does that fit into his standards? Or is consistency a part of excellence only when it's convenient?

He rolls his eyes in playful exasperation. "Great. My wife's abetting the civilized drug culture."

Solange stirs the air as she whisks past me. With a noisy crinkle, she plunges her hand into the bag on the counter and produces a plastic bag stuffed with gossamer shelled crustaceans. "I bought shrimp. Enough for the three of us." My hand goes to my stomach. Last summer after eating shrimp, I broke out in hives. The emergency room doctor suggested I stay away from shellfish until I'd been tested for shellfish allergies. But I'd been so busy completing the summer school credits I needed that I'd never gone to my doctor. If I break out in hives, I won't be able to start my Community Service Program tomorrow. And I'll have to go home to my doctor in Granville to get a written "all clear" order. This is mega-serious; I can't let anything interfere with my court-ordered program. If Solange's shrimp don't give me hives, this panic-attack-in-the-making will surely bring them on.

"Solange…" I start to explain, but she's digging in the back of the refrigerator.

"Let's not forget our champagne and the apple cider I bought for Hummingbird," she says, closing the refrigerator door with her bum.

Jake hands me his suit jacket, same as he used to do with my mother. "Hang it in the closet, would you?" When I return, Solange dumps her brown alpaca coat into my arms and murmurs, "Thanks, hon," kisses my cheek, and begins peeling the foil from the cork. *I'm on my way to becoming a doorman.*

Solange aims the champagne bottle toward the far wall and wiggles the cork back and forth. Absorbed by her task, she furrows her brow and purses her lips. "You showed me how to do this, but you didn't tell me how stubborn a cork could be."

Jake runs cold water over the shrimp, smiling like I've never seen him smile. I can't blame him for being thrilled, happy, and bust-his-Brooks-Brothers'-buttons-ridiculous. But

I wish he'd fooled around like that when he was home with Mom. He was always serious. And annoyed with Mom for depositing me in his lap.

The clock on the stove reads seven—Sukie is probably brushing her teeth, getting ready to go to bed without the alarms she needs to keep her safe. I hang Solange's coat in the closet. If I mention Sukie now, Solange will want to know what's going on. If she knew Sukie was in danger, she'd hop all over Jake until he did what he promised. She might even get mad at him. They'd have a fight. And that would ruin her celebration.

If I could get Jake alone and quietly mention the problem, he could make a quick call to Highfield and remind the night staff to put the alarm mats by Sukie's bedside. I peek around the corner into the kitchen. "Hello?" I call, signaling him to join me in the hallway. But he's running the water full blast, letting it splash all over the wall while he eyes Solange wrestling with the champagne cork.

"Here, let me help with that," he says, drying his hands on a dishtowel and moving to Solange's side.

"Afraid I might shatter the window, are we?" They share a look—his, knowing; hers, impish—that says that's exactly what she'd done. He rocks the cork back and forth, slowly, and ever so gingerly. I can't wait any longer.

"Hold on a sec. I need to tell you something."

Jake raises his left eyebrow, a disapproving gesture of maximum proportions. "Is this related to what we're celebrating *right this minute?*"

"I have to talk to you. It's important." I sound frightfully serious, as serious as the day he'd brought me to meet with the Juvenile Community Corrections Officer. That alone should draw his attention from Solange, who is now in the dining room, getting champagne glasses from the cabinet.

Mom warned me my father wouldn't take kindly to my interfering with his new life. That he isn't beyond sending me back. If that happens, my Service Learning Project at Highfield will be history. There'd be no substitutions; the program is so competitive that by now every Service Learning site in Granville has been filled. Taken. I'd have nowhere to go to earn the last credits I need to graduate from high school and to fulfill the agreement I made with the Juvenile Community Corrections Officer.

Because this was my first offense, and because I admitted to breaking and entering along with theft, the Juvenile Corrections Officer agreed to divert my case and treat me as a "Youthful Offender." It was the break I needed. *If* I fulfill the terms of what he calls my IAP—Informal Adjustment Program—"that means cross every last 't' and you know what to do with the dots," is the way the Corrections Officer put it—my offenses would be treated as though they'd never happened. Gone. Therein was the rub.

When I asked Jake if I could live with him, I explained I planned to target two very important birds—the Community Service hours I owed the court and the Service Learning Project required for graduation—with one huge stone. A boulder is more like it. My having presented him with "carefully considered goals" and an "action plan"—double-spaced, Times New Roman—showing the steps I intended to take to achieve those goals was better than his being crowned King. "An exceptional plan, exactly the quality I expect from someone of your ability," he said.

Problem is, receiving credit for my Community Service hours is tied to completing my Service Learning hours: if I don't fulfill one, I'll earn an incomplete for the other, and my plan to go to Tufts will dissolve. So, I need to live here in peace. That means I can't upset Jake.

To my surprise, he senses that something is wrong. He wraps his arms around me and whispers, "Listen, Solange worked long hours so she could land this contract. It's huge for her. Go along with her celebration for tonight, okay? We'll have lots of time to catch up later, I promise." As he squeezes me and pecks my cheek, I suspect he's being his manipulative old self until he says, "I'm glad you're here, Birdie."

Too shocked to say anything else, I murmur, "Me, too."

Birdie. Jake calling me his pet name eases the panic rising inside me. It had been two weeks since Sukie was admitted to Highfield and during that time she'd not had one accident. So why worry? The little voice inside me sounds an alarm. *Terrible, horrific idea*, it screams. But I'm not one to listen.

"Do you mind if I fry a couple of eggs for myself? I love shrimp, but it doesn't love me. I'm allergic to shellfish," I fib.

Jake gazes down his long nose, assessing the truthfulness of my story. "I've been trained to detect lies," he once told me when he'd caught me doing just that. Satisfied that I'm not engaged in a plot to sabotage Solange's dinner, he takes a second frying pan from the overhead rack and motions for me to use the first pan, the one with sizzling butter.

"Oh, if I'd known that, I'd have bought steaks," Solange says as she takes two eggs from the refrigerator door and hands them to me.

"It's okay," I say. Being alone with newlyweds is exhausting. All I want to do is go upstairs to "my" room. With one thwack, I crack one of the eggs in half and watch the albumin-surrounded yolk slither down the side of the frying pan.

"How about some toast to go with your eggs?" Solange asks.

The atmosphere in the kitchen takes a sober turn. Jake's gaiety gone, the circles under his eyes seem darker, more pronounced. Solange's hair is undone in limp walnut tangles that she tucks behind her ears. What little appetite I had has disappeared. The last thing I want is a mouthful of dry toast.

"Thanks, that'd be great." *That might be what the perfect guest would say, but what about the perfect daughter?*

Upstairs, alone after dinner in the guest suite, I sit at the library table in the bedroom and record my impressions of the day's events. I draw a huge zero. I think back to my grandmother in that horrid old bathrobe, not caring a hoot about anything except her new friend. If Sukie had been here sitting beside me as she used to do while I worked on my homework, she would ask, "What has gone right today?"

The sheer curtains dotted with flocked hummingbirds—one of Solange's sweet but silly welcoming touches—are reminders that someone besides Sukie is trying to comfort me. That's what Sukie would have pointed out. If she could befriend Hazel, shouldn't I do the same with Solange, the woman who makes my father's eyes shine? My heart tells me one thing, my head another.

I open my journal on my laptop and type: What went right today? First, I learned that the staff at Highfield is too busy with ailing patients to spend time with someone as independent as Sukie. That's important to know and understand. Second, even though both towns are in Maine, I don't know my way around Bellesport as well as I know Granville, where I can get around blindfolded. I'm new here, and it will take time before I feel comfortable. The same applies to my father.

I hope coming here doesn't turn out to be another of my famously bad decisions.

I glance at the computer screen and in a burst of typing confess: MY FATHER AND I ARE STRANGERS. I wonder if he knows.

Chapter 4:

The telephone in my dream sounds its brittle tone as I swim in my polka-dotted wet suit through tinkling shards of glass. I reach shore and slap my fins down a winding path toward Sukie, splayed facedown on the floor. I fall before I can reach her. The phone rings again. I wake with a start.

The door to the master bedroom creaks open. Jake barefoots down the hall to his study. Half asleep, I check to make sure there's no shattered glass on the floor before slipping into my flip-flops. My nightmares usually mean someone is in trouble. Ever since I can remember, they warned me whenever something was wrong. One time late at night after my parents were asleep, I woke to a nagging sense that drew me to the living room, where Marion's date had pinned her to the floor and was practicing an angry Braille on her body. I'm upset now, same as I was then. Grabbing my bathrobe from the hook behind the door, I scuff down the hall toward Jake's voice.

"Who, who did you say you are?" Jake is sitting at his oversized desk, perched on the edge of his chair, head in his hand, tufts of tousled gray hair protruding between his fingers. Muted yellow rays from a solitary desk lamp cut the room's darkness.

I clear my throat so I don't startle him. "Dad? What's going on?" This is the first time I've called him Dad since I got here.

He absentmindedly scoots over on his chair and waves for me to sit beside him. Maybe he's mistaken me for Solange, but I don't care. After dreaming about Sukie, I could use some comforting. Haunch to haunch, I drape my arm around my father's muscled back—I haven't squished in beside him in years—and press my ear to the phone. He puts it on speaker and adjusts the volume so I can hear a woman's soft Indian accent. *This is the father I want back.*

"Mr. Windsor? This is Jhumpa, the nurse on the Anne Fitzgerald Unit. Sorry to call you so early in the morning, but your mother—"

"What's happened to my mother?" The fear in his gruff voice upsets me more than my dream.

"She's on her way back from the Emergency Room at Bellesport Med. She's been there for the past few hours—"

"Emergency Room?" He stands abruptly, dislodging me but not for long. I scamper onto his chair and, steadying myself with my hand on his shoulder, draw him close. Once again, he makes room for me as he asks, "Is my mother all right?"

"She needed six stitches above her right eyebrow—"

"Wait a minute, let's back up. Why stitches? What happened?"

"Near as I can tell, she tried to get out of bed, lost her balance and fell." She's speaking very quickly now. My father leans toward the phone, straining to catch the words buried within her thick accent. "On the way down, she hit her head on the corner of her night table. I found her face first on the floor with a gash over her right eye. She needed stitches, so I called an ambulance."

"Why didn't you call me earlier? I would have met her at the hospital."

"I'm sorry, Mr. Windsor, it's been so crazy here tonight—two other patients had to go to the hospital, too. This is the first I could get to the phone."

"Did my mother have any other injuries?" The pronounced bob of his Adam's apple is his way of keeping himself from yelling.

I imagine Sukie's paper-thin bones hitting the hard linoleum floor. My father and I exchange frightened looks.

"Has she broken anything? She has osteoporosis, you know."

"Yes, I read that in her chart. I checked her while we were waiting for the ambulance. Nothing is broken. They checked her at the hospital, too, and gave her a CT scan. No fractures, no concussion."

"Does she have any bruises?"

"Not that I could see. But she'll probably turn black and blue. And the area around her right eyebrow, where they stitched her, will swell."

"How much?"

"You don't have to worry, Mr. Windsor, I've given her an ice pack. I'm afraid this happens all the time with the new patients. They think they're at home, get up to use the bathroom, become disoriented and fall."

Fuming, I jump to the floor. I should have interrupted Solange's celebration. It would have taken Jake two minutes to call Sukie's unit and remind them about the bed alarms. And if he refused, *I* should have called, should have put Sukie first. I missed my cue.

I remember a ballet recital during which I'd been so busy searching the audience in hopes of finding Jake that I'd missed my cue. That confused the other dancers, who slammed into one another and fell. If only I hadn't been so preoccupied with how Jake would react, Sukie would have been safe. *I'm such a screw-up. No wonder Jake left me.*

Looking gloomy, he settles back into his chair and covers the receiver with his hand. "Can you believe this?" His expression changes from that of an angry bulldog to a mutt being hauled to the pound.

I run my fingers over my right eyebrow as if doing so will magically heal Sukie's. "I just wish Sukie hadn't fallen—"

"Oh my gosh, your mother fell?" Hair flattened with sleep, knuckles jammed against her teeth, Solange stands in the doorway, one bare foot warming the other.

Jake jumps from his chair so fast it rolls toward me and sends me shuffling out from between him and Solange.

"We thought she'd be safe at Highfield. I'm not impressed," he says, pressing his fingertips together and holding them to his lips. I've seen him perform this routine with my mother. Painful to watch, I close my eyes. He repeats his conversation with the nurse, his modulated voice a combination of annoyance and distress, and, as I open my eyes, he takes hold of Solange's hand without finishing his sentence. Without admitting that he failed his mother.

"Aren't you going to go there to make sure she's okay?" is how the incredulous Solange, now nose to nose with him, responds, her silky pajamas colliding with his Fruit-of-the-Loom cottons.

He opens his eyes wide; he never intended to rush over.

His delay in answering adds to her shock. Disappointment shades her gold-flecked eyes. She withdraws her hand from his. "Let's get dressed and drive over." Now she's carefully modulating her voice.

Embarrassed, I clear my throat. "I can be ready in five minutes."

They stare.

"My orientation classes start at 8:00. If we go right away, I can see Sukie and still get to class in time." I work my way past them into the hallway away from the place where, for the first time in years, Jake drew me into his life and, for a few heavenly moments, returned to being my father. His and

Solange's eyes pop with surprise—they'd forgotten about me. The curtain comes down on this act with a heart-withering clatter. This part of my nightmare never changes.

Chapter 5:

I hurry by patients wandering in the hall on the Anne Fitzgerald Unit and past the nurses' station, where staff, bowed over their paperwork, are so focused on reading the doctors' orders they don't think to offer a reassuring word about Sukie. Jake and Solange were arguing when I taped a note on the coffeemaker, saying I would ride my bike to Highfield. Truth is, I wanted to get here as quickly as possible—Sukie needs me.

I find her outside her room, in her nightgown and a sweater dribbled with egg yolk. Hazel holds Sukie's hand and stares at her blackened eyes. Cawing softly, she strokes Sukie's double chin as though she were calming a frightened puppy.

Sukie sees me, raises her hand in a limp wave and, recalling her injury, pats the bandage on her forehead. Her hand trembles. "Thank goodness you're finally home. I was afraid you weren't coming. Look at me. What happened? Why does my head feel so bad?" Gulping increasingly frantic breaths, she studies her outstretched arm as if the answer is there.

I don't mean to gasp, but between the inky swells around Sukie's eyes and that vicious lump, I can't help myself.

Quick to read my reaction, Sukie wells with emotion. "My face... it's ruined...it'll never come back..." Then she remembers. "I fell, I fell," she chants as though she'd lost a precious gift, one she'd never thought to question. Despite her confusion, she senses the sad truth—accidents aren't supposed to happen. Not here. Not in the place that's supposed to keep her safe.

I gently finger her forehead. Sukie winces. "That must have been awful. Let's ask the nurse to give you something for the pain. Don't worry, we'll make it better." Validate. Empathize. Speak with your heart. That's what the geriatric social worker had taught Aunt Elizabeth to do to keep Sukie from working herself into a screaming pitch. Which is what I want to avoid.

A petite woman with dusty blond hair and emerald eyes comes out from Sukie's room. "That bump looks fearful, but don't let it scare you. I've been watching Cynthia to make sure she's all right. You're her granddaughter—the one in the birthday party picture by her bed, right?"

I nod. The woman's tone turns confidential and I strain to catch her soft bursts. "I can't believe the nurses let this happen. I've been telling them to alarm the newbies. But I didn't finish my college degree, so my suggestions don't count."

I'm so overcome, I forget to breathe. "You and I must be the only people who think bed alarms are important. Can I ask you something?"

The woman glances right and left as if worried we'll be overheard, then murmurs, "Sure."

"At home we gave my grandmother a medication that calmed her when she was getting upset. Do you think she should have some now? She's awfully shaken up about her forehead." I glance at Sukie, absorbing every word, most likely hoping I'll help her make sense out of all this.

The woman raises her armload of rumpled sheets. "Give me a minute to dump these and I'll get the nurse." Turning to face Sukie, the woman includes her in the conversation, "And I'll get more ice for that bump. You're going to feel better soon, Cynthia, I promise."

"Promises, write them on the wind," my grandmother says with a dismissive flick of her wrist.

The woman glances at me, then at Sukie. "I know exactly how you feel," she says, then hustles toward the door marked No Admittance.

At last! A staff member who calls Sukie by name, who takes the time to speak directly with *her*. Someone who treats her like a real person, not a PWA, person with Alzheimer's. Someone who eases aside my jumbled guilt and disappointment.

Sukie taps my arm. "How can I go to the mall looking like this? My friends will laugh."

I point at Hazel. "*She* isn't laughing."

Sukie loops her arm through Hazel's and coaxes her forward. "This is my friend, Hazel. And this is—" Her face goes blank.

I gasp a belly-breath of air. Her forgetting my name makes my heart hurt. But I don't let on. "Hummingbird, my name is Hummingbird. When I was a baby you held me in your hands, like this," I cup my hands together, "as if I were a tiny bird. So you named me Hummingbird." I repeat my name three times, twice to make sure Hazel and Sukie catch it, and again, to connect it with a gesture, just like my sister Marion does with her patients who have dementia.

"Silly me," my grandmother says, cupping her hands. "This is my granddaughter, Hummingbird."

A middle-aged nurse joins us. "Cynthia, how do you feel?" she asks. Without waiting for Sukie to answer, she turns to me, "I've been trying to get Cynthia to rest, but she insists she has too much work to do."

"My grandmother worked from the minute she got up until she said her prayers at night. She ran her own business, designing women's clothing, and helped my grandfather with the farm, too." From the corner of my eye, I catch Solange rushing toward us, trench coat cinched around her waist.

Her high heel snags a frayed loop in the carpeting and she stops for a nano-second, yanks herself free and charges forward. Her sleek hairdo has a weary second-day-without-a-good-washing look that matches the dark circles under her eyes. "Robin, I see you've met my beautiful stepdaughter." I figure the edge in her voice is from the fight she just had with Jake. Still, she wraps her arm around me and draws me close. "Hummingbird, this is Robin, the nursing supervisor from the admitting unit."

"Not any more—the supervisor who's usually on this unit started her maternity leave early. This is my first day filling in for her, and so far too much has gone wrong."

A part of me feels sorry for her; being new is tough enough without having to face a worried family.

I glance down the hallway, "Where's my father?"

Solange lets out an exasperated sigh. "He had to appear in court..." She turns to Robin, "His schedule is insane, so I'm usually the one who checks on his mother." If Robin picks up on the anger shadowing Solange's words, she's kind enough to not let on.

I check Sukie to see how much she understands and am relieved to see her shuffling toward her room. I don't blame her for losing interest. Jake's sticking Solange with the tough duty is old news. Two weeks ago, when he was supposed to have admitted Sukie here, he flipped the same routine—arranged for Solange and Aunt Elizabeth to hand Sukie off to Robin at the door.

Robin steps into the family void. Her worried blue eyes take on a new alertness as she gives Solange the once-over, sizing up her emotionally fried appearance. Then she says, "By the time I got in this morning, your mother-in-law had already returned from the ER. I checked her over. She was a little disoriented, which is to be expected, but she claimed she had no pain."

"I'm afraid she just told me her forehead hurt. Is there something you can give her?" I ask. Robin nods sympathetically. "And something to help her calm down? She won't tell you—she has this thing about not complaining to anyone outside the family—but she said she remembered falling. Actually, my grandmother . . ." I pause, hoping my resentment doesn't slip out, " . . . seemed very anxious when I first got here. When she was like that at home, the littlest thing would cause her to "escalate" is how her doctor described it."

"Between what she was given at the ER and our routine morning med pass, she's had more medication than usual." Robin looks at her watch. "The next med pass isn't until one o'clock, but I'll check her chart to see when it's safe to give her another PRN."

If it weren't for my sister, Marion, a geriatric doctor, I wouldn't have understood Robin's hospital-speak; terms like "med pass"—the scheduled distribution of medications—and "PRNs"—initials for the Latin, *pro re nata,* medications that are given as the patient needs them. I sigh. If I hadn't gotten myself into trouble, I'd be in Wisconsin doing my Service Learning Project under Marion's expert supervision. Maybe it's just as well; I'm the one who knows Sukie best.

Solange and I follow Robin into Sukie's room, where Sukie is sitting in a soft vinyl-covered chair. Robin sets her clipboard on the nightstand and checks Sukie's eyes. She turns to Solange. "Your mother-in-law's aide, Iris, was holding an ice pack on Sukie's forehead but the minute she left, your mother-in-law set it aside. That's the way they are–they all forget."

My shoulders droop; for a while I thought Robin really cared about Sukie, but now she's talking as though Sukie isn't here. Sukie may be forgetful about everyday events but emotionally charged experiences stay with her—falling out of bed is one. Not being kept safe is another.

To her credit, Robin notices I'm upset. "I've assigned staff to check your grandmother every two hours. Those bruises will fade in a couple of days. If anything changes, I'll be sure to call you, I promise." She picks up her clipboard. "See you later, Cynthia."

"There's something else," I say. Surprised by my boldness, Robin steps back.

"Wouldn't it help my grandmother if we placed alarm mats on both sides of her bed? That way, if she gets up in the middle of the night, the alarms will alert the nurse." Solange edges closer—steady, silent, encouraging. *There's a lot about this woman I could love.*

"I'm afraid alarms of any sort are considered mechanical restraints. Our policies don't allow them and our auditors are always looking for violations—"

"My father will sign a consent saying he requested them."

Such a confident request from such a small voice flusters Robin. Her clipboard clatters to the floor. I pick it up for her.

Solange steps forward. "Robin, we'd be grateful if you would help us with this. We all want to keep Mom safe. This will be a step in the right direction." She adopts a mellow appeasing voice, the "deal closer" tone I imagine her using whenever she's talking Jake into something he'd rather not do. "And if there's a form that gives consent for two alarm mats, one for either side of the bed, that would be perfect." She smiles at Sukie. "It's just that we don't want Mom to go through this again—"

"—Of course not," Robin cuts her short. "But that won't guarantee that an ambulatory patient like your mother-in-law won't get out of bed before we can get to her. We have one nurse and one aide on duty during the 11 to 7 shift, and there are forty other patients here. I hope you understand."

I worry that she thinks we're being demanding. I'm tempted to repeat my earlier argument, but don't want to sound like a smart-mouth kid. So I shut up.

"I have to look in on a couple of patients before I can get your forms. Do you mind waiting? I could fax them if you like."

"We'll wait," Solange and I say in unison. Robin hurries out of the room as Iris bustles toward us.

"Hi, Cynthia. Now that my hands are free, I want to introduce myself to your family. Is that okay with you, Cynthia?" She smiles and looks directly into Sukie's eyes as she speaks. I like that. More importantly, Sukie's smiling. She likes it, too.

Seconds later, her smile melts. She places her hand on the young woman's arm. "Do I know you? I should know your name but I have trouble with my memory."

"Oh, no, Cynthia, it's my fault, I lost my nametag." She scrunches her face into a comical forlorn look, then brightens. "I'll get a new nametag, so you can read my name: Iris."

"Oh yes, I need as much help as I can get." Sukie's discolored face has taken on a somber appearance, as it usually does whenever she mentions her increasing dependence.

Wizard that she is, Iris doesn't feed into Sukie's sadness. Instead, she distracts her with a change in topic. "Weren't you here yesterday?" Iris asks me.

I nod.

She looks at my grandmother who is listening carefully. "Sorry about Cynthia's clothing. I was hoping the family wouldn't see her that way. I was on another unit or I would have changed her into something real pretty. Sandis, the aide who was just assigned to Cynthia, was having a really rough day."

"I wondered about that bathrobe." I glance at Sukie's rumpled nightgown. "My grandmother likes to get dressed before she eats breakfast. Would you let the staff know that Sukie never hangs around in a bathrobe or her nightgown?"

"I'll try."

Before I can ask her what she means, Iris sees Robin coming toward us and starts walking away. "Good to meet you. See you later, Cindy."

"Sorry to keep you waiting." Robin hands Solange a consent form requesting alarm mats on both sides of *fill-in-the-blank's* bed.

I bristle; *my grandmother's name isn't blank, it's Sukie.* I'm tempted to tell Robin, but something, I'm not sure what, makes me stop. I hope I won't be sorry.

Chapter 6:

Traffic drones past Highfield's front doors as I describe the details of Sukie's accident to Elliot. "The basic thing is this: Even though Sukie can't always tell you what happened, she remembers the feelings that go with events. So, after her new aide messed up Sukie's morning routine, Sukie felt upset, but wasn't sure why. That made her feel uncared-for and unsafe. She had a restless night. Thinking she was home, she got out of bed and fell. That, ladies and gentlemen of the jury, is my closing argument. A skill I learned by listening to my father, Jake, rehearse his closings." I sweep an imaginary hat from my head and curtsey in front of Elliot's wheelchair.

He leans forward. He's shed his oversized Hell's Angels jacket in favor of a blue fleece that matches his eyes. He's cuter than the first time I met him. "Your father's an attorney?"

He's intensely interested in my father, and I regret having mentioned him. "Yes, but forget it."

His face brightens; he's more curious than ever. I want no part of this conversation; I'm afraid I'll slip and say something about my problem with the court, which I'm not ready to discuss. His coffee steams as he opens the top and sips. "Really? Why?"

"Come on, I asked you to forget it."

"It's just a question. You don't have to get pissy."

"Sorry, I've been awake since four. Plus it seems like I'm always apologizing to you. And it's not because you lost your legs."

"Ouch. You're brutal today. It'd be good for your grandmother and for me if she never got hurt again."

"It's not just my grandmother that bothers me. It's Jake, too. Seems whenever I need him, he disappears into his black hole of a schedule."

I'm looking for a drop of sympathy here, more than I got from my mother, who, during this morning's phone call, said, "Sukie's behavior is sadly new. Your father's is just sad."

Elliot squints, his eyes fixed in thought. "I've been here two months. Take it from me, your grandmother's fall was just the tip of a slippery iceberg. Robin has already admitted that she's short-staffed, so you can bet *she's* not checking on your grandmother's new aide or your grandma. If my grandma were a patient here, I'd watch that aide."

"And how would you suggest I do that?"

He rests his ski jump nose on his knuckles. "Easy. You'll be doing volunteer work on that unit, right?"

I nod. "And taking classes, so I can't be there every second." I am careful not to mention my court-ordered group therapy sessions for victims of sexual assault. In those sessions, I learned that I'm in no way obligated to him or any other guy. That there's no point in becoming a doormat for a guy—what the one black girl in my group calls "a holla back girl"—which isn't quite what I'd been. Still, I'm proud of myself for not telling Elliot what he doesn't need to know.

"No problem. With your charming personality," he winces, "the staff will fall for you in no time. Chat them up. Get them to open up. Believe me, they'll be so happy to have someone they can talk to, they'll tell you all kinds of stuff."

"Is that what you do?"

He beams. "What else do I have to do? After tutorial sessions, physical therapy, readjustment therapy and occupational therapy, the only thing left is homework and gossip. Homework's easy. Getting people to trust me so they'll gossip their brains out is a real art, one I've perfected."

"You can be a real jerk, you know that?"

He laughs. "I love it when you talk dirty."

"Okay, I agree with some of what you're saying. I was planning to spend as much time as I can on my grandmother's unit. Problem is, my schedule includes going to lectures and shadowing other staff."

"That's where I come in." His imitation of a villain, twisting the ends of his moustache makes me giggle.

What he says made sense: persons with Alzheimer's often have difficulty holding a conversation. So the staff would crave a normal conversation, a smart piece of gossip, a good chuckle. Anything to overcome the monotony of trying to talk with folks whose personalities are hidden treasures.

But the part about getting people to trust him reminds me of Bruce Talibert, the last guy I dated, and startles me sober.

I think back to last December when I was still at Granville High. If Maggie Forester hadn't been "having a little fun," hiding my clothes while I was in the shower, I would have been the first one out of the locker room. That was my plan. I'd been studying hard and was looking forward to taking my exam in AP invertebrate biology, an exam I expected to ace. I'd planned on getting to the lab a few minutes early so I could settle in, do some deep breathing, and get my head around the material. Early on, I'd found my focus was better during gymnastic competitions when I stepped away from the others and spent a couple of minutes alone. The same applied to school. I'd mistakenly shared my strategy with Maggie, and she obliged me by making sure everyone else left the locker room before me. Not quite what I'd had in mind.

I hated the empty sounds of that dreary old part of the building. The spooky way the dripping from the showers echoed when no one was around. Or the way the overhead water pipes rumbled when someone in another part of the building called for hot water. I pulled on my sweater and tights, zipped my short denim skirt, fixed my rhinestone comb into my hair, and angrily winged my backpack onto my back. If my future wasn't dependent on a high school diploma, I would have become an epic truant, anything to avoid Maggie. But I was stuck. My friends in my AP classes wanted me to see Mrs. Falon, the guidance counselor, to complain that between Maggie and her gofer, Bruce, I never knew when I was going to get slammed. But I figured I was smart enough to handle the situation alone. I swore them to secrecy. Told them I'd never been able to rely on adults, why should I start now?

As I turned the corner on my way to the staircase, Bruce stepped out of nowhere, grabbed my pack and spun me around and around. "So you're dumping me?" he growled, letting go. I slid across the freshly waxed linoleum floor and crashed, pack-first into the lockers. Air whooshed from my lungs.

Ordinarily, a crash landing of that magnitude would alert our burly gym teacher that "the guys were at it again." But that morning, "Brain Drained Dotowitz," as the kids called him, was no where around. And Bruce knew it.

He leered while I yanked my skirt down from my hips and pulled myself to standing. The locker-lined corridor led to the gym that Mr. Dotowicowski kept locked. The stairwell leading to the labs was at the other end of the hall and to the left of that, the girls' bathroom. Bruce spread his long arms and legs in a four-point star, splaying his feet against the sides of the stairwell. I was trapped. I could try to dodge his blockade or head into the girls' room and lock the door behind me. If I screamed, surely someone would hear me.

Behind the heavy wooden door, I fumbled with the lock, only to find it had been jimmied open. *Shit.* I checked the windows in hopes of squeezing out of them, but they were too small. I listened for Bruce's footsteps; there weren't any. The hallway was eerily quiet. This was vintage Bruce; games were his thing. He wasn't about to let me go so easily. I planned to hide in the middle stall, figuring if he came into one stall, I could escape from the other one. I was banking on being smaller and more agile than big-boned wrestler Bruce.

Other than my banging heart and the rumbling pipes, the bathroom and the hall were terrifyingly quiet. It wasn't like Bruce to give up, especially when he had me cornered. Still, there was no sound coming from the hallway. I wondered why the next gym class wasn't thundering down the stairs, until I remembered it was Thursday, the day Mr. Dotowicowski left early.

I was alone.

I stuffed my shoes into my pack and left it by the door, where I could grab it on the way out. I ran past the row of sinks to the middle stall. Even though I was sweating, the cold from the tile floor numbed my feet and shot shivers up my spine. After locking the stall door, I climbed on the toilet seat and waited.

I was breathing hard, thinking about what I could do to protect myself if Bruce came into the girls' room. I could push his nose into his skull with the palm of my hand like my brother, Timmy, had showed me. OMG, I didn't think I could do that, despite Timmy's guarantee that it would "work." Kick Bruce in his privates? Other than the tights I was wearing, my feet were bare. And small. I swallowed gulp after gulp of air, hoping I wouldn't yif.

The bell that announced the change of classes rang loud and shrill. Once it stopped, the bathroom was more silent than ever. I listened for Bruce. Maybe he'd had his share of bullying for the day. Like a drug addict who'd had his fix, maybe slamming me into the lockers had satisfied him. I wasn't sure. When I broke up with him a few days before, he'd freaked out. Without realizing it, I'd become his property. "It's all or nothing," he hissed, a super hard glint in his eye. I didn't dare ask what he meant by "nothing," but it scared the bejesus out of me.

My head ached from being slammed into the lockers, not to mention my shoulders. I listened again to the terrible stillness and decided to take advantage of the lull to get comfortable. I stepped to one side of the slippery toilet seat, carefully positioning my feet to balance the best I could. I looked up. Peering down over the top of the next stall was Bruce.

"Oh," I gasped, stepping backward and slipping off the toilet seat, scraping my backside on the toilet paper dispenser as I slid down the wall. Pain like I've never felt before charged up my spine. I ripped the lock open and darted for the door. But Bruce caught my arm, hurled me against the wall, and moved in close. I could smell alcohol on his breath.

"I got you," he said. "Now you're gonna beg." My nose was twelve inches from the middle of his T-shirt, four inches above his belly button. My insides quivered. I wanted to cry but wouldn't let myself; as long as his pants were zipped, I was safe. Kinda. I couldn't help imagining what he would force me to do while he pinned me against the cold tile wall. I tried to twist my wrists from his grip but couldn't. "You heard me: Beg."

"Don't do this, Bruce." His smile grew more sadistic. He loved being in charge. "Please, Bruce. Don't."

"That's what I like, Beggin' Birdie," he laughed.

That's when I did it. Channeled my brother Timmy and jerked my knee solid into his groin.

***

Elliot taps my hand, "So how about it, are you okay with my helping you?"

I almost scream, 'Get away!' until I remember this guy isn't Bruce. And that's the point—Elliot doesn't creep me out. He pays attention, never checks his email or takes "an important call" while I'm talking; he listens and gives me thoughtful answers and, best of all, he challenges my geeky ways and afterward, when I act more bizarre than ever, likes me just the same.

Because he's honest *and* accepting, I'm comfortable with him. And, scary as it is to admit, I trust him more than I trust Jake. My therapist would tell me to watch out—trusting too soon is an enormous red flag.

Chapter 7:

Before slamming me with a serious question, Jake usually settles into the proverbial quiet before the storm. Today is no different. He sets his coffee mug down soundlessly, no easy accomplishment for a man with hands as large as his. Also a bull's eye indication that I'd crossed his do-not-go-there line, again. "Really, Birdie, I taught you better. What happened to marshaling your facts before you accuse me of wrongdoing?" He folds the front page of the *Bellesport Sentinel* and puts it aside.

I swallow a mouthful of toast. The facts seemed clear to me, until now. The clock on the stove sounds its anxious electronic clicks. "What do you mean?" I ask, taking advantage of his preoccupation with breakfast to review the accusation I just hurled his way.

He plunges his spoon into a mountain of Honey Bunches of Oats, then into his mouth, skittering bits of cereal on the granite island top. He chews and chews until, like everything else he bears down on, the cereal gives up its crunch.

"Damn it, Birdie, I did call Highfield about those alarm mats for your grandmother. I faxed the social worker—what's her name? Corki?—a signed letter on my office stationery, giving consent for alarm mats, two of them." He leans forward, "If there's one thing I've learned over the years, young lady, it's how to write a letter of consent."

Now it's my turn to chew thoughtfully. From high on my stool safe at the far end of the shiny black slab of granite I come back with, "Robin didn't seem to know a thing about the mats. And if she did, why weren't they where they were supposed to be?"

He rises from his stool—given the charged atmospherics he makes a remarkably smooth liftoff for someone who occupies airspace six feet six above size fourteen feet—and pours himself more burnt smelling coffee. Situating himself the distance he'd stand if I were on the witness stand, he starts: "I have no clue of what's going on with Robin. But your assertion that I don't care enough about my mother to protect her is"—the last two letters roar at me from the back of his throat—"indelicate at best. If I were you, I'd work on getting the facts straight before I cast aspersions. How's that for a novel idea?"

I puff my lips into my best pout. I've been sitting, feet resting lightly on the stool's cross bar, but now I need whatever height I can muster. I push gently against the stool and pull myself up. "Okay, I get your point. But you've got to see mine, too. Robin didn't have a clue. Why else would she have tooled off to get a consent form for you to sign? What would *you* have made of that?"

"Given that the mats weren't by your grandmother's bed and she'd already incurred an injury—"

"But if you'd heard Sukie, you'd have gotten angry, too. She was so upset, all she could talk about was not wanting her friends to see her bruised face."

"Robin was worried. Backpedaling. Covering her you-know-what."

"Then, you can see why I . . ." I swallow the rest of my words. My father's graying eyebrows arch angrily, same as when my mother used to hammer him about the latest family problem. I know how that feels; I'm a lot like him in that regard. Once someone points out my mistake, I'll do anything to avoid having my nose rubbed in it. And now that I'm losing this argument, the most I can hope for is a distraction.

With one hand flat against the island, I push my feet against the rung of the stool and reach for the comics. *A few giggles ought to do it, but the paper is just little too far. I* stretch a bit more. My hand slides on a dribble of melted butter, my stool scrapes out from under me, and before I know it I'm headed face-first toward the granite. Just like Sukie...

"Got you," my father says, enclosing me in the crook of his arm.

"Put me down." But he jiggles me on his hip. "You know I hate that," I giggle.

"Then why are you laughing?"

In his arms, I tower above the stovetop, the counter, the sink, and the island. "Stop or I'll yif."

"Ah, that's my girl. Yiffing as a defense." He sets me down on the hard tile floor and checks his watch. "I've got to get to work, but let's get something straight. From now on, if something makes no sense to you, don't make me into your piñata." He looks me in the eye. "What's the cardinal rule?"

"Ask, ask, ask . . ." I chant, sliding my hand along the smooth, glistening island toward the door, " . . . about anything?"

He slips into his suit jacket and feels for his car keys. "Anything."

I reward him with a triumphant smile. "You realize you just signed a pact with the devil."

He sighs. "How well I know. See you tonight, Birdie." And he kisses the top of my head like he used to. I give him a little smile, but inside, I'm grinning ear to ear.

I hand him his briefcase, open the kitchen door, and wait until he's almost out the mudroom door before saying, "Tonight, Jake."

He looks back over his shoulder and points at me with his key. "Dad, to you. Got that?"

"Got it . . . Dad."

I close the door behind him and lock it. I figured he wouldn't let me get away with calling him Jake, and he hadn't let me down. I unearth my spiral bound notebook from my backpack and turn to the back page. Across the top, in large print is written: *DAD DESIGNATION CHART FOR JAKE WINDSOR*. Beneath it, the rating system I developed for him. So far, I've made one entry, yesterday's, dated October 11th with a full ten points for the sweet way he treated me during Jhumpa's phone call about Sukie. But later, after he didn't bother to visit Sukie, I drew a huge X through his ten points and penciled in big fat zero. *The daughter giveth and the daughter taketh away.*

With today's indication that he wants me to call him "Dad"—desire being the basic, first step towards being awarded the Dad Designation—he's earned a solid five points, a good start for a guy who's been wallowing for years in negative numbers. On the next line down, I write today's date, draw a diagonal line beneath it, and pencil in *5 points*. If he offered to call Robin to discuss the missing mats, he would have earned five more points for a perfect rating. While saving me from a face plant, then soaring me around the kitchen was decent, it wasn't decent enough.

Deep down inside, I feel like a tool. I'm being really tough on him. Pushing the eraser end of the pencil into my cheek, I reconsider. I *had* liked his playfulness when he caught me, and my giggling proved it. I erase '5' with slow deliberate strokes and in its place, write '6.' Then, I add another point for making his expectation clear: he's not about to put up with me calling him by his first name, and I like that. Despite the ugly things my mother says about him, he still thinks of himself as my dad.

He has tons of work to do before I'll feel good about honoring him with the title, DAD. Until then, I'll encourage him by calling him "Dad" to his face, and give him plenty of chances to act like a real father. In meantime, he's "Jake."

Chapter 8:

Elliot wheels across the Highfield employees' parking lot toward me, his face scrunched into a grimace that says he's not sure what to make of me. "Halloween is three weeks off, so what's this, an early costume?"

"I was afraid I'd be late, so I wore my jeans under my jumper. I'll take it off after I lock my bike." I unfasten the chinstrap from my helmet, then slip out of my backpack and take a quick look at the blue and white gingham Elliot is poking fun of.

"You haven't answered me. What's today—Dorothy revisits Oz day?"

"Don't be stupid. Just because I'm writing a reconstructed twenty-first century version of the *Wizard of Oz* doesn't mean I'm vying for a Dorothy dress-alike award. If you must know, this morning was the first time in *mucho* months that I've had breakfast alone with Jake and I wanted to wear something special." I unzip my backpack and take out my lock and cable.

"Something that makes you look like a little girl?" He lights a cigarette and blows the smoke to the side. "Most kids want their folks to think they're older and smarter," he says, then toasts me with his Coolatta.

I uncoil the bike lock cable and weave it through the spokes of the back wheel and around the aluminum frame. "My father claims I'm too smart for my own good. But that's not the problem." I glance up at him. His Red Sox cap softens the neo-Nazi impact of his shaved head, and his red fleece pullover gives his cheeks a healthy glow. Ordinarily, I wouldn't talk about something this personal with a stranger—especially a guy—but something about this guy makes me feel super safe. Red flags pop up all over the place, but I ignore them. Again.

"Have you ever seen a play?" I ask. He rolls his eyes and nods. "Then you've seen how costumes send messages that make the actress's work easier."

"You're kidding. You were playing the part of a little girl? Why?"

One end of the bike lock cable recoils. I start over, uncurling one coil after the other. "The other day, you wore a Hell's Angels jacket. Which role were you playing?"

He studies the dented fender on a nearby Toyota Prius, the morning sun glinting off the rim of his glasses, a new addition to his costume. "What's with you, asking such bizarre questions?"

"That was rhetorical, which means it's supposed to get you thinking. But you get my point. I dressed like a little girl to remind Jake that that's what I am."

"Did it work?"

"He started out being mad at something I'd said to him, then saved me from hurting myself big time, and a few minutes later got annoyed all over again when I called him by his first name."

Elliot's eyes are on me again. This time they glow with admiration. "I'd say you did okay for yourself."

I loop one end of the cable through my front wheel, weave it through the bike rack, then position it over its twin loop, and lock them together. "That ought to do it." I get up, unroll the legs of my jeans, and peel my jumper over my head. Beneath it, a tangerine jersey arrayed with blue sequined waves dancing along the hem.

Elliot gawks at my sequins. "Now you look as normal as someone like you possibly can."

"I was thinking the same about you, especially without your leather jacket."

He leans forward, cigarette bobbing between his lip, and twists an imaginary mustache. "But you're still afraid of me, right?" Overhead, a seagull screeches.

"Terrified." I force myself to sound sassy, but actually I am afraid. Bruce was as nice as Elliot at first, nicer even. But after he'd hurt me one too many times, I started keeping a list of the "accidents" I'd had when I was with him.

One time, he stuck out his gunboat of a foot and tripped me, but I regained my balance. Another time, he bumped me so hard—called it a "love-tap"—that my shoulder turned black and blue. Another time, he claimed he was "just playin' around" when he ripped the sleeve off my blouse.

Elliot, who has every reason to be mean and angry, is just the opposite. So far. In the back of my mind, I wonder if he'll turn out to be like Bruce: a guy who gets off preying on lonely girls, who hides his creeper self until later when he gets the girl to like him more than she should. I could save myself a heap of trouble by applying Jake's "ask anything" advice to Elliot. But I don't want to sound like Jammi, a cute girl in my group therapy session, who thinks all guys are as bad-assed as the one that broke her arm. Besides, it's getting late.

Elliot and I stroll-roll quickly along the sidewalk around the health center to the front lobby. Rouged maple leaves sputter on the breeze. Up ahead, ambulances are lined three in a row, waiting to transport patients. Their drivers stand in a circle, gossiping, two-way radios protruding from their hips, crackling with urgency.

An older driver with smooth blue-black cheekbones and a wide smile steps out from the circle and greets Elliot with a high-five. Their palms, one thickened from lifting and lowering gurneys and the other callused from propelling two-thirds of his former self, meet with an upbeat smack. "My man, how you been?" A gold tooth twinkles behind his grin.

"Better every day, thanks to you." Absentmindedly stuffing his cigarette through the sipping hole in the lid of his drink, Elliot looks up at me. "If it hadn't been for Gentleman George, I wouldn't be here. The day of the accident, he fished me out of Sebago Lake."

George waves no, puts his fingers to his lips to get Elliot to stop talking, then lifts his walkie-talkie from its holster and shrugs a relieved apology for the interruption. "Be seeing you," he says, turning his attention to the barking dispatcher.

"You didn't tell me you were in a boating accident. Is that how . . ." The automatic doors gape. Before I can finish, a crowd of visitors sweeps us into the lobby.

"You never asked."

My eyes open wide; he read my mind!

"One of these days, when I've downed one too many Coolattas I might tell you about it. But for now, I'm better off when I don't talk about it. Besides, I've got to get my sorry bones to Physical Terrorpy." He shoots me that lopsided grin of his and rolls off past the receptionist, down the hall by the atrium, in and out among speed-walkers and stragglers alike.

He's like the sun, I think as rays pour through the pollen-streaked windows to warm the side of my face. *Determined to get through.*

Lydia Charles from the Volunteer Services offices isn't at the nurses' station on the Anne Fitzgerald Unit, where she promised to meet me. After waiting for fifteen minutes, I check the clock mounted above a pile of orange and brown construction paper leaves taped to the wall: 9:00 exactly. Mrs. Charles is late.

The smell of cold eggs, stale bedclothes, and warm bodies too sleepy to budge fills the unit. If I could find a nurse, I'd ask her to tell Mrs. Charles that I'll be visiting my grandmother. But no one is around.

I could leave a message, but where? The nurses' side of the station is festooned with notes of all sizes, dangling from the undersides of the counters far from patients' wandering hands. On the back wall, the staff bulletin board is papered with reminders for staff training classes, annual flu shots, and a solemn Note of Thanks. Even if I wrote Mrs. Charles' name in screaming bold letters, I doubt she'd find it.

I peek down the corridor leading to Sukie's room. A med cart against the wall means a nurse is nearby, but where? A supply cart rests idly beside an unoccupied wheelchair at the junction of the two corridors. The unit looks like a movie set prepped and ready for the actors and actresses to take their places.

I go into the recreation room, where the television has lapsed into the same weary silence that fills the unit, and call Highfield on my cell phone. When the receptionist answers, I ask for Mrs. Charles.

"Oh, Mrs. Charles is out for the rest of the week."

"Is anyone else in the volunteer office?"

"Sorry, hon, Mrs. Charles runs the office solo. Would you like to leave a voice mail message?"

"No, no message," I say and click off. I called last week and reminded Mrs. Charles that I'd be starting on Columbus Day. We agreed to meet here at 8:45. Then she complimented me on recommendations my guidance counselor and teachers had written. "Congratulations on being accepted to Highfield for your Service Learning Project site. We're delighted to have you with us." If she was so thrilled, how could she forget that my placement started today?

Mrs. Charles had no idea of the hell I'd gone through to get here. Of the hours I'd spent in summer school classes and, each day after they'd ended, in the library, earning credits for the classes I would miss while I volunteered here at Highfield. But that was only part of it. Summer school had been my hiding place, where I'd be least likely to run into members of the "Society of Bling," Maggie and her elitist clique of girls, jingle-jangling keys to their fathers' Mazdas.

"Blingers" were some of the most insecure kids in Granville High. While I can say that with certainty now, last spring when I was desperate for their protection, I kept this to myself. To them the school day was boring, and after school hours, deadly. Rather than joining athletics, theatre, or photography clubs, which is what they'd told their parents they were doing, they broke into the homes of one another's mothers, women who wore "their kind" of clothing, and stole from them. Just for fun. A designer scarf here. A blouse there. Items the owners would assume they'd left at the dry cleaners.

Maggie, the leader of the Blingers, hatched her "high stakes" game and invited only the most "promising" girls to join. Soon they had the reputation of being tough, unruly, and on the prowl for new projects. So Maggie's Blingers voted to take on the girl most in need of a "nerd-purge": me. By then, Bruce had nearly raped me, right there in the girls' bathroom; I needed the Blingers more than they could imagine.

So far, the decisions I've made in math and science were advanced placement caliber, while those I made about other kids sucked big time. I tend to like the wrong people for the right reasons and no one knows it more than me. Take Bruce for instance. He was charming and sweet, the kind of kid who charmed my mother with a bouquet of flowers the first time he picked me up for a date.

Definitely not a sixteen-year-old guy thing; that alone should have tipped me off. Sure, I liked him all right, but I wasn't as gaga about him as my locker-mate, Maggie, thought

I should be. Anyway, by the time I worked up the nerve to tell him I didn't want to go for another of our walks in the woods, where he wouldn't stop groping me, he'd accused me of leading him on. As luck would have it, Maggie asked me to join the Blingers and that's when I hatched a plan of my own.

Thinking about this makes me want to cry. During my group therapy sessions, I learned to identify myself as a victim of bullying. God, how I hated that! I had to admit in front of eight other girls that I was angry about what had happened to me (duh) and later, role-play ways to manage my anger. I would have agreed to eat raw liver, swallow a mouthful of fish eyes, anything to get through those sessions.

I draw a deep breath and think back to the promise I made to Jake: ask tons of questions, get the facts, and tread softly when it comes to drawing conclusions. He'd be disappointed to learn that I'm a victim of the assumptions that worm their way into my brain. They slink up and down, back and forth, looking for a crack in my promise. Then conclusions elbow their way front and center.

A woman with shoulder-length gray hair and a pretty brown beaded necklace shuffles out of one of the bedrooms, hands clutching her walker. Her blue-gray eyes sparkle with what might have once been seeds of laughter, but now look more like tears. She spies me instantly. "Nurse," she calls, "Nurse," and hurries over.

"I'm not a nurse, but I'll find one for you. What do you need?"

The woman looks up one corridor and down the other. Seeing no one, her pleasant features collapse into frantic wrinkles. "I have to go to the bathroom. I need a nurse."

Hearing the distress in the woman's voice, I forget my problems. "I'll find one for you."

"Hurry, please hurry."

I search the corridor where the med cart is parked, poking my head in and out of the rooms. Some patients are watching television, some stare out their window, and others are still in bed. Finally, I see Sandis go into Hazel's room. I hurry toward her. As I pass Sukie's room, I peek in. She's sitting in a chair, elbows on her knees, head in her hands. My heart does a triple flip into my throat. "Sukie? Sukie, are you all right?"

She looks up and grabs my arm. "Hummingbird, thank goodness you're here." The bump on her forehead has almost disappeared and her eyes, rimmed in blacks and blues, are less swollen than yesterday. Within them is a different shade of despair.

"I don't know what to do, Hummingbird. I've been shopping all morning. I must have become tired. All of a sudden I looked around and found myself in this bedding department." She points to the pile of fresh linens beside her rumpled bed. "Now I can't remember how to get back to my car. You know what a good shopper I am. I know my way around the mall as well as I know my own face."

That awful lead-apron is back, wrapping its suffocating self around my heart, sinking my hope that Sukie would win out over Arlene Alzheimer.

I take Sukie's hand and help her out of the chair. "Come with me, we'll find your car."

Her eyes widen with surprise. "You remember where I parked my car?"

I kiss my fingertips and, gently touching her cheek, plant my kiss in a ritual I hope she remembers. I'm not disappointed. Her face lights up. She tugs me to a stop and kisses me back.

"Let's go," I lilt, hoping she's forgotten the mall.

The woman in the walker is still waiting by the nurses' station. I wave. The woman moans, "Won't you help me?

Please. I have to go to the bathroom." Her voice is more desperate than before.

I wave again. "I'm working on it."

"Who's that old woman?" To hear Sukie's words, peppered with scorn, you'd think she is years younger than the woman.

"She needs our help. Let's see if we can find a nurse for her," I say, walking as fast as I can toward Hazel's room.

"A nurse?" Sukie's frightened realization. "Am I in a hospital?"

I stop and face her. I'm not sure what to say. I don't want to lie because if I do, Sukie will know. Despite Arlene Alzheimer's constant presence in her life—the stupid nickname makes it easier to say my grandmother's name and her diagnosis in the same sentence—Sukie can still sniff out a lie faster than a beagle in search of a bone.

"You're not in a hospital." That much is true, kind of; Highfield is a health facility that specializes in rehab.

"Then where am I?"

My stomach flip-flops. Oh, God, how I wish Solange were here to help me through this one. I can't think of a kind way to explain the Anne Fitzgerald Unit and I don't want to use the diagnostic term. Years back, when Sukie had just crossed the dementia threshold, her geriatric psychiatrist had explained her diagnosis to her in the gentlest possible way. Sukie came home and didn't speak to any of us for days. "Grieving," was how the psychiatrist described Sukie's reaction, "...a vital response, one that will allow her to move on." Since then, Sukie had moved on.

Careful not to say anything that would drive her back into that dark cave, I launch into my explanation: "You're in a place that's helping you with your memory." Because there are plenty of people to talk to and activities for her to do, it's as close to the truth as I dare come. My heart speeds up as it typically does when I'm bending the facts.

"Something's the matter with my memory?" She stares blankly at me. "Oh dear, that's awful."

"But you're getting lots of help, and I'm very proud of the excellent work you're doing."

She blushes with pleasure. "Thank you. That's so good to hear." Like me, she loves praise. I make a mental note to praise her more often, stretch onto my tiptoes to kiss her again, then guide her toward Hazel's room. The lead apron pressure in my chest disappears; my heart pulses as usual.

The woman by the nurse's station wails again, "Somebody, please help me."

I peek in Hazel's room and, not seeing Sandis, start back down the corridor. Except for the woman, the place is quiet. By the time Sukie and I reach her, her eyes have widened like those of a cornered animal.

Miraculously, Sandis and an older aide appear. Expressionless, they ignore the woman. I wait, thinking they're about to take her to the toilet just a few feet away. Instead, the graying aide with the name badge, Timtiere, takes her cue from Sandis and heads for the utility cart, where she loads up on towels and sheets.

"Aren't they going to do something?" Sukie asks loudly enough for them to hear.

I can't stand it any longer. "This lady has been asking to go to the bathroom." I glance up at the clock: 9:20. "She's been waiting for twenty minutes."

Without warning, the woman droops over the front bar of her walker, her head and arms limp. Having lost interest, Sukie wanders down the hall.

"She's fainted!" I say to Sandis, too disgusted to hide the accusation in my voice.

"Don't mind her. She does this all the time . . ." As if to convince me, she adds, "...whenever she can't get her way." Her mean words tumble out of her mouth so casually, she scares me. I try not to stare at the strip of fiery orange hair that outlines her moon-shaped face.

I feel a little off, as though I just entered a scene from an old movie, *One Flew Over the Cuckoo's Nest.* I check the woman's pulse—steady and strong, although now she smells of urine—and hesitate before leaving to make sure Sukie is all right.

Sukie is sitting in shocked silence in the small day room with Hazel and another woman with doe-like eyes and childish braids. "I have to go to a meeting. I'll be back later," I tell her.

She looks uneasy about being left with staff who wouldn't bother with a woman who told them exactly what she needed. The fear in her eyes says, "What will happen to me when I need help and my words won't come?" Remembering her manners, she musters a half-smile. "All right, dear. You go to your meeting. But please, don't forget I'm here."

Sukie has a right to be worried. If the staff can blow off an old woman while I'm standing there, what will they pull when no family member is around? I get the feeling that Sandis and Timtiere hate old people. "I won't forget for a second," I assure her, a big, aching smile cracking my lips.

Chapter 9:

Between the smells, the eerie stillness, and the problems on the unit, I want to escape. Sukie living as one among dozens of other equally broken eggs makes me want to scream, 'It's not fair!' I key in the combination to the door that will take me off the unit. Nothing happens. No shrill whistle to alert staff that someone is leaving, no welcome click-click as the locks on the double doors release. Perspiration dribbles from my temples down my cheeks. Did those aides flip a switch that mistakenly locked me in, too? I hear Sukie in the next room, telling Hazel she is going to take care of her. "Would you like that?" Sukie asks, her voice brimming with the same devotion she once offered me.

I long for a return to the happier days when my sister, Marion, said Sukie's forgetfulness was nothing more than "a mild case of short-term memory loss." Mild, as in not dependent on medications to control her behavior. That July, I asked Sukie if it was okay to take the dusty dead Christmas poinsettia from the dining room table and put it on the compost heap. Though I hadn't touched the plant, Sukie started ranting, "Hummingbird tried to steal my plant." Shortly after, her diagnosis spiked into the serious range.

"Sukie thinks if she keeps everything the same, she'll stop changing, too. That sounds irrational to us, but it makes sense to her," Marion suggested.

Sukie ranted until Aunt Elizabeth gave her a powerful white pill that left her so lethargic and gape-mouthed I worried that she'd had a stroke. That's about when I began needing something powerful, too. Unfortunately, I turned to Bruce.

I tap the combination onto the keypad once more. Finally, the heavy steel fire doors buzz open. But the elevator takes forever to come up to the third floor. I can't wait a second longer. I key my way into the nearby stairwell and gallop down the stairs, one flight after the other without stopping, until I see a sign for Business Offices/Main Lobby. "Thank goodness . . ." I burst into a wide hallway dotted with love seats and artificial ficus trees ". . . civilization."

Women in business suits bustle past me, laptops tucked under their arms. Some smile warmly and others, walking two and three abreast, never break from their serious conversations. I follow them into the bustling ladies' room and just as quickly leave in search of another more private bathroom.

As in a busy airport terminal, if you look a hundred feet beyond the crowds, you can always find a vacant restroom. True to my prediction, down the hall and around the corner, I spot a sign with the international symbol for restroom. I lock myself into the "oner" and lean against the door. When I finish crying, I pull a handful of toilet paper from the dispenser and blow my nose.

If the aides on Sukie's unit can't make time for a woman who had to use the toilet, who's going to stop to answer the type of questions Sukie asks? I study my damp face in the bottom half of the mirror; the answer glares back. "I can't, I'm just a kid," I say out loud.

"Age doesn't matter." Sukie's words thunder in my head; she's counting on me.

Weighted by this load, I consider calling my mother and begging her to take me home, until the problem-solving part of my mind fans out. I remind myself that I'm tough and fast, strong enough to pull into a tail-tuck, or reverse a downward plunge into an upward lift. If Sukie can befriend Hazel and the woman who looks like a graying child, I can find answers to Sukie's questions.

I use the toilet, this time for more than a crying station, wash my hands, anchor my rhinestone comb through my springy waves, and leave. The first thing I have to do is find the administrator, Mrs. Perducci. Hopefully, she'll be able to tell me how to break into my new and now more-important-than-ever volunteer job.

"Well, let me think," Mrs. Perducci says, unbuttoning her tailored navy-blue suit jacket and seating herself in the chair alongside mine. "If I were your age, what volunteer jobs would I feel comfortable doing?" She taps her rouged cheek with her index finger, its short nail filed to match the shape of her slender fingertips, exactly like I wear mine. "I tell you what. My daughter volunteered here last year." She glances at her wristwatch. "Sarah's in study hall. Let's ask her."

She reaches over a stack of files for her iPhone and texts her daughter. Within seconds, her daughter fires back a list of duties, which Mrs. Perducci shows me: dlivr linens, fil sop + papr towl dispnsrs, whl patients 2 + frm hairdresr, dlivr meals, hlp rec aide, stuf lik that. No time 4 +. Got 2 run. XX, S.

Mrs. Perducci sets the iPhone on her desk beside a smattering of memos, scribbled notes, and photos of her with her husband and children. She has five, ranging from a tall dark-haired girl wearing a UMAINE sweatshirt down to a little boy in shorts and a cock-eyed baseball cap. Red Sox.

"We have five kids in our family, too," I tell her. "I'm the youngest."

"And the smartest, no doubt." Mrs. Perducci taps her little boy's picture. "My youngest has the advantage of having his older sisters and brother as teachers."

"Our family is older. I was my mother's surprise baby, the straw that cracked her back, as she likes to say." Mrs. Perducci titters appreciatively. "My oldest sister is a doctor. She runs a geriatric clinic and teaches at the medical school in Madison, Wisconsin." For the first time in what seemed like forever, I'm free to be myself. I relax into the blue velvet wing chair. "She's why I came here. I want to specialize in geriatrics like her."

"So, you're headed to med school?" Mrs. Perducci's iPhone rings. She presses a button to silence it and says, "He'll have to wait. We're having a real conversation. Do you know how few real conversations I've had lately? We're in such a rush nowadays that we speak as though we're texting—in the shortest and fastest sentences possible. And later, when things go wrong, we wonder what happened."

"I think a lot about those kinds of things. My father says I'm his youngest-oldest daughter. That I was born old." I stare at the photo of the Perduccis with their five kids. I'm so envious of Mrs. Perducci's kids having two parents living under the same roof, I could die. If I were the kid in that photo, sitting on Mrs. Perducci's knee, no one could rip me away.

"That must be hard for you. My middle son is quite brainy, and when his chess-whiz buddies are busy, he's pretty much alone." She rubs her left eye, smearing her mascara down her cheek.

"Mrs. Perducci, if you had just smeared mascara down your cheek, would you want a complete stranger to say something about it?"

She throws her head back and laughs, a rich warm sound that makes me laugh, too. "Yes I would," she says, pushing herself out of the chair and stepping to the side of her desk, where her purse gapes open on the floor. She hoists it up by the leather handles and takes out a small silver-rimmed mirror.

I start. Beside the mirror rests a small opened box of tampons, a painful reminder that I have yet to get my first period, the "ticket to womanhood," as Maggie Forester liked to remind me. I blame hours of gymnastics training for my flat-chest, meaty shoulders, small hard butt, and screwed up hormones.

"Thank you. I have a meeting this afternoon, and I need to look decent." Mrs. Perducci dabs a tissue on her tongue and scrubs her face. "Mother's spit, cleans just about anything . . ." she turns toward me, "How's that?"

"My grandmother has a mirror like yours that slips onto a tube of lipstick. I didn't think they made those anymore."

"You're right, that mirror belonged to my mother. They don't make them like her anymore, either." She returns to the chair beside me and as she lowers herself ever so gingerly, suddenly looks fragile. "My mother had Alzheimer's."

The image of Sukie, upstairs chatting with her odd companions, the women she probably thinks of as the "girls" in her old bridge club, returns. "Is your mother what brought you to work at Highfield?"

Mrs. Perducci tilts her head and gazes appraisingly at me. "I'll bet your parents are very proud of you."

"Not as proud as my grandmother. Actually, she's an important part of the reason I'm here. She's on the Anne Fitzgerald Unit." I consider telling her about the aides and the old woman who fainted, but decide against it. I don't know Mrs. Perducci and I don't want her to think I'm a trouble-maker. Still, my decision doesn't feel right.

Mrs. Perducci's eyes soften with understanding. She rolls her lips into her mouth and studies her fingernails. I look around for a box of tissues in case she starts to cry. She takes a few halting breaths. Moments slip by before she can speak. "I'm very sorry to hear that."

"Ever since Arlene elbowed her way into our lives, our family has been stranger than ever. And that's saying a lot."

Mrs. Perducci perks up: she doesn't look so fragile anymore. "Arlene? I don't understand."

"Sorry. My mother gets annoyed when I forget to tell her what I'm talking about. She's always telling me to stop living in my make-believe world. But Arlene isn't pretend, she's very real, at least to my grandmother and me." Mrs. Perducci still looks puzzled. "Arlene is our name for my grandmother's disease, because whether we like it or not, it's become her companion."

Mrs. Perducci's face brightens. "Oh, I understand. Befriending your Alzheimer's by naming it—I like that twist of wisdom. Do you mind if I use it during my meeting today?"

I flash her a weak smile. "Sure." But befriending is just one way of looking at Alzheimer's; it's more complicated than that. Sukie asking me what went wrong when she added French salad dressing to the apples she was preparing for a pie and hearing the despair in her, "I'm afraid I'm losing my mind . . ." forced me to either smother misery in a mound of humor or drown in Arlene's lava-like spew. Self-pity is crippling when it comes to helping Sukie tame the beast.

Mrs. Perducci phones Robin, the nurse supervisor, to check that the activities her daughter recommended were "a good fit for the A.F.Unit" and arranges for Corki Goodale, the bubbly social worker I met the other day, to introduce me to the unit staff. She dials another number to find out what happened to the volunteer coordinator and apologizes for her absence with, "She's come down with the flu."

"Before you meet Corki, you should get some lunch. Do you know your way to the staff cafeteria? Snacks, drinks, and meals for volunteers are on us." For the first time today, I feel welcomed. I wish I could say the same for Sukie or the lady wearing brown beads.

After downing a complimentary bowl of tomato soup, a yogurt, and a chocolate chip cookie, I wait for Corki on the unit. Compared to this morning, the unit feels lived in. Patients sit in the television room, listening to a live concert. A jovial bristle-haired young guy with vines tattooed up his skinny forearms plunks out jaunty Steven Foster tunes on a scuffed baby grand. Several ladies sitting with Sukie join the pianist in singing a sporadic measure of *Camp Town Ladies*. The sunny wraparound windows frame views of traffic flowing past tidy two-story houses with fluorescent three-wheelers on the front lawns, a Sudanese grocery on the corner, a neighboring barbershop, and Vinodha's Auto Detailing—Voted the Best Rub in Town!

The pianist waves at Sukie, urging her to sing, and though the words of the song she once sang aren't there for her, Sukie's eyes dance along with her bare feet. Unlike this morning, she wears a flirtatious little smile.

"Your grandmother is having a good day." Corki's lips part into a brilliant white-toothed smile.

"I'm staying out of sight so I won't distract her," I say, backing away from the wall by the doorway. "We've swapped places—my grandmother watched me sing when I was in kindergarten," I say sadly as Corki and I settle by the nurses' station. A handful of patients, the sparrows whose wings have been clipped, nod drowsily in their wheelchairs. "Will our talking bother them?"

Surprised, as though she'd never considered this possibility, Corki shakes her curly henna head, carefree and breezy like we were at a picnic. "You don't have to worry about them. They've eaten their main meal of the day. They often nap here, where the staff can keep an eye on them."

I quickly scan the far-reaching arms of the corridor. Other than Corki, there's no staff. A med cart topped with plastic cups and half-gallon containers of orange juice and a high protein milkshake type drink Sukie likes, is in the same place as this morning. A nearby toilet flushes. A woman wearing a headscarf, pushing a cart loaded with stacks of toilet tissue, scrub brushes, and a large swishy mop comes out of one room and shuffles her way into the next. "I expected this place to be busier," I say.

Corki glances at the clock. "Just wait until three-ish. Everyone gathers around the nurses' station. We can never tell how our residents will react then. We call it 'sundowning,' the worst time of the day."

"For a while, late afternoon before dinner was the 'witching hour' in our house. My mom would try to make dinner while I showed her my 'big threes'—tired, hungry, and cranky. Sometimes, Mom got just as cranky." I roll my eyes.

"What did your mother do?"

"She's a CPA. She runs her business from her office at home." I stop short of telling Corki that since my parents' divorce my mother sips one eight-ounce glass of wine after the other and calls each morning to check that I've not left my most important school project until last minute. I know what's really on her mind: she's getting a read on my progress with Jake. She's afraid I might not want to come home to her. Sometimes, I think she's right.

"No, I meant what did your mom do about your 'big threes?' Your sundowning?" The make-up around her eyes creases when Corki smiles.

"Oh..." It takes me a second to get back into our conversation. "My mom bought me snack packs—raisins, crackers, peanuts—miniatures a kid likes to handle. Then she'd pop an old movie like the *Wizard of Oz* into her old VCR for me to watch. As I watched, I'd make a raisin and peanut stew on my little stove, and Mom would cook in peace, until the Wicked Witch threatened Dorothy. Then I buried myself under the sofa cushions and waited for Glinda, the good witch, to save Dorothy. That's when Mom would come and get me."

Corki listens intently. "That's kinda what happens here. Only our residents were the ones who were making the meals or coming home from their offices. Between three and four o'clock their inner alarm goes off, reminding them they're supposed to do something, only they can't remember what. Even if they did, everything here is done for them. Anyway, the point is, they become anxious, which makes them surly."

My mind churns. Sukie often complained in the late afternoon that she felt "like a nobody," especially when she would try to help Aunt Elizabeth fix dinner. Unless Aunt Elizabeth guided Sukie's hand while she peeled potatoes, Sukie couldn't figure out how to make the peeler work. One day, Sukie got so frustrated she threw the potato across the room. I tried to help Aunt Elizabeth by taking Sukie for a walk.

Walking was one of the few activities Arlene Alzheimer hadn't poisoned. And Sukie loved how the fresh air and exercise made her feel young and strong, like her "old self." Before Sukie started getting lost, she walked by herself every day. She enjoyed seeing her neighbor's gardens, chatting with the neighbors, and patting their dogs. By the time she headed home, she glowed.

Corki interrupts my thoughts. "Before our dayshift goes off duty, I want to introduce you to a few people."

"When does their shift end?"

Corki checks her watch. "Three," she says absently.

"Lots of things happen here at three, don't they?"

Corki starts; she'd never thought about how confusing this must be for the residents. I cringe. *I need to be more careful. Adults don't like having a kid point out the obvious.*

I clear my throat. "You reminded me that I'd like to introduce you to a friend who'll be visiting my grandmother."

Corki brightens. The bouncy melody from *I Could Have Danced All Night* leaps from the keys of the baby grand into the hallway. "Oh sure, I'd love to meet your friend."

We search for staff in one room after the other, looking past teddy bears with "I Love Grandpa" on their little shirts, a quilted twin bedspread pulsing with primary colors, an occasional bouquet of dusty silk flowers, bathroom doors with simple black and white sketches of a toilet taped to the outside, and the mahogany bureau a family trucked over in hopes of cracking the room's institutional glaze.

We come to a single room, smaller and more intimate than the others. Velcroed across the doorjamb hangs bright red netting with a huge STOP sign. On the other side, the tall, graying aide from this morning slides the sidebars on the patient's bed upward into a position Robin, the nursing supervisor, would classify as a "restraint."

The room smells of feces, soap, and antiseptic lotion. A host of birthday cards to Our Dad, My Favorite Uncle, Our Brother stands on the windowsill by the bed. A man's thin body sleeps beneath a flannel receiving blanket over which the cleft in his chin rests. Teeth marks from a comb have yet to disappear from his damp white hair. The light outside the window says it all: both it and the man are dimming.

Timtiere is at the bathroom sink, washing her large hands. Despite the fatigue that lines her eyes, she manages a surprisingly gentle smile. "You look very familiar," she says after Corki introduces us. "But then we have lots of students on this unit."

I choose not to remind her that we first saw one another this morning when the woman who begged to be taken to the toilet fainted. Besides, I don't feel right starting a conversation while the man in the bed is sleeping. "Nice to meet you," I murmur while Corki leads me out into the hallway, where *Somewhere Over the Rainbow* wafts our way.

"Poor Mr. Hartwell is on hospice care. He was so sweet, I'm going to miss him." Corki whispers as though he's already gone. "When a person like Mr. Hartwell is on hospice, the doctor often stops his meds. More often than not, once the drugs are out of the person's system, the person sits up and talks as if nothing had ever happened. It's a shame that didn't happen with Mr. Hartwell."

I'm amazed Corki doesn't recognize this as a valuable observation, one that might help others. I make a mental note to call my sister, Marion, and ask if she's tried reducing the medications of residents in better shape than Mr. Hartwell. If medication makes it harder for people with Alzheimer's to talk, why not adjust their meds so they can act and feel more normal? Restoring their ability to tell others what they want and need seems ridiculously simple. *Is that too simple?*

"Do you have time to meet my friend?" I ask Corki.

"Of course I do," she says all chirpy.

The music ends and, as with any crowded event, there is one person intent on being first to get out, rudely jostling others, elbowing her way through the concert-goers. My breath clots in my throat when I hear a familiar voice snarl, "Get out of my way. What's the matter, don't you hear me? I said move." Although I'm out of her range, I imagine her angry spit landing on my cheeks. Even at this distance, it stings. I hope against hope the voice doesn't belong to Sukie.

Chapter 10:

The squabbling draws Timtiere out from a patient's room into the corridor. Almost half of the unit's forty patients have managed to roll themselves into the hallway. At the counter that separates them from the nurses, they jam the hall with their wheelchairs. Patients, who were peacefully enjoying their musical reveries, now snap as Sukie grabs their wheelchairs, jerks, and bumps a path through their steel maze. Hazel caws in distress. A tiny greasy-haired woman covers her head with her arms and chants, "I live at 87 Pine Street. Please take me home."

Hearing the commotion, Iris pokes her head out from behind the kitchen door. "Oh no, it's Cynthia," she says. Pain registers on her pretty face. She peeks behind the door to make sure none of the eagles are standing there, then bustles into the crowd. "I'm going to move your wheelchair aside. You'll feel a little lift," she says, telling each bewildered person what she intends to do before she does it. I admire her even-handedness as she makes her way toward Sukie.

The pianist closes the lid of the piano, then edges his way into the middle of the ruckus. "Here we go, Mrs. Millford, this way to your room," he says in usher-like tones. "Come this way, Mr. Samuels. Manny, the walker with the red balloons is yours."

Two men and a woman who just arrived for the three to eleven shift see the disturbance and immediately deposit their belongings behind the nurses' station. Without taking their jackets off, they sidle into the tangle of wheelchairs and rescue a couple of terrified eagles.

I slip quietly to Sukie's side. "What are all these people doing here?" she demands of me, as though I were responsible for them filling the hall. "You know I don't like unexpected company. There's not enough dinner to feed you kids and them, too." The rage in her voice has gentled; in its place, the anxious tone of an overwhelmed grandmother.

Hoping to relax her, I rub her clenched fist. She doesn't give me a sliver of recognition. Not knowing what she's going to do next frightens me. I try to make eye contact but her blackened eyelids are like those of a broken doll—rooted in place. It's as though my Sukie has run off and a stranger moved in.

Sandis joins Timtiere behind the nurses' station. More stuck than the Sugar Daddies some snot-nosed kid plastered to my mother's front door last Halloween, they ignore the unfolding crisis. It's a couple of minutes before three and their shift is almost over; as with the woman with brown beads, they don't want to get involved. I can't believe they're not helping; they may as well roll up their Certified Nurses' Aide credentials and smoke them for all the good they're doing. I want to scream at them, until Iris puts a reassuring hand on my shoulder. "Can I help?" she asks, much to my relief.

"I think the crowd frightened my grandmother. If we give her a couple of minutes, I'm sure she'll be all right." I slip my hand in Sukie's. "You're safe. Everything is quiet now." Sukie's hearing aid shrills.

"That awful noise is back. It makes me feel crazy." The fear in Sukie's eyes intensifies as they dart from me to Iris. "Can you make it stop?" She is shouting again and every time she moves her head, the whistling grows more shrill.

"I'm going to take your hearing aid," I exaggerate the enunciation, slipping the flesh-colored comma out of her ear and flicking off its miniature switch.

Sukie's expression changes so quickly, if I didn't know better, I'd think I'd imagined the entire scene. Without her hearing aid, she relaxes. She's like a two-year-old who bellows with frustration because she doesn't have another way to make her needs known. "That's better. Thank you," she says. Her tone returns to normal, as pleasant as ever.

"I put both her hearing aids in just before the concert," Iris says. "She must have taken one out and left it somewhere. No wonder, if it was screeching like that one." She gestures toward my hand.

She positions herself directly in front of Sukie and smiles. "Are you feeling better, Cynthia? That noise must have hurt something awful."

I cringe. How I wish Iris hadn't gone there. My therapist—required by my Informal Adjustment Agreement—always reminds me that negative memories stick with us longer and stronger than positive ones. Take it from me, she's right: Sukie reacts to the angry memory of her hearing aids ruining the concert for her.

"It was awful. I feel awful." She turns to me. "Get me out of here. Let's go home. Pop-Pop is waiting for his dinner." The sharpness has returned to her voice.

I think of Pop-Pop in the sun-flooded old farmhouse he and Sukie had lovingly decorated. He was the only one Sukie trusted to take care of her more personal needs, bathing and powdering and dressing her every morning and night, until his giant exhausted heart stopped. Alzheimer's is a bigger bully than Bruce Talibert. And like Bruce, it ricochets from its victim to hurt others as well.

"Let's see if we can find your other hearing aid, okay Cindy?" Iris speaks into Sukie's good ear.

Sukie strokes Iris' cheek. "That would be wonderful, dear," she says, linking her arm in Iris's and walking toward the now empty TV room.

Iris glances over her shoulder at me. *Thanks,* I mouth, ignoring the scramble of feelings that never fail to appear after one of Sukie's incidents. The two-year-old in me insists a full-blown tantrum will release the tension I've built up. If that would change things, I'd throw myself on the floor and make a fool of myself. Instead, I try to wrap my arms around what this afternoon must have been like for Sukie:

As the concert progressed, she stopped enjoying it. She heard music that was filtered through a watery amplifying system into a brain stiffened with plaque. Her hearing aids started screeching. Frightened, she wanted to escape. By the time the concert ended, she was so upset, she'd forgotten where she was and why. The wheelchairs and walkers surrounding her seemed like a thorny hedge—she felt trapped. That's when she panicked. Who could blame her?

If Sukie could, I'm sure she'd compare living with Alzheimer's to being stuck in the middle of an old-fashioned game of pick-up sticks. She has no choice but to play even though the floppy cotton gloves she's wearing put her at a disadvantage. Still, she does her best to pick the tangled sticks apart. After several unsuccessful attempts, her once bright eyes grow dull. She doesn't care about the game, but *hates* feeling inept. Her spirit shrinks. That's what I fear the most.

Alone, Sukie and I sit in the TV room at the table, folding washcloths. Comfortable with the feel of fabric, her fingers read the bleached terrycloth, taking in every nub as though it were Braille. She concentrates just as she had when she set the darts on one of the high-fashion dresses she once designed.

Lucien, a male nurse on the three to eleven shift, breaks the spell. "I've got something for you, Cynthia," he singsongs. His refrigerator-size physique casts its shadow over Sukie's work. I wish he hadn't interrupted, but Sukie returns his bright smile.

He's about to deposit three pills—one lavender, another white, and the third, orange—into her uplifted palm. I've never seen Sukie take these, much less take them together. Marion warned me about elderly patients being overmedicated; I bristle with worry. "So many pills at once? What are they for?"

Lucien pours juice into a small paper cup and hands it to Sukie. I mush my face into my fiercest scowl. His massive round eyes twinkle; he's not taking me seriously. He probably wonders what kind of kid would be interested in an old woman's medications?

"If those are to keep my grandmother calm, she doesn't need them. She *is* calm."

"Ah, that is precious wonderful," he says, pouring the pills into Sukie's palm. Fuming, I fold my arms across my chest.

I'm usually better at "intellectualizing." That's what my therapist calls my habit of creating theories to separate the crappy things that happen to me from the feelings *she* thinks I should have about them. She should see me now: emotions 1; theories 0. Not being taken seriously by adults makes me furious. Admitting this is supposed to make me feel better. Believe me, it doesn't. Sukie's situation is spinning out of control. And that's "precious" scary.

"That was delicious." Sukie smiles politely and hands her empty cup to Lucien.

"Good job, Cynthia. I'll see you later."

Sukie turns to me and says, "What a nice man."

"I suppose," I murmur, plopping back against my chair. "Do you think he can play pick-up-sticks with his gloves on?"

Chapter 11:

My resentment toward Jake is ballooning. This time he's begged out of giving me a lift to the Halloween Ball at Highfield. "Something's come up; I've got a slew of calls to make." He closes the door to his study, cutting me off just as I'm about to accuse him of breaking his promise. He's forbidden me to take the bus at night because the area around Highfield isn't safe after dark. "Besides, if I recall the terms of your Informal Adjustment Agreement, you're not supposed to go out at night unsupervised."

He's right, but dumping me last minute plunges his overall "Dad" rating into the "weak by any standard" category. I make a mental note to award him a rating of five for worrying about my safety and for reminding me about my agreement, and add two more points for not laying a guilt trip on me for going out instead of working on my project. Then I subtract six for breaking his promise. Again.

"Thanks for taking time out of your evening," I say to Solange, then slam her car door harder than I'd planned. The damp wind nips at my freshly rouged cheeks and stockinged legs. Highfield's lobby glows with strings of orange and yellow lanterns suspended over bales of hay dotted with pumpkins large, small, and in-between. I take a couple of seconds to balance myself over my impossibly high stacked heels and totter toward the entrance.

The passenger-side window makes a *zerring* sound. "Your Dad just called and offered to pick you up whenever you're ready. Call him, okay, honey?" Solange pleads. Since she and my father married, Solange has championed the cause of easing Jake and me into an authentic father-daughter relationship. Having lost her family at a young age, she works

84

doubly hard at bringing whatever is left of ours together. I can hardly blame her; once upon a time, I, too, dreamt the three of us would become a happy family.

Three weeks into our family-living experiment, I detect a weakening of the family pulse, though the body hasn't cooled enough to pronounce it dead. If Jake's dumping me is any indication, I've failed to inspire the rhythm needed to produce a strong steady beat. More often than not, Jake keeps me from getting too close. *How much of a Tin Man-like heart actually beats inside him? Can that be what he's protecting?*

Solange wrenches the gearshift into park and scoots over the center console toward the passenger side window. "Try not to worry about your dad, he'll come around. This is your night, concentrate on having fun. Elliot won't believe what you've done for your costume—Hummingbird goes retro and in the process looks fantastic."

I don't know what comes over me, but my wobbly legs carry me as fast as they can to the car, where I dump my things on the sidewalk, open the door and throw my arms around Solange. "I couldn't have done this without you," I blurt, sniffling back tears as I recall the hours she and I spent together while her seamstress adjusted my dress to perfection.

"Whoa, careful now or you'll ruin that fabulous hairdo we worked so hard to put together." Solange gently pries my arms from her neck. She tucks a strand of hair into my 40's hair style, then straightens the oversized fabric peony gracing my shoulder. "If I were a betting person, I'd wager those calls could have waited until your father dropped you off. My guess? He's home wishing he were here right now."

"My father has regrets, feelings of remorse? Really?"

Solange ignores my sarcasm. "He's not perfect, but he's the only—"

"He makes me so angry, it's impossible to think about how he feels."

"Give him time, he'll come around," she says softly. "Did you bring your lipstick?"

Relieved for the change of subject, I hand Solange the tube of Passion Red. She daubs the sticky red paint over my lips, then pulls a tissue from her jacket pocket. "Here." I press the tissue between my lips, producing a sensuous full-lipped blot. I cringe. My last kiss came from Bruce the day after I'd told him I didn't want to see him anymore, when he pinned me down and mashed his disgusting mouth onto mine. Not the type of memory a girl dreams of. I crush the tissue in my fist and am about to toss it into the Bellesport Recycles bag when Solange makes a brushing gesture over her front teeth. "Not so fast. Check your teeth."

Sukie had always gone through this ritual before leaving her house. First applying lipstick that matched her nail polish, then blotting, then glancing in her silver mirror at her straight white teeth. Holding the silver mirror at half an arm's length, I scrub an offending dot of red lipstick "What do you think?" I part my lips, imitating the posed smiles on the plump-lipped beauties in Solange's magazines.

Solange nods. Disappointment lines her tight smile. I understand—she's waiting for me to acknowledge Jake's offer.

I check my fake alligator clutch bag for my cell phone. "Okay, I'll give Dad another chance. I'll call him later."

I'm supposed to meet Elliot in his room so we can make a grand entrance into the gymnasium-sized recreation room, where the Highfield Halloween Costume Ball is being held. I decide it's okay to meet him in his room because, well, this is Elliot, not Bruce. *Besides, I move faster than he can.* The minute this thought pops up, I feel ashamed. Completely, thoroughly ashamed. Or worried. This is my first date since Bruce, although Elliot didn't call it that. Still, the entire thing, right down to dressing in costume, was his idea. What else could this be?

Before meeting him, I stop on the third floor to show Sukie my costume. Other than the muted sounds of canned laughter coming from a resident's television, the corridor basks in luxurious silence. A young blond nurse with a ring in her right nostril sits behind the nurses' station thumbing through a cumbersome file. When she looks up, I introduce myself.

"Oh, I know who you are." The nurse waves her forefinger at me. "You're the spitting image of your grandmother. And let me tell you, she's a hoot."

I don't know what this woman, someone my brother would dub a Hare Krishna wannabe, means. "Has she done something wrong?"

She drops her head back and lets out a throaty chortle. "Not on your life. Your grandmother stopped here about fifteen minutes ago. I didn't know she could be so funny. She set her elbow right here on this counter . . ." she gives the counter a couple of friendly taps, "and looked at me real serious, like my nose was where my left eyebrow is supposed to be. I figured she was about to say something hysterical about my nose ring, but she didn't. Instead, she asked, "Shouldn't you be out on a date tonight?""

"No kidding? My grandmother said that?" I shake my head in disbelief. I might have laughed out loud if Sukie hadn't said the same thing to me twenty-four hours after I'd nearly been raped. I take a deep breath and try to hold it, but it escapes with a *whoosh*. Well, tonight I *am* on a date. *Is it normal to be this nervous?*

"Before I forget, these are for my grandmother." I hand the nurse a plastic shopping bag. "I bought her two dozen pairs of socks."

The bag rustles as the nurse takes out a pair of blue, orange and purple striped anklets with slip-proof soles. "How cool are these?"

I shoot her an appreciative grin; when I use slang at home, my mother calls me "common" and threatens to ship me off to live at the Y. "Ordinarily, my grandmother doesn't wear loud colors. But with the way the laundry loses her socks, I figured loud was good,"—*I can hear my mother dialing 621-YWCA*—"hopefully the staff will recognize them as hers and return them."

"You realize we can't stop residents from walking in and out of one another's rooms. If something attracts their eye, they take it. Things are mucho communal-like. Once a week one of the aides goes from room to room, returning things that have strayed. But that doesn't guarantee they'll make it to their rightful owners."

"That's why I bought this." The only good thing about wearing high heels is that I can reach over the counter without standing on tiptoes. I dig to the bottom of the bag and pull out a mesh laundry bag. Across it in enormous letters, I've written: ***CYNTHIA'S SOCKS***.

"If the staff would agree to put her socks in her laundry bag and keep it in her closet," I turn and point in the direction of my grandmother's room, "each morning she'd have a fresh pair of socks. I hate seeing her walking bare-footed. It reminds me of Anna, her friend who just died." Even though Marion warned me that Alzheimer's leaves no survivors, I tell myself that isn't going to happen to Sukie. *Wearing these socks will keep her alive.* "What do you think?"

The nurse hesitates. Her face scrunches into a skeptical wrinkle that makes her nose ring stand on edge. "We can try. I'll leave a note for the day shift and ask them to tell the night shift to keep her clean socks in her laundry sack." The hair at the back of my neck stands on end. Getting information from one person to the next is like playing telephone, the game where the first player whispers her message to the next person, who whispers it to the next, who repeats it to the next. By the time the message reaches the last player, it's so mangled the first player can't recognize it.

The game is supposed to be funny, but thinking about its impact on Sukie makes me sad. The nurse is trying to help me understand that the likelihood of staff following through on a special request like mine is low. The little voice inside me warns that no matter how hard I try to keep Sukie's feet in socks, someday what happened to Anna is going to happen to her.

Halfway down the corridor by the TV room, Sukie spots me. "What are you doing here so late, young lady?" Her eyes twinkle as she hurries toward me.

"I'm going on a date and I wanted you to see my dress. Are you ready?" Still walking toward me, Sukie nods. I step back and pivot, slowly modeling the inset dolman sleeves, the fitted bodice with a wide violet belt that matches the dress's rich rayon fabric. Then I point to the sleek straight skirt with a kick-pleat that goes from my knee to my thigh and shows off the black seam on my stockings. Solange and her seamstress thought of everything, right down to my fake alligator pumps with stacked heels.

Sukie's expression changes from surprise to faint recognition. I hold my breath, hoping she'll say something about the dress design. She approaches me, one thoughtful step at a time. When she reaches me, she takes my shoulders and turns me around for another look. "Hmm," she murmurs appreciatively, "you're quite the looker." The nurse giggles.

Sukie pats my shoulders, wide with padding, and runs her fingertips over the double-stitched seams, the telltale mark of one of her creations. "I like this: let's keep it," she whispers as though she were back in her studio above the barn, evaluating each feature of her latest design, keeping some, discarding others.

"Most of all, I like this." She cups her palms around the fuchsia fabric peony on my shoulder. "Where did you get such a beautiful flower?"

This is the Sukie I miss. More than anything, I want her back for good. I'm afraid if I say the wrong thing, I'll break this magical spell. "A wonderful seamstress made it for me."

Sukie regards me with awe. "I made flowers like that one. I sewed them on hats..." she runs her fingers over my hair, slicked tight to my head, rolled and pinned into a golden brown sausage at the nape of my neck, "on dresses, and on beautiful girls like you..." her voice drifts off, taking memory along. Sad now, she stares at the wall clock as though expecting its tick-ticking to bring back her glory days.

Something precious has just happened.

That burst from memory's corridor vanishes with a *whoosh* so real that I shiver. I flex my fingers hoping to catch it, but it's too late. The wondrous moment has passed. My chest aches with guilt for having made Sukie sad and from greed, because I long for more of these moments. From the expression on Sukie's face, she does, too. Memory's glimmer has twin faces: that of delight and of loss. Treat and Trick.

Unlike Sukie, Elliot is getting better and will one day leave this place. No matter where he lands, his room will always be a mess. "A reflection of me," he likes to say. And he's right. Resting on a portable steel sawhorse by the window is a disemboweled lawn mower engine. Strewn along the wide marble windowsill, projects in varying stages of repair: two blenders, a portable sewing machine, a dark greasy mass of gears that reek of lubricating oil. On the ceiling above his bed, a poster of a moto-cross rider, feet firmly planted on pedals, legs angled like a prize-winning jockey's, butt high above his air-bound bike. Tacked to his bulletin board, 8x10 glossies of the fiberglass racing boats Elliot built. Taped to the bottom-most part of the bulletin board's frame, a new photo: an 8x10 of the remains of the boat that chewed off his legs. Across its destroyed bow, lettered in somber black: MOBY DICK.

I've been through enough psychological test batteries to estimate that Elliot and I are intellectual equals, both in the gifted range, maybe higher. He has an amazing capacity to latch on to mathematical and spatial concepts. Between his muscular build and the outdoor hobbies he participated in, he is, or was, a natural athlete. As far as his ability in the social arena, he has potential as a sociopath, con man, or a politician, I'm not sure which.

He can charm his way past the plainest nurses, not to mention the handful of retired Marines moonlighting as Highfield Security Guards. He confessed to distracting them by chatting them up, then watching as they keyed their way into the Anne Fitzgerald Unit. Later, he let himself in and made himself at home, munching popcorn and watching re-runs of *Jeopardy* with Sukie. He can imitate the janitor's Indian accent, the way the head nurse on his unit pops pills out of blister packs, and Barack Obama on an oratorical roll. He is a master impersonator if ever there was one.

All of which makes me question whether any part of his Mr. Congeniality, I-Can-Do-Almost-Anything-and-Convince-You-to-Do-the-Same personality is original. It occurs to me that I have yet to see the true Elliot, uncluttered by his Velcro-like ability to adopt other people's likes and dislikes as his own.

I settle my eyes on him and take him in, ridiculous grin and all. Thanks to the spray-painted silver cardboard box he's sheathed in, he sits straighter than ever in his wheelchair. A papier-mâché heart dangles from the silver ribbon around his neck. The same expandable silver tubing that carries lint from my mother's dryer encases his arms from his shoulders to his wrists. From his waist down, a pair of sweatpants, legs stuffed and lifelike, match his breastplate.

My thoughts swarm like angry bees. I plant my fists, fake alligator clutch and all, on my hips and glare at him. "How dare you dress like that?"

"What? Because you have this thing about the Wizard of Oz, you own the rights to the costumes?" He's not smiling anymore; he's clutching his papier-mâché heart.

"You could have told me you were going to do this." Our voices are dangerously loud.

A nurse with squeaky shoes stops in the doorway. "Everything okay in here?"

"Fine" is our answer. Simultaneous. Abrupt. Pissy.

I wait until the squeaking fades. "You could have asked before you—"

"Before I created the most imaginative version of the Tin Man known to Highfield? Have some respect, Birdie. You're speaking to the sure winner of first prize—a week's worth of Dunkin' Donuts coffee coupons, compliments of Highfield. Besides, I thought you'd come as Dorothy tonight, and I wanted to surprise you."

"Oz is the world *I* escape to, Elliot, not you. I may talk about it every once in a while—"

He rolls his eyes. "You talk about it a lot. More than you know. More than I'd expect for someone . . ."

"Go ahead, say it—for someone my age. I don't care." I fold my arms across my flat chest and look around. The place is filled with other people's stuff. "If we're going to talk about things that don't fit—what's the deal with all this junk? This isn't a garage, it's a rehab center."

His face softens. "That's right, and that's why 'all this junk' is here. It is rehab. What's your excuse?"

"I know what you're doing. You're trying to make me feel like a tool. But I won't let you. And you're not going to horn in on the place I escape to, even if it seems childish. I've got my reasons for hanging on to it, no matter how ridiculous it seems."

He's gazing at the floor, nodding like an old man struck by a special memory. One that brings back a sadness he tries to bulldoze aside. "And you're not going to take my hiding place from me," he says quietly.

I see what he's driving at—I never imagined a guy needing a safe place like the one I keep for myself. I feel like dirt. But I'm still angry with him for flipping my escape place and morphing it into his. "I think you're . . ." I start to say, until he places his hands on his sweat pants and crinkles whatever he's stuffed them with.

The other day he told me he can feel his legs as if they still exist and that every once in a while his body jerks like it's about to get up out of his wheelchair and walk away. That more than anything, he wants to believe what it's telling him. That one day he forgot, tried to get up and nearly fell. Ghost memory—the body's way of hanging on to the past it holds dear. It's what we two have in common. It's why I've chosen him to be my first date of this, my new life.

Elliot pats his sweat pants gently as though they were pet retrievers. "This is the first time since last summer I've looked down at two whole legs."

"You planned all this," I scan the room with my finger. "You made a big deal about gathering all this junk. You schmoozed the staff into letting you get away with your schemes. You're doing all this to prove to everyone, yourself included, that there's more to you than . . ." My eyes drop to his sweatpants. If I'm not careful, I'll cry.

"Okay, Miss 1940's super model, and a terrific looking one at that, you've figured me out. I'm like you. I need to pretend, too." I agree with him, though he's closer to the truth than he knows: I fit better as a 40's super model than I do as a twenty-first century kid.

He takes my hand and gently plays with the little finger that healed with an inward curve after I'd broken it. It's as if he's reminding me the only true way to comfort is by going inward. I check him over from the inverted funnel on his head to his silver sneakers. "Okay, I'll share my special place, but you're not done yet."

"I was hoping you'd help me with that." He hands me a tube of *Thompson's Theatrical Make-up, Silver. Safe and easy to remove. No scrubbing required.*

I've never touched his face before. After all the trouble I got into last spring, I thought I'd never want to be this close to a boy again. But this boy is different, and not because of his legs. I start at the round of his broad forehead, daubing gently over the scar from his accident and work outward, easing the cool silver cream around his honest hurting eyes, down the root of his nose to its upturned bulb—stopping when he asks me to hand him a mirror so he can watch—in and around his dimples, over his strong angled jawbone and chin. My shins tingle as they press against his stuffed legs. I bend over and kiss him lightly on his lips. He kisses me back, smearing silver cream over my red lipstick. We look in the mirror and laugh. I can't help myself; I kiss him again, only this time longer.

I haven't felt this happy in forever. Yet, he hasn't asked why I'm wearing this costume. Why instead of coming as Dorothy, I chose to dress like Sukie would have when she was young. In admitting his need to have a place to hide, he shared something special. Something he doesn't tell everyone. I like that. I want to tell him something special in return. As I finish his makeup, I tell him about the socks I delivered to Sukie and my plan to stop her from going barefoot. At first this doesn't sound as personal as what he told me, but as I finish, I realize how bone-biting personal it is.

So does Elliot. His head jerks to a skeptical tilt. I pull back, a gob of make-up on my fingertip. "Don't fool yourself, Birdie. Your solution to your grandmother's losing her socks isn't going to do what you want it to."

"And what is that, exactly?" I sound like a smart-ass, but I'm terrified of what he's about to say.

"You hope your grandmother is going to get better because you've come up with a handy idea, but she won't. Face it. Your grandmother's like me, she lost something that isn't going to grow back." Except for the in-out sounds of the oxygen machine across the hall, the room is silent.

"I've been thinking about that," I say bravely, which is a lie. I'm not ready to let him know he plunked his finger on a tender spot that makes me want to crawl onto his lap. The red flags my therapist warned me about flap madly. I distract myself by smearing silver cream over his blabby lips. "Just because your life and Sukie's are different now doesn't mean they can't be good."

That skeptical tilt of his head again. "You really believe that?"

"I'm trying to." I thump his papier-mâché heart. It's as hollow as my father's promise to come get me the minute I call.

Chapter 12:

My feet are on fire. My stacked heels may have matched my Halloween outfit, but in the process they mangled my toes and knotted my calves. I hike my bottom onto a kitchen stool by the island. One by one, I drop the torture instruments in double thud somersaults to the tile floor. Each clatter to a satisfying death. "Shh, you'll wake your father," Solange whispers as though that would undo the noise I've already made.

Besides, I could care less about my father's sleep patterns. He was supposed to be up, standing here beside me, asking about Elliot, the dance, whether I had a good time, and when he was going to meet "this Elliot fella." I'm still digesting all that happened tonight when I realize how bratty and ungrateful I must seem to Solange, who has gone silent. I could kick myself. I owe her a lot, but can't stop myself from feeling annoyed with her, too.

If she hadn't been so willing to do my father's errands for him, he would have *had* to come to get me. If not for her, he would have *had* to keep his promise. When I called him, which is what he'd asked me to do, Solange answered. Apparently, Jake had scratched his name from my birth certificate and replaced it with Solange's.

"Why don't you change into something more comfortable?" By way of suggestion she pinches the shoulder of her baggy sweatshirt, stretches it a couple of inches, and releases it cockeyed onto her shoulder. "In the meantime I'll make you a cup of cocoa. How's that sound?"

It's hard to stay angry with this brand of kindness, especially when the person offering it has little to do with the fact that your father doesn't give two honks about you. From what my mother told me, he'd been the one who'd tagged me, the baby who was supposed to revitalize their flagging marriage, "our last mistake."

My introduction into their life had the opposite effect. Their petty arguing swelled, taking up more space than their shaky household could spare. Depleted after pouring energy into raising four wildly successful kids, by the time I showed up, their parenting cupboard was bare. Not one crumb left.

So, my finger-painting with red-and-green striped toothpaste on an important legal brief propelled my father's temper to the top of Mount Vesuvius. And, yep, he erupted. That morning as he set his lukewarm mug of coffee down, he lifted my tiny shame-faced chin from my chest and said, "I forgive you because you are and always will be our most beautiful and most enduring mistake. E.M. for short." But couching my new tag within his typical soft-spoken humor did nothing to offset a little girl's hurting, guilt-ridden heart.

"Cocoa sounds good," I mumble. As I pick up my shoes, I wonder whether Jake told Solange about my nickname, the initials that sounded more like an advertisement for used cars than anything you'd label a little girl with. Thank goodness, Sukie put a stop to those bruising letters. Crackling with intolerance, she suggested that Jake call me by my baptismal name, Abby, or "Hummingbird," the confection of a name she'd come up with. Incapable of arguing with Sukie, from then on he called me "Birdie."

After scrubbing the pancake makeup from my face and combing the sausage roll out from the nape of my neck, I slip into my sweats and fleece-lined scuffs. They lap comfortably at my heels as I enter the kitchen. Solange stirs the warming milk, her wooden spoon creating swells of sweet-smelling cocoa.

I'm angry with Jake for not picking me up and with myself for believing tonight would be different. On the way home, I took my disappointment out on Solange, giving her the nastiest of punishments—the full-fledged silent treatment: arms locked across my chest, lips glued, shoulder mashed against the passenger side door.

To Solange's credit, she's not a bit like Jake: no slouching behind the wheel, no snorting with each angry thought, no shooting the bird at drivers stupid enough to cut her off. She possesses an uncanny tolerance for silence, the kind a daughter retreats into when she doesn't know where else to go with her hurt. But Solange didn't deserve to be treated so poorly.

"The costume party was fun," I say, taking the wonderfully warm mug from Solange, breathing in the velvety aroma, then sipping. "Mmm, good. I've never had cocoa with a peppermint stick in it. This is delicious." Solange doesn't have any make-up on, which I hadn't noticed until now. Without it, her pretty features are softer, less ferocious than the sales rep persona she projects during her working day. "Thank you, Solange. For everything. For helping me with my costume and for chauffeuring me back and forth from the dance." She blushes. "Really, you're one of the best things to happen to me today."

"Was it that bad a day? I thought you said you had a good time with Elliot."

"I did, but not until we had a go-around." Solange settles on a stool while I tell her that Elliot accused me of being unable to accept Sukie's Alzheimer's. Reluctantly, I admit, "The awful thing is—he's right." I sip my cocoa before going on.

"Sukie wasn't in the TV room having coffee with everyone early this morning, so I went to look for her. I overheard a couple of aides whispering about a woman who died unexpectedly. I thought they meant Sukie. I nearly mowed one of them down as I bolted toward Sukie's room, promising God if He spared Sukie, I'd try harder with Jake."

Solange sucks in a startled breath, closes her eyes, and moves her head from side to side. Her reaction is awful and wonderful at the same time. She knows what it was like for me, running down that hallway, bargaining with God, and her reaction is as painful as mine. My heart pounds with relief—I was entirely wrong about Solange; there is more to the big pharma queen than she lets on.

I feel badly about upsetting her.

"It wasn't Sukie," I explain, "it was another woman who died." A cascade of ice cubes rumbles into the automatic dispenser. I twist toward the stainless steel door half expecting to see the woman, staring at me. "Her name was Anna and she was beautiful in a fragile sort of way. She had long gray braids and sat still as a statue in her wheelchair. She was much younger than Sukie and had been the vice president of a bank.

When I finally found Sukie, she didn't say a word about Anna. She grabbed my arm and pulled me away from Anna's room. Sukie knew. She gripped my arm. Her dilated pupils said it all—she didn't want that to happen to her." I pause. "Neither do I."

Solange reaches across the counter and squeezes my hand. "I don't know what's worse, the helpless feeling you have as you watch a loved one being dragged through a cruel disease, or having your entire family snatched from you in an instant." Her fingers slide off mine.

She studies her hands, glances at me, then checks her hands again—she's debating whether or not to talk about the accident that claimed her family. I dread hearing about it. Not that I haven't heard bits and pieces about the tragedy; I have. Large families are fertile grounds for gossip. In my family, I'm the least interested in gossip; I have a hard enough time wrapping up my own grief and tucking it deep inside. When I hear about someone else's tragedy—especially someone I care about—it rips the gooey protective scab from my emotions and makes me ooze.

Solange opens her mouth as though she's about to say something, then presses her lips downward into a scowl. The faucet drips in a one-two-three-splatter rhythm that drums more loudly with each passing second. Solange's eyes narrow with thought. I wish I hadn't reminded her of death. I don't mean to sound unsympathetic, but I consider leaving her with her memories; I don't think I can handle another sad story, not with Sukie the way she is. Just as I slip my foot off the upper rung of the stool, Solange stands.

"What bothers me most about losing my family is that I didn't have a chance to say good-bye." She clicks her thumbnail against the nail on her ring finger. "We were on the train from Chicago to North Dakota to visit friends who owned a llama farm. I had this thing about llamas and had collected every llama that I could fit into my room: magazine pictures, posters, ceramic llamas, stuffed llamas, llama pajamas, llama-print curtains, you name it. My mother let me have them as long as I dusted everything. Going to the llama farm was my seventeenth birthday present." She sucks her bottom lip in and nods as if to say, See what happened? I should have gone to a keg party with my friends.

I like imagining sophisticated Solange propped on her elbows on a sunny Saturday afternoon by the river, drinking beer, burping, and peeing in the woods like my brothers and their friends. At the traitorous age of seven I spied on such a scene, hightailed it home, and interrupted my parents' argument with news of my brother's party. Of all my attempts to bring my parents together, this was one of my most successful. The arguing stopped. "What did you say Benjamin was doing?" they asked in unison. After grounding him, he called me the fifth apocalypse after conquest, war, famine, and death, but he'd lived to take it back. Not so with Solange's brother.

Hands curled around the edge of the stove, elbows jutting just as my mother's had the day I ratted on my brother, Solange takes a deep breath. "I won't bore you with the gruesome details."

I shake my head in agreement, jarring my rhinestone comb loose.

"You've probably heard that the train derailed."

I murmur sorry, I had.

"And that I was the only one of my family to survive."

I nod.

Solange pulls her shoulders forward and drops them back in a helpless shrug. "I packed my llama collection into boxes, sealed them tight and stashed them in the attic." She glances at the ceiling. "For years I went around feeling guilty, as though I'd done something to cause the accident. My therapist tried to help, but the emptiness never went away. When I stopped seeing my therapist, I predicted the grieving would never stop." Her eyes travel appraisingly from the refrigerator to the sink, to the table by the window, to the butler's pantry, to the island. "If it wasn't for your father . . ." she pauses, "and you, I'd be alone. That's one of the reasons why it's so important for me to bring this family together."

She puts her arms out and gives me a delicious hug.

I offer to show her the project I'm doing for school. Pleasantly surprised, she says, "I'd love to see it."

We carry our cocoas up to my hideaway on the third floor. Once the servants' quarters, the small rooms spill like stars from a large center room. Under the eaves in each room are three long built-in drawers with wrought iron pulls shaped like half-shells. The adjacent ginger-colored walls are long enough to place one twin bed against each. Cocoa-colored spruce floors connect one wall to the next like a rippling blanket on a crowded beach. Opposite, a small rectangular window topped with an eyebrow window peers out over the back yard.

This is the first time I've brought Solange here, far from the distractions of the adult world, into my hideaway. Despite room after room of delicious space begging for clutter, this attic is, for the most part, vacant.

"So, you've made this into your refuge," Solange says with a giggle. "This space has been begging for someone like you to carve out a little den." She gazes approvingly at the old maple desk chair and matching desk I positioned under the window with a floor lamp between it and an upholstered armchair with a broken spring.

"You can sit in the armchair, if you don't mind the broken spring."

Solange slips one leg beneath her and, as she lowers herself into the chair, I wrap the afghan my mother gave me around her knees. "Between this and the heat from the lamp, you'll stay toasty warm."

"Hmmm, thanks." Solange's purring makes me realize that tonight was just as trying for her as it was for me, maybe more so.

I open the three-ringed binder decorated with photos of Sukie's tulips, her favorite flower. "This is the log I'm keeping on my activities on the Anne Fitzgerald Unit."

I flip the colored tabs one at a time and show Solange each section. First, the red tab labeled *Medications*. Behind it, a chart that lists the medications Sukie is being given, along with the date she started each one, its dosage, and any reactions and responses she has to them. "My sister, Marion, helped me decide which information I should track." Solange nods with appreciation.

I show her the blue tab on which I've lettered *Observations.* "It's my daily log of what Sukie says and does, the circumstances under which each event takes place, the date, time, and weather. This section has the most information."

Behind the orange tab is Sukie's *Weight Chart.* "Changes in weight are very significant for someone with Alzheimer's," I tell Solange.

Classes/Conferences is written on the green tab. "I haven't been to any Case Conferences—that's where the entire treatment team: nurses, social worker, dietician, recreation worker discuss Sukie—but one is coming up pretty soon."

I show Solange the yellow tab, last in my log, where I keep my questions. "It's getting longer every day."

Solange beams. "That's an impressive piece of work. Very professional. What will you do with all that information?"

"It'll be part of my final report. The teacher said I can't show him the binder itself unless Sukie or her healthcare Power of Attorney—that would be Dad—signs a release. That's to ensure Sukie's privacy, which is good."

"You sound like your father when you talk about your grandmother's right to privacy. You're learning a lot of useful stuff."

I blush with pleasure. That's exactly how I feel.

Solange leans forward, presses her mouth into an impish half-grin. Her eyes sparkle with mischief. "Now I have something to show you. I'll be back in a tad."

She tiptoes downstairs and within seconds the door to my father's study creaks open. A minute later, she's back. "You won't believe this." If it hadn't been for the fact that she was carrying a three-ringed binder, I'd have guessed that she had the winning lottery ticket. She presses the binder into my lap. "Take a look."

Super professional, the white binder has computer-generated section dividers. The topics on the dividers are the same as the ones in the binder I made for Sukie, plus a few I don't have: *Physician's Orders, Phone Log, Family Observations, Physical Therapy, Occupational Therapy, Speech and Language Therapy.* "Who's this for?" I ask.

"Look on the front page."

"Are you sure? What if this belongs to one of Dad's clients? It could be confidential."

"I don't think he'll mind if you take a peek."

By now, I'm getting nervous. Jake once gave me what-for for reading a file he'd left on his desk. That was long before Solange. I'm not sure about this. I plant my hands by my side.

"Go on," Solange urges. "Open it."

After helping me with my costume, coming to get me, then staying up to make me hot cocoa, I should have known this last surprise would be her best: Jake's binder. On the first page he'd typed in bold Times New Roman, **Cynthia Windsor**.

Jake did care. Kind of.

Chapter 13:

The oak tree in front of Highfield was the last to drop its leathery leaves. Other trees were done with theirs—the maples long gone, the ash's shriveled past recognition, and spiny skeletons all that remain of the Japanese pricker bushes. November's cold temperatures and the dwindling daylight had convinced the oak to give up its leaves earlier than usual. But not without a fight. I like a tree with attitude.

By now, most critters had taken the hint and departed. So had Anna, the lady with shoulder-length braids, the bedridden yet elegant Mr. Hartwell, and the crowing Hazel. Sukie then befriended Lucy, the little lady with greasy hair whose only words were, "I live at 87 Pine Street. Please take me home." But as of today, even Lucy was gone.

Sukie is understandably upset. My voice cracks as I try to soothe her with, "Lucy went to heaven to be with Hazel and Jesus," a version of what Sukie told me when my Cocker Spaniel, William, had died. She's so busy blowing her nose, she doesn't scold me for wiping my eyes on my sleeve. I wonder if she feels like Solange, guilty for being alive? Does she wish she'd kissed her friends good-bye? Told them how much she loved them? Sukie hurries down the corridor, slips into her room and slams the door. The sound reverberates, then fades into tense silence. From Sukie's room, an awful scraping sound, the screeching of furniture being dragged across the linoleum floor, draws Robin and Iris to her door. They signal me to stay behind. I feel more helpless than ever.

I try to concentrate on the last of my morning chores, but Sukie's agonized shouting knocks my thoughts into a tailspin. She's barricaded herself in her room and won't let anyone in. Robin said it would be best if I left her alone, that attempts to comfort her will only aggravate her. That eventually she'd calm down. It's all I can do to stay at this end of the hall when she's at the opposite end, hurting. Not physically, Robin assured me. Sukie has not been injured. But she is in pain. There's anger in her voice. Robin said she's confused. I hear loss.

During November, lots of things drop from sight—daylight, leaves, people, I muse as I sort through the notices on the staff bulletin board. I worry that Sukie might disappear, too, and, finding that too scary to think about, return to clearing the orange, blue, and green flyers from the bulletin board that announce outdated training sessions. A flowered clipboard with the vignettes I'd written about Sukie's life hangs on a picture hook to the right of the now tidy bulletin board. I've added lines beneath each vignette, so the person who reads it can sign his or her name. Mrs. Perducci liked this idea so much she offered employees additional training credits each time they read one of my stories. "These will give our caretakers the chance to see your grandmother as a person with a full life, not just as a woman with Alzheimer's," she said, her bright expression knotting when she mentioned the beast.

Outside Sukie's door, Iris waits with Sukie's lunch tray. "I don't want it. Stay out of my house," Sukie yells. Implicit in her snarl is the threat that should Iris open the door, Sukie would send the tray air-bound. I shudder at the possibility. Earlier that morning, when Iris tried to help Sukie tie her shoes, Sukie scratched Iris's arm. From inside the bedroom, the slamming of drawers and cabinet doors pounds a drumlike warning.

I clench my jaw and blink furiously. My throat aches from fighting the impulse to cry. Suddenly, more than anything else, I want to call Jake and hear him tell me he'll rush right over. I imagine him hugging Sukie, then me. It would be the first time since Sukie left home that he's visited her. Now, I really want to bawl, a real soaker.

The slamming continues. Iris returns Sukie's untouched tray to the meal cart and disappears into another room. I convince Robin to page the doctor on duty. She's learning just how pesky I can be.

"Dr. Len has 296 other patients here," she says when I complain about him taking too long to return her call. "The minute your grandmother started to escalate we removed her roommate and the other residents from that wing. We checked to make sure there's nothing in her room that can hurt her. I know it sounds strange, but that's how we do things here."

Robin tries to sound reassuring, but her anxiety oozes. "I gave your grandmother a dosage of Ativan, a medication that will help her relax. She'll calm down soon." Recently, Sukie had started pacing, grabbing other residents, and ramming their walkers with the one she now uses. Solange said Robin and the staff are rattled by the "contagion factor," the possibility that other residents will imitate Sukie.

As if Robin has read my thoughts, she adds, "I hope you understand, I can't allow three-year-old behavior in your grandmother or in anyone else on this unit. It's not safe." She suggests I'd be better off spending the day downstairs in Physical Therapy. "Do you have a cell phone? I'll call when your grandmother is ready to come out of her room."

I want to stay. "You may need me. When Sukie acted like this at home, I was the only one she would talk to." I don't tell Robin that Sukie never tried to hurt Pop-Pop or me. My stomach makes swishing noises, the kind that leads to a major bout of diarrhea; Sukie doing battle with the beast is making me sick. I take a stale peppermint from my pocket, unwrap its brittle cellophane, and pop it into my mouth.

Within the last few weeks, Sukie has morphed from a social butterfly who hovered around the nurses, asking what she could do to help, into a loner who paces the halls in her walker. If she isn't pacing, she's sleeping. Early last week, she woke to me rubbing her arm and calling her name. Her eyes fluttered open. "I must have taken a little snooze," she said as though it were an unusual occurrence. Toward the middle of the week, she complained of "feeling strange, like someone else is living in my body." By the end of the week, I found Sukie in the TV room slumped, sound asleep, her face on her knees. No matter how much I massaged her back, kissed her cheek, or called her name—all the things she loved—I couldn't rouse her.

A tear dribbles down my cheek; I'm afraid she's going to die, just like Lucy and Hazel and the others. I feel more panicky than ever. If I don't do something quickly, I'll lose Sukie. Then all the Ativans in the world won't calm me down.

"Something is terribly wrong. Please look at my grandmother," I complain to Robin.

Preoccupied with a new resident, she dismisses me with what I've come to think of as a textbook mantra: "The decline in your grandmother's behavior, her inability to function in a group, and her increasing agitation are functions of her dementia. Those things happen to everyone with Alzheimer's."

Fuck you, I silently fume. "A function of her dementia" explains nothing. Robin never bothers to ask what might be causing Sukie's agitation. Instead, she lumps Sukie's distress into "a function of her dementia."

But why? I get upset and I don't have dementia. Robin gets upset and she doesn't have dementia. Why doesn't Robin connect Sukie's agitation to Lucy and Hazel's deaths, or to something else, something we don't know about? Doesn't

Robin understand how hard it is for Sukie to find words to tell us what's bothering her? THAT'S PART OF DEMENTIA, TOO. Like a three-year-old, when Sukie's words fail her, she uses her behavior to tell us something is wrong. Which is exactly what she's doing now—signaling us that something is wrong. Terribly wrong.

My hand trembles as I clip this week's vignette on top of the others. So far, I've written about topics I'm sure Sukie will remember: the bridal gown she'd designed for Marion's wedding; her tradition of taking photos of the neighborhood kids in their Halloween costumes; her passion for bargain shopping; the trip she took on a Coast Guard buoy tender after she'd raised money for their morale fund; and today's topic: the elaborate meals she prepared for the holidays.

I'm grateful Mrs. Perducci didn't need a lengthy explanation about my clipboard project. She understood that brief, spirited stories would give the staff something specific to chat with Sukie about, which in turn provided Sukie the attention she craved, for a while.

After Hazel died, Sukie spent more time alone. She started making hostile statements, so unlike her. Yesterday, as I was getting ready to leave, she grabbed hold of my arm. "Get me out of this place. Take me home," she begged.

That bothered me. Not only because it ripped my heart out to leave her behind, but because a couple of months earlier, Sukie loved living here, where the circular hallways were long enough for her to enjoy her daily walk without worrying about getting lost. She loved the group activities that took place in the TV room. But best of all, she loved talking to the other residents, who never made faces when she chatted about whatever odd thing strayed into her mind. They didn't get upset when she interrupted them with stories about how Pop-Pop used to fry eggs for her lunch; they understood if she didn't tell them right then and there, that she'd forget what she wanted to say.

Not that she'd ever forgot Pop-Pop, she once told me, but she was so busy, she didn't have time to think about him. "I never thought I'd be happy without my sweetie," she confessed. And that led me to think that maybe, just maybe Sukie had found a different kind of happiness. I was wrong.

I press the latest in my series of vignettes against the clipboard and open the clip. Before I can slide the new piece in, the aide who dressed my grandmother in a man's bathrobe hisses, "Well, look who decided to join the world." Sandis points to Sukie, shuffling toward us. Papers drift to my feet.

"You keepin' these?" she asks as she scoops up my stories. The glare from the overhead lighting makes the thin jagged scar through her eyebrow look grotesque. I don't have a chance to answer; Sukie is walking down the hall, screaming my name.

The circles under her eyes are darker than usual. Her hair is still flattened from sleep. She'd buttoned her blouse halfway down and put her brown lace-up shoes on the wrong feet. She stops by the water fountain. "Hummingbird, would you help me?" The harshness in her voice disappears. In its place is a preoccupied tone.

She takes four plastic pill cups the size of shot glasses from her pocket. One by one, she wipes each with her sweater, fills it with water, and sets it on the edge of the fountain.

Without understanding what she's doing, I hurry out from behind the nurses' station. "Coming, Sukie," I call.

Sukie never looks up. "Go into the cellar and bring up a dozen potatoes?" she asks, as though we were home in her kitchen. "Make that two dozen—we're having a houseful of company for dinner." Sukie raises her voice, but not unpleasantly, until she eyes Sandis. "You're not invited," she says childishly and returns to her work.

Clutching her hand to her large chest and pretending to be devastated, Sandis sashays her way toward her friend, Timtiere. "Stop laughing, you know what that does to her," warns the older aide, who moves a shock of streaked orange hair that has slipped across Sandis' eyes.

Sandis shrugs Timtiere's hand off her shoulder. "Did you tell your granddaughter about last night, Cynthia?"

"Just because we got stuck doing back-to-back shifts doesn't mean you can take it out on the patient. Come on, Sandis, let's go on our break."

A curdled grin, that of a playground bully, tugs at Sandis' lips. She rests her arm on the top of the nurses' station, making her position clear: time clock or not, she isn't about to miss the show. "Cynthia, tell your granddaughter the nasty thing you called me last night."

The air ripples with tension. Had Sukie said something about Sandis' scar? She doesn't usually make unkind remarks, except when she's not herself, "agitated" as Robin would say. Even so, I can't believe Sandis is provoking Sukie, especially after she had such a tough morning. Had Sandis gotten into trouble the other day for dressing Sukie in a man's bathrobe? Is that what's made her so angry? Whatever it is, she reminds me of Bruce, and that scares the hell out of me.

"Sukie, I've got the potatoes," I call, hoping to steer her from the aides.

"Well, where are they?" Her voice is harsh and her eyes harden as she glances from my empty hands into my face. Her look says, Liar.

"The potatoes are in the kitchen. You said you wanted to make dinner. Come on, I'll peel them for you."

Sukie slips her arm under mine, and we start walking. "That would be helpful, dear. I don't function the way I used to, you know. Besides..." she looks over her shoulder, then quickens her pace, "there's more funny business around here than I can tell you about. Hurry, let's get going."

"How about going for a walk?" I come across as ridiculously enthusiastic, but Sukie doesn't notice.

I guide her away from the aides into the TV room, but Sandis finds an excuse to join us. "Cynthia, darling, you gotta be tired today," she says as she scatters an armload of magazines on the table, "'cause you stayed up all night. You've been doing that a lot lately." Her calling my grandmother "darling" grates more than fingernails raking a chalkboard.

"I'm not surprised." I wouldn't ordinarily tell someone like Sandis about Sukie's habits, but I chance it, hoping she'll realize Sukie didn't mean to inconvenience the staff. "Sukie's a night owl. At home, she watched Jay Leno every night."

"Well, she doesn't do that here. After the others go to bed, she hangs around with the night staff." Sandis licks her bottom lip, implying something dirty. "And I'm not talkin' about the women."

Standing a little too close, saying some, but not all, of what she means creeps me out; she's lifted this act from Bruce's modus operandi.

I pry myself from Sukie's grip and slip between her and Sandis. If this were about me, I wouldn't have the guts to come right out and say this, but it's not; it's about Sukie: "You have no right to say things like that."

Even though I'm smaller than Sandis, she makes a point of peeking around me at Sukie, but Sukie turns away. "Cynthia, your granddaughter doesn't believe me. Tell her how you talk to the night staff, why don't you? For an old lady you sure know how to make us blush."

Timtiere rushes in, grabs hold of Sandis' arm and tries to pull her away.

Sukie straightens. "You shut up, scar-eye." No longer the confused, loving grandmother about to cook a meal for her family, this woman sounds deranged.

My eyes widen. "Sukie," I gasp.

Timtiere slaps her palm over her gaping mouth, but Sandis erupts into laughter. Sukie spins around, eyes narrow, lips taut. "Laugh? Who's laughing?" she asks, loud and demanding. She gazes suspiciously first at one aide, then the other.

"That's enough!" Timtiere says to Sandis. "You know the rules—we're not supposed to tell family members what goes on when they're not around. Come with me before you land us both in trouble."

"But the girl's interested in her grandmother or she wouldn't be here. She claims she wants to learn everything about old people. She thinks she can do a better job helping her grandmother than we can. Well, this little lady needs to know her grandmother has a history." Sandis grins again, so wide that the gold crown in the back of her mouth flashes like light in a dark smelly cave.

Beaming stupidly, she shoots Timtiere a that'll-fix-her-wink.

"That's enough. You need to go, before I call the supervisor." My voice squeaks. I feel helpless, a tool of a kid, giving an adult what for. But Sandis is no ordinary adult. Guffawing, the aides stop at the nurses' station and shoulder their fat gaudy purses.

I look up and down the corridor, searching for Robin and, within seconds, remember she's downstairs, admitting another new resident.

My face burns with humiliation: Sandis knew Robin wasn't around. And that she'd just set me up, choosing words which, if repeated, would paint me as the hysterical granddaughter reading too much into what she would describe as everyday chit-chat. Other than Timtiere, the staff avoids Sandis and is so scared of her that they wouldn't dare stick up for me. This feels like Granville High all over again; I'm alone. On my own. Only this time I'm like the oak tree that refused to give up its leaves; I have an attitude.

Chapter 14:

I plop myself and my attitude into the easy chair in Elliot's room. "My grandmother's in trouble," I blurt. And when the horrified reaction I expect from Elliot doesn't come, I slap my three-ring binder open and stifle a gag; the room reeks of dirty motor oil.

Elliot's left eyebrow arches the way it usually does when anyone barges into his sanctuary. He interrupts whatever he was doing on the small outboard engine and glances at me. He's situated his knees, padded with pillows for protection, as they're not entirely healed, between twin sawhorses bridged with planking, and has scootched his butt dangerously close to the edge of his wheelchair. Like a gladiator's helmet, the engine's small shell with "Honda" embossed in silver letters rests lopsided on the floor beside his open toolbox.

I try again. This time I pull my attitude in on a short leash. "Whenever Sukie had an argument with my dad, or when her closest cousin was diagnosed with breast cancer, she'd start banging her pots and pans around the kitchen and before long the counters overflowed with roasted chickens, potatoes, green beans, the works. Even though she can't go into her own kitchen, that's where she was pretending to be just now."

"What are you talking about? Did Sukie get herself a job in the kitchen?" Elliot chuckles, stopping his work long enough to gauge how I'm taking his humor.

I tap the air with my knuckles as though it's his forehead. "Knock, knock. Anyone home? If you expect me to make sense, forget it. Not much makes sense, that's why I'm here. I was hoping you'd help me figure it out. Instead, you're making stupid adolescent-boy remarks." *Sukie cooks when she's upset, and I pick a fight with the one person I trust who happens to be an idiot.* I flare my nostrils, take a deep breath, and let it escape as prolonged and obnoxious as possible.

"Okay, let's have it. Tell me everything. What happened?"

"At first I thought she was reacting to Lucy's death—"

"That's pretty important. You could have told me that from the get go."

"True, but it's more complicated than that." I tell him about Sandis and Timtiere and the awful things Sandis said in front of Sukie. "Something happened during the night shift."

He scoots himself back against his wheelchair. "Come on, Birdie. Everyone knows Sandis spends her spare time following the guys around. She's telling you *she's* got a history, not Sukie."

I run my finger back and forth across my lips and nod. "Hmm, I didn't know that about Sandis. But that doesn't give her the right to rile Sukie." I pause. "And why would Sukie have become so overly focused—intense is more like it—when Timtiere tried to keep Sandis from laughing?" Elliot scowls and I offer specifics in hopes he'll get the picture. "When Timtiere told Sandis to stop laughing, there was something about the word 'laughing' that grabbed Sukie's attention and made her angry. She wanted to know who was laughing, and if you'd heard her demanding tone, you'd have thought there was a law against laughter."

"The whole thing's bizarre." His adolescent-boy expression melts into a thoughtful one. "Let me ask you something. This may sound foolish, but bear with me: was Sukie looking directly at those aides when they started this laughter business?"

I roll my eyes up to the left and think. "No, she was facing the other direction. She spun toward them after

Timtiere scolded Sandis. Why? What difference does that make?"

"Didn't you tell me even though she has a hearing problem, if Sukie's interested in what's being said, she pays incredibly close attention and hears perfectly?"

"Yes, if it's juicy enough, she puts every ounce of energy into listening."

Disappointed I haven't read his thoughts, Elliot screws up his face. "Don't you get it? Hearing the word 'laughter' was like sounding a gong for Sukie. There's something about that word that registers big time with her. Don't you remember doing something bad when you were a kid? You hoped your parents didn't find out, but you weren't sure. You were on heightened alert: every time you heard them mention your name, you jumped out of your skin. It was the same for Sukie, except she was on heightened alert for the word, 'laughter.' That's why she picked up on it. What we don't know is what it means to Sukie."

I clap my hands to my mouth. "Oh my gosh, that's exactly what happened." I sink back into the chair. "That means—"

"She's hypersensitive because they *had* been laughing. Probably at her. Over what I don't know."

I bite my lip and release a long sigh. *So something had happened to Sukie.* I'm shocked and I'm not—I knew something was going on. Suddenly, I relive the fear I felt at school, where I became a victim. Now, Sukie is, too. My stomach sloshes with rage. "Oh, no I think I'm going to be sick," I moan, running into Elliot's bathroom.

The tile is hard and cold against my knees and shins. My elbows rest on the toilet seat and my hands prop my head up, ready to fall away should my stomach turn inside-out again.

There's a hesitant tap tapping on the door. "Birdie, you're awfully quiet. You haven't fainted have you? Tell me you're okay. Okay?" Elliot has smushed his lips in the space between the doorknob and the lock and is whispering. If I didn't feel so awful, it would be funny.

"I'm okay. Just give me a minute." I take a gulp of mouthwash from the bottle on the shelf and swish it around my mouth. Then I wash my face and dry it on rough paper towels.

Ten minutes later, I open the door and bump into Elliot's wheelchair. "Remind me to never again eat egg salad sandwiches from the employee cafeteria."

"Had it turned green?"

I shake my head. "You mean like 'green eggs and ham'?"

"At least your sense of humor is coming back. But you look like someone dunked you face first in a bucket of ashes." I like that he sounds worried. "My nurse said you were probably dehydrated and that you should sip this." He toasts me with a can of Canada Dry Ginger Ale and pours it, spitting and sizzling, into a tumbler.

I want to hug him for being so sweet, but the memory of wrestling with Bruce stops me. "Thanks," I say, wrapping my fingers around the plastic tumbler. The damp coolness feels good against my palm. As I lift the tumbler, teasing bubbles nibble at my nose. Elliot leans forward, eyebrows raised in hopes of witnessing my cure. I hate to disappoint him, but one swish of soda isn't about to rinse the distrust that has taken hold of me.

Besides, I need to concentrate on how to help Sukie. Elliot's right, this is complicated. The only thing I know for certain is that Lucy died today. The rest doesn't make sense: Sandis, who should have ignored Sukie, provoked her; and Sukie reacted viciously. The word 'laughter' caught Sukie's attention and brought out a terrifying ugliness in her. I'm afraid Sukie is no longer "in love" with Highfield, she's "in hurt." That's what bullying does to you.

I glance at the clock—almost three. That the aides will soon leave for the day is a temporary fix. More than anything, I wish I knew what had happened to Sukie. The woman from the Alzheimer's Association warned us that although Sukie might not remember the exact event, the feelings—good or bad—surrounding that event would linger. Elliot's nurse is right, the ginger ale soothes my stomach; I wish Sukie's situation were as easy to fix.

Chapter 15:

The air smells of snow. At 4:30, a windswept darkness closes in like a lid on a soup pot. Traffic buzzes with the urgency of parents taking last minute trips to Shaws to stock up on the pretzels, potato chips, sandwich meats, and DVDs their kids would need should this freak storm—"a November anomaly" was what the weatherman called it—materialize into a day off from school. I clutch my backpack with one arm and wave good-bye to the white transport van that just dropped me off. Because Elliot is sitting in the back of the van, his wheelchair secured by cargo straps to the floor, he sits taller than the driver, Gentleman George. As the van inches forward from the deep granite curb on Bigelow Street, the Highfield Health Center logo—an enormous blue heron taking flight—trains its eye on me. An eye with a skeptical glint.

The staff assured me they would take special care of Sukie tonight. Still, I didn't want to leave her, didn't want her to feel that I was abandoning her. I remember my father driving away on Christmas Eve when he left our family for good and my insides ache. I don't want Sukie to feel that way, now or ever. Without calling attention to myself, I stick my tongue out, just a little, at the heron.

Gentleman George steers the van into the traffic edging toward the bridge, and Elliot, twisting so he can see me through the back window, waves one last time before disappearing. I huff my pack onto my back and follow the slate walkway toward the three-story gold Victorian with cranberry and green trim. Shaped like an oversized business card, the gilded gold sign by the front door announces *Jacob Bartholomew Windsor, Attorney at Law*. Ordinarily, my father's tendency to go for the ostentatious sends my annoyance meter to the top of the Richter Scale. Today, his heavy-hitting presence gives me a sense of relief.

Coming to my father's office was Elliot's suggestion. "What else can you do? You tried his cell; you've got no choice."

I hesitated. I wasn't sure my father would help. And if he did, I'd hear about it for not telling him sooner. Of this I was certain: trouble in one form or the other was spinning my way. My father would probably unearth complications in Sukie's situation that I should have known about, and the entire business would become my fault. If he were annoyed enough, he might even send me back to my mother's. That would leave Sukie alone to face those vicious aides. And deep-six my chances of an early acceptance to Tufts. I scowled at Elliot. "You're right," I reluctantly admitted.

Elliot speed-dialed Gentleman George's cell phone and asked if he would give me a lift across town. "All set," he said, looking downright proud of scoring another point for his Mr. Get-'er-done reputation. "Look at it this way: the situation needs serious muscle. Regardless of how astute our collective brains might be, you've got to admit, we lack the gravitas that comes with age and a well-tailored suit." He'd crossed his eyes and mushed his face into the goofy smile that always gets to me.

But now that I'm alone outside my father's office, I feel like an intruder, like the time my brother talked me into spying through a hole in the fence at our newly married neighbors, frolicking in their in-ground swimming pool. There was no disguising the fact: I was about to invade the place my brother referred to as "the whale's belly." The place that swallowed our father whole and carried him farther and farther from his caustic wife and us, his boisterous family.

I never told anyone before admitting this to Elliot today, but every once in awhile I rode the bus here without getting off. Needing a formal invitation to drop in to see my father was unnatural and awkward, not to mention bizarre. After he left, my parents never argued about who could take the kids on which weekends, for which birthdays or holidays. My father simply left us with my mother. Other than checks to cover the costs of birthday gifts, Christmas presents, and clothes for school, we rarely heard from him.

Oh, he'd accept my calls if he wasn't busy with "one of his precious criminals" as my mother put it, but he didn't call me, and he never invited me to visit. Never brought me to the office on Take Your Daughter to Work Day to which my mother said, "You didn't miss a thing."

I place my hand on the brass doorknob and peek through the full-length lace curtains, hanging smartly, barely touching the beveled glass. This is Solange's signature window treatment: fabric anchored between upper and lower curtain rods, stretched taut without distorting its pattern. The raised brass vines beneath my palm surprise me with their soft feel. They remind me again of Solange, who lived in this house before she converted it into an office for my father. I peek through the lace at the tiled foyer and a lonesome black umbrella propped against the wall. There are two inside doors: one looks like the opening to a small closet, and the second, a tall and imposing panel of frosted, wood-encased glass, the entryway to my father's world.

My sneakers barely make a sound on the hexagonal black and white tiles. I don't mean to interrupt the receptionist, sitting at her desk by the fireplace, clacking away at her keyboard, but I can't stop the glass door from catching and sticking on the oriental carpet. An enormous draft wafts in. I bend over to straighten out the carpet, and as I stand, my backpack smacks the doorjamb, nearly knocking me off balance. My hands jerk upward and I scream, "Whoa!" The receptionist looks up and takes in my lame smile.

She's about Solange's age and she's wearing a short tight skirt and bright pink sweater that clings to her lanky figure. She pushes away from her desk and hurries over. "Are you all right?" she asks, reaching for my elbow. "I'm sorry about the door. Everyone has trouble with it. We've ordered a new carpet but for now, it's a beast."

That this bright-eyed woman uses the word 'beast' strikes me as a good omen and, despite associating it with Sukie's Alzheimer's, helps me relax. "Other than looking like a doofus, I'm okay, thanks. I usually make my entry with a little more…" I stop to search for the right word.

"Grace?" the woman laughs, and I giggle nervously.

"That would be one way of describing it. I'm sorry about barging in like that." *That's the second time I've apologized today. First Elliot, now this woman.*

She ushers me into the reception area, once a parlor, and motions for me to take a seat. I slough off my backpack and am about to lower myself onto the comfortable-looking leather sofa when she says, "You must be here to see your father."

My face goes slack with amazement. I hope I don't look dumbfounded. Or just plain dumb. "How did you know? I mean, we've never met before, have we?"

"You're right, we haven't." She extends her hand. "I'm Antonia, Toni for short. It's nice to finally meet you." Her hand is soft and warm, her handshake firm and kind.

"I'm Abby, but they call me Hummingbird, and to my dad I'm Birdie." Toni nods as though this is nothing unusual.

"To answer your question, Hummingbird, your father has a photo of you by the parallel bars the day you won first place at the gymnastic competition."

My jaw drops. "Real-ly?" Wildly delighted at his show of fatherly pride, I singsong the word. He'd agreed to come that day, but with all the people milling about, I couldn't find him and, believe me, I looked. Combed the bleachers. Searched each row until my coach stopped me from distracting myself. That's when I vowed to put on my best show so my father would feel extra awful for not showing. I make a mental note to ask my mother if, by chance, she'd given him that photo. I glance up at Toni, who takes in every nuance of my reaction, and quickly change the subject. "I tried my father's cell phone, but he must have turned it off."

"Did you leave a message?"

I shake my head. "I couldn't think of what to say that wouldn't upset him. I need to talk to him about my grandmother. It's kind of involved."

Toni tilts her head. Her eyes narrow with concern. "Has something happened that your father ought to know about right away?"

I'm not sure how much Toni knows about Sukie or whether I should impose on someone I just met. And I don't like the feeling that I ought to apologize for wanting to see my father. This is all too weird. Normal kids in normal families don't have to ask.

"I'm not entirely sure that I have all the pieces to a very long story. I just know that my grandmother gets very upset when she's with two aides in particular. And that they've said very nasty things to her, stuff that would make my father furious."

The last phrase hit hard. Toni lifts her head. "Sounds serious. How about I try to contact him for you?"

I take a deep breath; my insides quiver. "My dad is the only person who can help." I don't call him "Dad" very often, but it spills out so naturally that a surge of belonging shoots through me—him to me and me to him—that tells me I have every right to track him down. For the first time in a long time, I feel like his daughter. It's a feeling I could get used to.

Toni checks her watch. "He should be on his way to an appointment. After that he has another appointment followed by a dinner meeting. He's at the tail end of an overloaded day."

She walks toward the front door, then skillfully dislodges the carpet from under the door. I panic. *Hey, don't go, you said you'd help me,* I almost cry out.

Toni reads my mind. "It's late. Give me a second to lock the front door, then we'll go upstairs and make a few calls."

I sigh. Toni hears it and smiles. "Sorry," I say. "I guess I'm more nervous than I thought."

"Don't worry, I'm feeling a little nervous myself. Your father is very close to your grandmother. Whenever an update comes in regarding her condition, your father has asked me to interrupt him, no matter what he's doing or with whom. If he has questions, I call your grandmother's unit, then put the call through to him. I also type the content of the conversation, print it out and insert it in a three-ring binder that has your grandmother's information in it."

Without thinking, I place my hand over my pounding heart. "So that's how he does it." Toni looks puzzled. "Oh, Solange showed me his binder," I say by way of explanation. "I love that he collects information on my grandmother, but couldn't figure out where he found the time. I mean his records are sooo detailed." I blush; I sound like I'm my father's biggest fan, which is insane. "Anyway, now I know. Depending on what happens during the day, it might take me an hour to update the binder I keep on Sukie."

"You keep one, too? Really?"

As we start up the stairs, I reach over my shoulder and pat my backpack. "I carry it to and from the unit every day. If I have time at lunch, I jot a few notes and write them up when I'm home—I mean at my father's house." *Whoa, that was the first time I called my father's place, "home."* Do I mean it, I wonder? I glance at Toni to see if she notices my mistake. She hasn't. That's the third time something having to do with my father has taken me by surprise. What's more surprising is that I'm thrilled.

On the second floor, my father's office occupies a room that was once the master bedroom, running the full length of the house from front to back. A tall wide window frames the view of Bigelow Street below with neighboring Victorians occupied by other lawyers, accountants, and a few doctors. Placed to afford him a window side view, my father's antique desk, oversized and ornately carved, seems at ease in its gingerbread surroundings. Opposite it, on the other side of the room, between a pair of windows is a long sofa upholstered in zebra skin fabric and a couple of black leather chairs. Oriental rugs cover the oak floors.

Behind his desk is a rogues' gallery. With the exception of my mother, everyone is there: my only sister, Marion, in her cap and gown, reaching to receive her degree from the dean of Tufts Medical School; my oldest brother, Charles, squinting into the sunshine in Washington, D.C., after having argued and won his first case before the Supreme Court; Benjamin, second oldest, and the only engineer among us; and Timothy, just a few short months ago, unloading his car in front of his apartment near Boston University, the choice that wounded my father's ambition to land at least one of his sons at Harvard, his alma mater. And, blown up larger than Tim's photo, matted and framed to look bigger than any of the family photos, a picture of me—my father's enduring mistake—one hand resting on the parallel bars. I can't begin to say how deliciously happy this makes me.

I wander around while listening to Toni making call after call, thanking the person on the other end, then asking them, "If Jake happens to contact you, please have him call Toni at the office, or later, on her cell phone."

"I've asked your father to tell me when he changes his schedule," she says, clearly annoyed, "but he forgets." Toni shrugs her shoulders in apology for not locating him. I'm tempted to tell her not to be surprised; he's forever saying one thing and doing another.

The sick feeling that hit me earlier returns. The last thing I want to do is waste time in the bathroom. "Can we make one more call?"

"Absolutely. Who?"

"My sister, Marion. She's a geriatric doctor, she'll understand what's going on with Sukie." As she seats herself on the sofa beside me, the fading scent of Toni's citrusy cologne eases my queasy stomach. She hands me the phone and I punch in the numbers, starting with a Wisconsin exchange.

Marion doesn't believe in the kind of ring that calls attention to the person, who then dives to answer a silly rendition of Beethoven's fifth—da, da, da, daaa. Hers is a no nonsense, old fashioned noise—br-ing, br-ing, br-ing. I hold my breath and so does Toni, to whom I give a quick recap of the aides driving Sukie into a frenzy. I omit the part about the men. "During orientation, I learned every resident has a right to be respected and cared for. Judging from the way Sukie reacted to those two women, I'm afraid what I saw is just the tip of the iceberg." Toni purses her lips. She's awfully serious, and that scares me.

As the phone rings, I make a mental note to tell Marion about my discoveries: that Dad keeps a log on Sukie; that his office is loaded with family photos; and that he may have been at my gymnastic competition. The thought of him watching without letting me know he was there thrills and angers me at the same time. Why can't it be one emotion or the other? Why do they come in pairs? And why are they so sticky and complicated? The phone cues me to leave a message for Dr. Windsor. "It's 5:45. Call me on my cell, no matter how late it is. Sukie's in trouble."

Chapter 16:

Minutes after Toni drops me off, I stand in the doorway of my father and Solange's bedroom, talking way too fast about Sukie and the two aides. Solange listens while she hangs her suit in the closet, steps into a pair of jeans, and zips. Her effortless movements make her look as though I'm delivering a standard daily report, but the wariness in her eyes says otherwise. She shoots a slew of questions my way: What condition was Sukie in when I left? What was she like the day before she had this "exchange" with the aides? What are their names? When did all this occur? Who was there besides you, Sukie, and the aides? Have I spoken with my father?

She grabs the first sweater from her bureau drawer and slips it over her head, then opens a second drawer, pulls out a pair of fuzzy knee socks, and sits on the bench at the foot of their king-sized bed. Her hands drop between her knees and her socks dangle. She squints at the honeycombed window shades, closed to the sleet pummeling the glass, and thinks. The more she ponders, the more restless I become.

At last she says, "This kind of thing always gives me the willies. This isn't a case of teasing that turned into taunting. I'm afraid this sounds like abuse."

She tells me she's dealt with abuse issues at work, and that it brings out the ugliest in people. She scowls and takes a breath as though she were about to lift a fifty-pound sack of manure. "Those aides had no business talking to your grandmother like that. I can't believe they said those things to Sukie, but to do so while you were there is beyond stupidity."

"Elliot told me the two aides are cousins and that they're related to some bigwig at Highfield."

"That makes it worse," Solange moans and motions for me to hand her her oversized handbag. "No matter whom they're related to, we need to let their supervisor know what they've been doing." She plunges her hand into the gaping brown leather maw and lands her iPhone.

My stomach rumbles as rudely as the radiator, gurgling furiously as it tries to warm the room. "So it's true then." The foul taste from this afternoon returns to my mouth. "I wasn't sure how big a leap it would take before the aides crossed the abuse line."

"You're right, it's tricky." Solange leans back and studies me, sitting beside her. "You need to remember, it's not your job to prove that abuse is occurring, but you must alert your supervisors when something is amiss."

I'm close to tears. "I should have paged Robin, or Mrs. Perducci."

"You said you let the night staff know you were worried about Sukie's having been so upset. That's a start." She pulls me in for a hug. "Everyone, even smart kids, need help figuring this kind of thing out. You and I need to talk about how to know when strangers and friends have gone too far. Not tonight, but soon. I promise."

She's referring to Sukie and to my brief but life-altering encounter with the Blingers.

"Highfield will have to treat this as an allegation of institutional abuse." Solange is unusually intense. Seeing me grimace, she pats my knee. "They don't have a choice—it's the law: anyone who witnesses a questionable interaction between an employee and a patient is obliged to report it to the person in charge. It's to protect people like Sukie, who rely on others for their care. Jake deals with this type of thing at the jail, where you expect..." Her voice trembles. She sounds as stunned as I feel. We can't believe that anyone would do such a thing to a person with dementia, much less to our Sukie.

Solange paces, massaging her neck, iPhone crushed to her ear. I draw my feet up, wrap my wool pea coat around them, and rock from side to side. No matter how insistently the radiator hisses, I can't get warm. This business with Sukie makes me feel inside-out and now that Solange is involved, I'm downing a mouthful of déjà vu juice. My mother's voice had a similar intensity when she called to tell my father about "your daughter's initiation into The Society of Bling." With Sukie less capable of fighting back than I was back then, her abuse registers volcanic.

Getting through to the unit takes forever. "Can you believe this?" Solange mutters. The phone at the main switchboard rings and rings. "No one's answering." She raises the shade and presses her nose to the window. "If it wasn't so god-awful out, I'd drive over." She frowns, covers the phone, and whispers, "Jake is out in this mess. I hope he's okay."

I'm about to say something reassuring about what a careful driver he is, but Solange starts talking to the operator. Telling her that she must speak to the supervisor on the unit for the memory impaired; that this is the second time she's called; that this is extremely important. The operator puts Solange on hold.

She takes one look at me, shivering under my coat, sits down and puts her arm around me. "Everything's going to be all right, honey. Don't worry," she whispers, "we won't stop until we're sure Sukie is okay."

When the call finally goes through, Solange identifies herself—she uses her maiden name, so whoever is on the other end doesn't know she's related to Sukie—but doesn't state her business. "To whom am I speaking?" She's switched from her kind voice to her business tone.

"Sandis Doyle, I'm one of the CNAs."

With the speakerphone on, I hear a commotion in the background—several excited voices, two coaxing, the third loud and harsh. I slip out from under Solange's arm and frantically mouth: *That's Sukie yelling.* Sandis and Timtiere were supposed to go home after their early shift. I assume Timtiere is with Sandis and wonder what they're doing there.

"Sounds like you're having a party." Solange's tone is deceptively casual.

"Just one of the residents, having some fun."

"First snowstorm of the season. Makes everyone nervous. By the way, I'm trying to reach the nursing supervisor, is she there?"

"I haven't seen her in a while. She's covering three units tonight. A couple of supervisors couldn't make it in on account of the snow. Last time I saw her, she was on her way to the second floor. I'll put you through."

Solange marvels at how people love to sound like they're in the know and at how much they'll tell you, if you just take the time to listen. Sandis is no exception.

I press my face to my knees. I don't like that Sandis is there. I hate the condescending tone in her voice, the flippant way she spoke about Sukie. And hearing Sukie snarl, "Give me that Kleenex, it's mine," rips at me. Sukie's behavior has changed so drastically over the last couple of weeks, it doesn't take much to imagine her tugging on a box of tissue until whoever is holding onto it gives it over. Box in hand, Sukie then pulls the tissues out one by one and tosses them on the floor like the three-year-old I used to baby-sit for.

Solange drums her fingernails on her dresser. "I've never heard Sukie so angry. Have you?"

I lift my head and shake, no. "That's what's scares me. Something's happening to her, something that's never happened before. She's been acting awfully strange."

I pull my binder out of my backpack and flip it open. Before I visited Elliot, I'd listed Sukie's behaviors. I read them to Solange: "a) getting into spats with the other residents, then isolating herself; b) scratching Iris, then barricading herself in her room; c) pretending to cook a family meal, a sure sign of stress; and d) reacting suspiciously when the aides mentioned the word, 'laughter.' On top of all that, Sukie's friend, Lucy, died this morning." I slip my notebook into my backpack. Not that I need to be so all-mighty neat, but this small action distracts me enough to keep me from crying. "Lucy was Sukie's last friend after Anna and Hazel died. Losing her had to get to Sukie, big time."

Solange straightens; someone comes on the phone. "Yes, I've been holding for the nursing supervisor." She sits beside me.

After introducing herself and her relationship to Sukie, Solange explains her concerns.

Nursing supervisor, Louise Dominick, murmurs, "I see, I see." She apologizes for the gaps that occur during their conversation and explains that she's taking notes. When she finishes, she says, "If I follow our procedures manual to the letter, after I hang up, I should send Sandis and Timtiere home on administrative leave, pending the results of an investigation. But that would leave the Fitzgerald Unit short-staffed—I'll never be able to get anyone to come in, not with this storm—and that wouldn't be safe for Sukie or anyone else on the unit."

Solange rolls her eyes. "The way I look at it, Mrs. Dominick, we've got two situations going here—one with the aides and the other with my mother-in-law. I've already told you about the aides. When I called the unit a few minutes ago, my mother-in-law was clearly upset. I could hear her yelling. Since no one has contacted me to say they were about to give her a PRN medication..." *That's one of those meds the nurses can give as needed.* "...I'm assuming my mother-in-law's issue has yet to be dealt with. Am I on the right track here?" Never once does Solange raise her voice, she doesn't need to; her words scream on their own.

"I'm on my way now to the Fitzgerald unit. I'll assess your mother-in-law's condition myself and test her for a urinary tract infection. We may have to give her a PRN to calm her. I'll also call my supervisor about having the two aides swap places with staff from another floor. When the aides have finished their shifts, I'll place them both on administrative leave. I'm not sure my supervisor will like my idea, but it would take care of the 'two situations,' as you put it, and avoid leaving us short-staffed. If not, we'll come up with another plan. I'll call you as soon as I have more information. Can I reach you at this phone number?"

"Yes," Solange says. "I know you're very busy, but I'd appreciate your calling as soon as you assess my mother-in-law. Her granddaughter is here with me and she's—both she and I are very worried." Solange nods. "Yes, that'll be fine. Thanks, Louise." The call ends, but for me it's just the beginning.

"Louise Dominick, she's a cut above the rest," Solange says. "She thinks outside of the box without ignoring policy and procedures. That's why she's a supervisor. She recognizes an impending crisis and acts. I like that." Solange stops talking long enough to glance at her watch, 7:15.

She ducks partway under the bed for her sneakers, talking all the while. "Sukie might need a dosage of Depakote to calm her plus an antibiotic if she has an infection. We'll have to wait and see. Working with someone like Louise makes me feel better." Her muffled voice lilts with hope for reasons that aren't entirely clear to me. "At least I know someone with brains and authority is going to sort this out."

Her phone rings. "That can't be Louise. It's got to be Jake. Answer it, will you?"

Without so much as a hello, my father barrages me with questions: "What's happened to your grandmother? Is she all right? Where is Solange? Has she seen Sukie?" I hold the phone at arm's length, draw a deep breath, then bring the phone to my ear. "Hold on a second, Dad. One thing at a time. Yes, I asked Toni to locate you. The nursing supervisor is checking Sukie for a urinary tract infection. Yes, yes, I know it's called a 'UTI.' Where are you? Are you all right? When are you coming home?"

My last question launches yet another round of questions. "Wait a minute, here's Solange." I hand the phone over without asking the question I want to ask most: Why is it you're never around when we need you?

While Solange rattles off an ultra-efficient summation of her conversation with Louise, I picture all the scraped knees, baths, bedtime stories, weekend trips to the zoo, vacations, birthdays, holidays, and honor-roll announcements my father had missed, and roll them into one flimsy ball. I'll never forget him stealing a photo of my gymnastic competition without stopping to give me a hug. Now that Louise Dominick is caring for Sukie, he ought to call her for details about what was happening to the mother he so cleanly deposited in the capable hands of Toni, Solange, and his youngest daughter. Then he should add Louise to the list of women who are doing his job!

Four hours after my father was supposed to be home, he hasn't called or showed. Solange calls the local hospital and the state police to ask if Jacob Windsor had been admitted or was in an accident. With each "No, that name is not listed here," she breathes a sigh of relief and shakes her head to relay the message to me.

Just as she rings Jake's office for the umpteenth time, our power goes out. Downed electrical lines don't help her nerves or mine. We bury ourselves in our respective beds to keep warm. I hear Solange tossing and turning. Exhausted after imagining horror scenarios—for Sukie and Jake—I finally close my eyes at 4:00 a.m. only to be awakened at 5:30 when the reading lamp by my bed floods on. Solange pokes her head in my room. Her face is drawn and pale. "Jake never came home," she whispers. I understand why she's afraid to speak out; a normal voice would make his absence frightfully real.

My stomach swishes again, same as it did during Sukie's incident. "Don't worry, he can take care of himself," I say, as if my father was a favorite old dog. "Besides, he's been AWOL before." As soon as the words tumble from my mouth, they feel sadly familiar; my mother said the same thing when my father took to spending nights away from his family.

Chapter 17:

Dressed in last night's rumpled clothing, Solange dumps mounds of French Roast into the coffee maker. Within seconds, pungent puffs of brew burst into the kitchen, where the thermostat registers 56 degrees.

I hand her a fresh mug of coffee.

She sips. "I tried calling Jake before I came downstairs but couldn't get through. I bet he hasn't charged his phone in days." She sets her cup on the island and studies the thermostat. "Brrr. Once this behemoth of a house cools down, it takes forever for her to warm up, even with a new furnace. I told Jake we should have had insulation blown into the walls, but no…" she sing-songs, as she presses the thermostat, holds it for three seconds, then presses three more times, calling for more heat. The furnace purrs into action. A couple of minutes later, the cast iron radiator gurgles. Despite their promise of warmth, I think about Jake and shiver. *At least we know where Sukie is,* I figure, demoting her to second place on my fret list.

I pull my fleece hoodie over my head and wrap my hands around my mug. While I don't care for the taste of coffee, its heat radiates into my fingertips, which makes up for its bitterness. Solange pulls her phone from her pocket, swipes it once, and presses it to her ear. Her red-rimmed glasses magnify the worried lines around her eyes. She lets out an exasperated sigh.

"Still no service?" I ask weakly.

She doesn't speak. Her left hand wanders to her pale lips; one by one, her fingers wilt over her chin and down her throat. That says it all. If Solange loses it, so will I. I gulp a few mouthfuls of coffee. My stomach churns. I'm more worried than ever.

Last night, I dreamt the snow had stranded Jake's car by Highfield. With traffic at a standstill and nowhere else to go, he headed inside to the third floor, where, seeing Sukie safe in her bed, he seated himself in the uncomfortable vinyl chair in her room and dozed off. He'd not visited her since she moved to Highfield, and though neither was awake, at least they were together in the same room. It was a good start, but I want to make it real.

"Solange?" My voice stirs her from her thoughts.

"Hmm?" she murmurs.

"It's after 7:00. Would you call Highfield and ask how Sukie is? And find out what happened to Sandis and that other aide?"

"Sorry, I should have done that right off. I guess I'm more tired than I think." Within seconds, Solange is speaking to Robin, the nursing supervisor on the day shift.

Finished, she clicks off. "Robin sounded unusually somber. Everything happened just like Louise Dominick said it would. Last night, the aides were assigned to work on other floors in positions that didn't involve patients. As soon as the aides left, Sukie quieted down. The charge nurse gave her another Ativan to help her relax. Sukie slept all night. Now, she's up, has had her breakfast, and is sitting quietly by the nurses' station. Robin said she's doing well, a lot better than some of the staff. As soon as Corki gets in, Robin will ask her to conduct an investigation of our allegations. Until that's resolved, the two aides are on administrative leave."

"What's that?" I ask through the relief of knowing Sukie is okay.

"Administrative leave means the aides aren't allowed to return to work until the investigation is over. They'll be paid to stay home. And…" Solange removes her glasses and rubs her eyes, "if they're found guilty of wrongdoing, they may be dismissed."

"They might lose their jobs?"

"Exactly." The finality in her voice rings with angry judgment.

What started out as an incident involving two aides has affected two other workers on two different floors. By now, the gossip mill on the Fitzgerald unit is churning out all kinds of stories. Sukie's experience was revolting, and the outcomes for the aides might be just as destructive. Maybe more so. The entire situation should never have happened. "Inexcusable," is what Jake will say when he hears about Sandis. The iPhone vibrates. Without bothering to see who's calling, Solange mashes it to her ear. "Hello, Jake?" Her knuckles turn white from holding the phone too tightly.

She's so deflated as she hands the phone over that I put my arm around her shoulder as I greet my sister, Marion, finally returning my call. She tried several times, but couldn't get through. Ever the sleuth, Marion clicked on the NOAA Internet site, saw the storm over the East Coast, and understood. Being a doctor who works in a hospital, she also knew that Highfield would have power, no matter what.

She called the Fitzgerald Unit and spoke with Louise Dominick, who checked Sukie's file to make sure Marion Strauss, DO was approved to receive information about Sukie. Then Louise updated her on Sukie's behavior with the aides. Sukie's urine test results are "within normal limits" so that wasn't contributing to Sukie's behavior, Louise told her. Clean test results didn't soothe Marion, not one bit; she was incensed.

I hold the phone at arm's length—that's how loud Marion gets when she's furious—while she repeats the questions she fired at Louise: "What's the name of the supervisor who was on duty at the time? Did anyone tell her that Cynthia was having difficulty when she reportedly approached the night staff? Do staff understand if they fail to report incidents like these, they are as much at fault as staff who are directly involved?"

"Only if the investigation finds that the allegations are true," Louise told her.

"Whether or not this incident occurred the way it was reported, *something* happened. Surely the nursing supervisor must understand that all behavior—hers, mine, Sukie's—conveys meaning? Distressing as it may have been, Sukie was using her behavior to tell us something was wrong," Marion pauses. "Very wrong."

For half a second, I actually feel sorry for Louise. My sister is not one to take no for an answer, which is one of the reasons she's such a good doctor. Still, she isn't the type of person you want to tangle with.

"I insisted that Louise review Sukie's medication chart with me," Marion says, and I imagine her closing her eyes in disgust.

"What did it say?" I'm curious to know if anyone else had noticed the changes in Sukie's behavior.

"To put it in layman's terms, the nurses wrote that Sukie had become very nervous, especially in the evening. She had a short attention span and was unable to follow directions. The nurses were worried about what Sukie might do to the other patients, and to them."

"You mean they were *afraid* of Sukie?" It was hard to believe that the kindest, most fun-loving adult I know scared people. Like Bruce Talibert scared me.

"I know it's hard to hear all this, but..." She pauses. During that slice of silence, I sense how painful this is for Marion, who'd specialized in geriatric diseases so she could help elders in other families, hoping she'd never be called on to do the same with our precious Sukie.

I can feel Marion pulling back, reeling in her heart's strings. A breath later, she speaks in the controlled thoughtful voice of Dr. Marion Strauss, "That's why I asked which medications were ordered. Unfortunately, Sukie is being given too many new medications too quickly. It happens all the time in nursing facilities." In the background, I hear Marion being paged. Before I can tell her that Jake is missing, she hurriedly says good-bye and promises to call later.

"Marion says Dr. Len doesn't understand that the five meds he prescribed have never been tested for use with geriatric patients. That between Sukie's age and her Alzheimer's, Sukie's neurological system is fragile."

"Oh dear," Solange paces back and forth across the kitchen. "I feel awful—I sell Highfield those medications."

"Marion said if the meds are given in small dosages *and* if the docs wait to see how the patient responds before increasing the dosage that they can be very helpful. But she also said that docs should introduce only one new medication at a time. I told Marion that Dr. Len is the only doctor at Highfield and that he has 300 patients, not counting his private practice," but Solange had stopped listening.

"So Marion thinks Sukie is having a reaction to her medications? A med reaction can cause some very bizarre behavior." Solange pauses. She looks as though she's face to face with the devil. "Does Jake know that Sukie's doctor has that many patients?"

I shake my head no. "I haven't talked to him about Dr. Len. There's no way the doctor can oversee all the medications he's prescribed. I doubt he'd recognize Sukie if he bumped into her. Wait until my father finds out."

A hint of satisfaction glows within me—I was right to ask if Sukie's meds were being increased too quickly. But no one listens to a kid, even if she is smart. *Not that smart,* I tell myself. *A smart kid would have called Marion right away.* My list of "should haves" is getting longer.

There's more to worry about: with the aides on administrative leave, the rest of the staff must know what happened. How can I show my face on that unit? And when I do, how will the staff react? More importantly, how will they react toward Sukie? Will they take their anger out on her, do little things out of spite? It would be easy to let shampoo dribble into Sukie's eyes when they give her a shower. They could blame the misbehavior that would surely follow on her dementia.

A scraping thunderlike roar reverberates along the far side of the house, rattling the bank of triple-wide windows in the living room. A double-bladed snowplow rumbles down the snow-clogged hill alongside the house, spraying snow higher than a fireboat dieseling down river on the Fourth of July. Its white spray arches and falls, creating parallel mounds that pile three feet of packed snow on top of the three feet of snow that had already fallen.

The parking spaces along the side of the house and the driveway leading into the garage at the top of the hill, where Jake usually parks his car, are plowed in. Mounded more than four feet high, snow blocks his entrance. The hill alongside the house and the street in front are now clear, but between the snow walls packed around the front, back, and side, there's no way Jake can reach his turreted castle.

That Sukie is okay and the power is on do little to console Solange, who wanders into the living room and stares out the front window. "Jake should be home by now," she says. Fatigue vines itself through her ordinarily confident voice,

143

giving it a drifty tone that unnerves me. Solange calls his cell phone again. No answer. She gets through to Toni, who had to wait an hour in her car until their plow-guy had blown a pathway to the front door. While Solange is talking, the landline in the kitchen rings.

I run to answer it. "Dad!" My shout brings Solange to my side. "Where have you been? Are you all right?" He sounds tired and upset, more upset than I've heard him in a long time.

He tells me he'd been snowed in while interviewing a client, "… a fellow named Harold Miller, a real piece of work, a legend in Bellesport criminal court. I had the choice of sleeping in his kitchen in a tattered chair with broken springs or in my car. I didn't know the storm would last as long as it did, so I chose the warmer of two evils. Believe me, I've never been so wrong."

"You probably want to talk to Solange," I offer, figuring she would update him on the incident with Sukie.

"In a minute I do. But, should you leave for Highfield before I get home, I want you to stay away from someone you know." His tone changes from weary, but relieved, to ironclad serious.

"Who's that, Dad?"

"Elliot Miller," he says, roaring into the explanation he intended to give, whether or not I asked: "Elliot's brother, Harold, is a genius with a record as long as the list of patents the U.S. Patent Office holds in his name. He's gotten himself into all kinds of legal trouble. His family is a walking disaster. You stay away from Elliot, you got that?"

I can't believe it! My father has made assumptions about the only *real* friend I've ever known. *I wish I'd never called him "Dad."* Besides, the Elliot Miller I kissed isn't that kind of boy.

"We'll discuss this tonight when I get home. Is Solange there?" I'm too upset to answer.

I slip the phone into Solange's waiting hand, follow her into the living room, and perch myself on the chair by the windows. By jumping to conclusions about someone he hasn't met, Jake is violating his own ethic: gather the facts before judging. Worse yet, he's intruding into my life.

I close my eyes and wish that the Good Witch of the North would appear and magically top our snow walls with an impenetrable glaze of ice.

A tapping on the windowpanes answers: sleet, granular and unforgiving, grazes the windows and trees, and bounces along the mountains of snow. At this rate, the approach to Jake's castle will be glazed with a slick of ice. Then, he'll never be able to get in. And I'll be glad.

Chapter 18:

"There are no excuses believable, creative, or foolish enough when it comes to missing a meeting with your probation officer," Phineas Barnes warned me the first time I met him, his oversized lips manhandling his words, etching them into my memory. "Not rain—by that I mean a monsoon—not snow—that would be a blizzard of biblical proportions—not sleet—you get my point?" As we sat in the untidy basement cubicle he referred to as his "penthouse office," he drilled his point home again and again. On my way out, I promised myself I'd never forget an appointment with Phineas.

If it hadn't been for my mother, reminding me during her usual morning call of my appointment with "that Phin-person," I would have missed the one meeting in the world I'd crawl through glass to get to. Two seconds after I thanked her for rescuing me, frantic Solange called Jake at his office. A hundred-dollar bill convinced his snow removal guy to leave the sidewalks half-finished and head for Madison Hill Road to release Princess Hummingbird from the confines of her ice castle. Forgetting something as important as this monthly meeting isn't like me. I phoned Phineas and told him I was on my way.

I sit in the mudroom at Jake's house on an overturned bushel basket, tugging thick rubber ice grips around the heel of my boot. I adjust the cleats—they're more like nail heads—over my sole and tap the concrete floor once, twice, three times, then repeat this tap dance with the other foot. I've dressed for the weather—ski jacket, hat and scarf, but my bare fingers ache from the cold. I slip into the thick woolly mittens Solange loaned me and loop my arms into my backpack.

Gripping the outside of the storm door for support, I place the sole of my right foot squarely on the ice, grind my cleats firmly into its unforgiving crust, and anchor my other foot. I feel as unforgiving as this ice. I'm still upset about Jake's edict to avoid Elliot and haven't yet decided what to do. I have to put all that aside if I'm going to put on my best face for Phineas, who doesn't want to hear that I'm flirting with trouble again. If I'm very careful, I can avoid slipping on the ice.

One of the conditions of deleting my attempt to fit in with a bunch of fashionista idiots from the collective memory of the juvenile corrections system is this monthly meeting. Maybe these get-togethers are more useful for the hardcore felons Phineas usually works with, but with an ingenue like me, he crosses his lanky legs and arms first one way, then the other, uncomfortable and bored.

Odd as it is, Jake has a sense of humor about a few things, including my having been arrested with a bunch of "society punks," kids so unimaginative they couldn't think of a more exciting crime than breaking into one another's parents' homes. "Amateurs, real amateurs," he said, baffled by the utter stupidity of their "stunts." Nonetheless, he let me know he wasn't pleased. He rubbed his chin, darkened by his five o'clock shadow, and said, "Now should you want to dabble in the legal system *after* you've attended Harvard Law, that'll be another story. One with a more acceptable outcome. But as far as this blip is concerned, it'd best be your last; otherwise I'll see that my criminally inclined daughter receives the justice she deserves." Fatherly love; it can revive a floundering father-daughter relationship or strip the enamel right off your teeth.

According to WTFB, the Bellesport Bus Company is "alive and running" on routes wherever the side streets have been cleared. Thank goodness Madison Hill Road is among the first to be plowed. I tiptoe across the now-cleared walkway in back of the house, where sleet ricochets off the floor-to-ceiling sunroom windows onto my unprotected face. I pull my hood over my hat and jerk the visor into place. Between the sleet angling at me from the top of the hill and the sleet bouncing off the windows, I feel like a car in a $10.00 beat-you-clean drive-thru. The last thing I need on a day like this is another beating. I vow to never again put myself in a situation where I would be forced to rendezvous with a cigar-smoking probation officer, no matter how goofy cute the guy is. That means I need to find out whether Elliot has a history like mine.

The bus stops a block away, which usually isn't a life-threatening walk. Today, however, between having to climb over small mountains of icy snowpack—when you're 4'9", scaling a five-foot peak of snow feels Himalayas significant—I wish I'd agreed to let Jake make out the juvenile last will and testament he teased me about. As the bus rounds the corner, I make my way down the side of what I hope will be my last snow mountain. The pack I've foolishly removed from my back, thinking it would throw me off balance, slips off my arm. Lunging for it, I careen into the slick sloppy road.

Positioned like a dead bug on its back with its legs up in the air, the former gymnast, once famous for doing back flips on the balance beam, hears Carlos, the Bellesport Bus Driver of the Year, struggle to bring his long blue bus to a slushy stop. I glimpse his tensed shoulders and beautiful brown eyes, widened with the possibility of the death of his favorite *señorita* as I glide toward his bus. I imagine his booted foot doing the all-points press on his computerized braking system, the kind that does the thinking for you as long as you trust it enough to keep your foot planted on its black rubber surface.

By the time Carlos stops the bus, jerks the doors open, makes his way between its large orbed headlights—always on for safety—and falls to his knees, tears stream down his smooth olive cheeks. The brave souls on the bus follow. They urge me to reach for the handles of the golf umbrellas they're poking at me, the girl the newspapers will report as "an imp athletic enough to stop her trajectory with her cleats."

I lie flat on my back between the front tires. "Grab on," Carlos says as a bearded fellow in a Peruvian ski hat and another fellow with bloody dots of toilet paper stuck to his chin hook their umbrella handles around my outstretched wrists.

Safe on the bus, my wet backside informing me that it is about to turn blue-black, I feel nauseated. My face color changes from petrified pale to crimson, starting from my neck and traveling up to the tips of my slightly oversized ears. I feel awful about almost having destroyed Carlos's flawless driving record and just as bad about the scene I created. So I have no choice, I let the passengers baby me. One woman gives me her cup of peppermint tea. "You look like you could use this. I haven't sipped from it, I swear," she says, pressing the double-layered cup with the Sunshine Health Foods logo and a recycled plastic sip top into my hand.

I force a smile. "Thanks," I murmur, my garbled voice not fully recovered.

As I settle into the seat directly behind him Carlos tries to make me laugh: "I was so afraid I'd made you into an *enchilada.* You sure you don't want me to call an ambulance?"

I yank my hood and my hat from my head. "Do you see any gray hairs?" I lean forward, positioning my head so he can see me in his overhead mirror.

Not understanding my attempt at humor, he draws back. Seconds later, after the other passengers laugh, his face brightens and the smile that welcomes me every morning breaks through to show off his gleaming gold crowns. "If you're joking, you are okay, then."

"Starting out under your bus isn't my favorite way to begin the day, but I'm good, thanks to you." I reposition my rhinestone comb in my tangled hair and tuck it all under my hat. "I'm sorry I caused so much trouble."

"No trouble as long as you're safe." He studies me a moment more, convincing himself that I'm as good as I claim. Satisfied, he releases the brake and puts the bus into drive. "Then we're back in business," he says and the bus eases forward.

Phineas cut me a break by meeting me halfway at The Town Line, a small café located on the boundary that divides Granville from its working class brother, the defunct factory-choked town of Bellesport. Being one of two juvenile parole officers in town, the guy is usually up to his eyebrows in appointments. The freak snowstorm caused tons of cancellations, he told me when I'd called, which gave him time to do me this favor.

A patch of sunlight breaks through the crystalline boughs of the blue spruce alongside the café, disappears, returns, vanishes, and reappears as if to remind me that no matter how severe the storm, the sun wins out in the end. It's the way I feel about this particular snapshot of my life, taken through a scratched lens: though clotted with clouds, the sun occasionally flickers on.

Phineas has become one of those flickers. "Hey, kid," he says as I ease myself onto the bench seat opposite him. "You look like a cat that's been punted down the stairs."

A Zulu-like vegetarian who runs five miles a day, he wraps his enormous maw around his tofu burger and chomps.

"No running in this mess, huh, Phineas?"

He leans against the back of the booth, jaws working in the kind of movement you'd expect after popping a wad of rock-hard Super Bubble gum into your mouth. Sidestepping his opening observation—his standard, earthy way of starting our meetings—is like waving a red handkerchief in front of a bull. "Oh, I got my five miles in all right. Just came from the Bellesport Y, where all the working moms were dropping off their kids for the dazed staff to look after."

A chubby waitress with purple streaks in her plaited hair stops by our booth, pad and pencil in hand. "Phineas told me he was expecting you, so I put a fresh pot of coffee on. How do you like it?"

Not wanting to offend by telling her coffee is my least favorite drink, I say, "With cream, please. And, I'd like a grilled cheese sandwich."

The waitress looks skeptical. "You look like you could use the entire pot of coffee, straight-on black." She turns toward Phineas. "She's kinda green around her gills, Phin. You better work your magic on her, like you used to do with me."

She leaves and Phineas sets his elbows on the table and rubs his eyes. When he removes his hands, his blue-ringed eyes seem older, more tired. "Sorry about that. She's one of the reasons I don't usually meet clients outside my office. Confidentiality is hard to maintain in a small town."

I shrug. "We could hold hands if that would put her off our scent."

"Now where did that come from, young lady?"

It's my turn to lean against the table and rub my eyes. "Promise you won't tell a soul, including our Java-slinging waitress?"

He nods over the lip of his cup of tea.

"I just got two aides that were making my grandmother act crazier than ever suspended from their jobs." Phineas drops his jaw and is about to speak when I put my hand up like a traffic cop, "Then my father didn't come home last night."

His eyes pop open. "Attorney Windsor on the prowl?" he whispers.

"Don't be a dork, Phineas. Turns out he stayed with one of *his* unsavory clients, the brother of a sweet guy I know who's a patient at Highfield. Right off, my dad, Mr. Always Be Reasonable, jumps to conclusions about my friend, Elliot, and warns me to stay clear of him. But I don't see how I can. Elliot's like you—one of my few real friends." Phineas rolls his eyes up beneath his dappled-gray eyebrows; he hates when I say things like that. "Then, upset and hustling to get here on time, I fell on the ice and slipped under an oncoming bus, praying all the while that the driver would stop without skidding. That, Phineas, is the story of my past twenty-four hours. Stay tuned for the next edition of Hummingbird Sings Her Blues."

"So, how did all that feel?" He blows on his Fair Trade Organic Green Tea and takes another sip.

"Unloading my saga?" I raise my right cheek off the hard bench, cushion it with my folded leg, and grimace as I set my weight down.

"Hmm," he murmurs in the middle of another sip.

"It drips with self-pity."

"What about annoyance tinged with good old-fashioned self-righteous anger?"

The waitress appears, plate and creamer in one hand, coffee mug in the other. She sets the slightly burned grilled cheese sandwich plate clattering to the table, slides it toward me, then eases a brimming mug of coffee into place. "There's your joe, and here's your cream. Anything else you need?"

I shake my head, as does Phineas when the waitress looks his way. "Okay. But I've got your favorite, pumpkin pie with whipped cream." Phineas taps his stomach to indicate full and shakes his head again. "Okay. If you change your mind, just holler."

Pushing his half-eaten tofu burger aside, Phineas folds his hands on the table. His face settles into his let's-get-serious expression. "All of what you told me is important. And we're going to unpack every part of it, in detail. But first I have to ask you the question Juvenile Services, in its wisdom, is overpaying me to determine—has your friend, Elliot, been in trouble with the law?"

"The poor guy lost both legs in a boating accident." I'm trying to hold my exasperation in check, but it spills. I can't help myself and I don't want to. I'm feeling moodier than ever.

Phineas unfolds his fingers and fans his fingers into a whoa gesture. "Let's be calm about this. You've had a hard night. I'd be edgy, too, if I were feeding from your menu. I'm not trying to put Elliot in a bad light. I'm trying to protect you. If you recall the first time we met, I told you"

"—that I was under no circumstances to associate with anyone who was on probation or who has a record." I purse my lips in satisfaction. Memorization has always come easy.

"Right. So, are we on the same page here? Are you going to let me help you rid yourself of your Youthful Offender status? Is that what you want? Because if you don't—"

"Yes," I interrupt. Given my circumstances, I'm amazed that I never wondered whether Elliot has ever been in trouble. I assumed he was "clean" like most normal people. I knew he came from the rough side of town and that his interests and hobbies didn't make much sense to me, but those aren't reasons to call in a background check on the guy. But seeing Phineas jump out of his skin when he mentions Elliot makes me doubt. What if I have made a mistake about him, then what? Not knowing could cost me *mucho*. I'm dying to ask Phineas to find out from the other juvenile parole officer whether Elliot is one of his clients, but I'm too scared. Something tells me I don't have to bother. I'm afraid my life is over.

Chapter 19:

Highfield's main entrance glistens with the watery aftermath of snow removal and a dousing of calcium chloride, which melts snow and ice and the undercarriages of unsuspecting vehicles. Ambulances and transport vans occupy their reserved parking spaces as though nothing had happened. Mounds of snow along the medians in the parking lot and puddles on the lot surface are all that remain of the freak storm. Even the gold and orange mums in the urns on either side of the entrance have had their snow jackets cleared away. Upon entering the mighty glass doors that whisk visitors and staff into the foyer, people wipe their boots—hastily resurrected from attics and basements—before crossing the threshold into the busy reception area.

That's where I meet Mrs. Perducci. "My goodness," she says, excusing herself from the conversation she's having with the receptionist, "You're as good as the Postal Service—neither rain, nor wind, nor snow keeps you from your duty. I never expected to see our star volunteer on a day like today." Her welcoming expression becomes serious. "You're so pale. Is something wrong? Are you coming down with the flu?"

"Other than eating the worst grilled cheese sandwich in my life, I'm okay. Just a little tired maybe."

Mrs. Perducci checks the purple wristwatch that matches her tailored pantsuit. "It's 1:00. Do you have a few minutes? I'd like to speak to you." Her tone is pleasant enough, but its underlying gravity makes me wish she hadn't noticed me.

"Is everything all right with my grandmother?"

Mrs. Perducci gives my arm a reassuring pat. "Of course it is. I'm sorry, I didn't mean to startle you."

In the time it takes to wend our way down the corridor to Mrs. Perducci's office, she answers three "quick" questions and puts off two phone calls.

"This is a busy day for you, isn't it?" I ask in an effort to make small talk.

"Snow events are bad enough but when we have an early storm…" her gaze drifts to the snow on a window sill, "people act as though it's the first time they'd seen the stuff."

The comfy twin wing chairs in Mrs. Perducci's office are situated to one side of her desk just as they were the first time I stopped in. Her desk is as cluttered as ever with files, family photos, pens, and sticky notes attached to her lampshade. But the vase of pumpkin-colored mums is new.

"Special occasion?" I ask, breathing in the funeral-home aroma that florist-delivered flowers give off.

Mrs. Perducci blushes. "They're from my staff." She seems unusually flustered. "Word got out that I've been selected Rehab Facility Administrator of the Year." She gives her eyes a modest little roll. "It's quite an honor, although, between you and me, I'm not one for the spotlight. There are plenty of others here who deserve recognition. I'd rather highlight their achievements." She steps back from the flowers. "But they are perfect, aren't they?"

I smile in agreement. "Granville High has a monthly citizenship award. They have two ballot boxes, one outside the cafeteria and another outside the guidance office. Nominations are open. A student can nominate a teacher, a student, or cafeteria worker, and vice versa, as long as that person has done something that serves the common good. It can honor someone who develops a new school-wide program or someone who does the tiniest good deed."

Mrs. Perducci nods. "What a wonderful idea. I bet we can do something like that for our staff. It'd be a way to recognize staff members who go the extra mile. We can call them 'Highfield Milers' and make them members of the 'Mile High Club.' Reward them with prime parking spots, first in line at lunch, that kind of thing. What do you think?"

"The kids at school—most of them that is—love being nominated. I bet your staff will love it, too." I feel seasick, as though I were on a breakneck boat ride.

"Oh, dear. You do look more peaked than before. Do you mind if I check to see if you have a temperature? I'm not a nurse, but having five kids taught me the basics." Before I can answer, Mrs. Perducci's cool hand is on my forehead.

"No temperature that I can feel."

"I think it's cramps, but I'm not sure."

Her face lights with understanding. She presses a few numbers on her phone and asks for a couple of ginger ales with ice. While we're waiting, she sits in the chair beside me. "I want to talk to you about your grandmother and the allegations against the aides."

My cramps worsen.

She scooches to the edge of her chair and turns so her knees almost touch mine. "I can't discuss the particulars, but I want to congratulate you on having the courage to speak out. As an adult, I find abuse a difficult topic to talk about. I can only imagine how hard it must have been for you. I want you to know that we take your allegation seriously. I've asked Corki to interview you about what you saw. She'll also interview the aides in question and the workers who were on duty with them. She'll bring a summary of her findings..."

There's a knock at the door.

"That must be our drinks," she says, heading for the door.

A young woman whose wavy hair is flattened beneath a hair net hands her a tray draped in a linen dinner napkin, two cans of Canada Dry Ginger Ale, and two glasses filled with crushed ice. "Thank you, Nina."

Using the tray to push a couple of photos aside, Mrs. Perducci sets it on her desk and cracks open the first soda can. The fizz and pop of ginger ale glugging over ice make me realize how thirsty I am. Mrs. Perducci steps backward and is about to hand me a glass when she suddenly loses her balance. The glass sprays an arc of soda and ice, bounces off my right shin, then drops to the carpet like a wounded soldier. "Oh no," I yip, bolting toward Mrs. Perducci and grabbing her lapels to keep her from falling into a heavy brass floor lamp. I step out of the way as she lurches toward her desk. The photo of her youngest son collapses, hitting the next photo, causing a domino effect of tumbling photos.

"What a...clumsy...thing...for me...to do," she says in between gasps. "Are you... all right?"

"Yes," I fib, ignoring the sharp pain radiating up and down my shin. "It wasn't your fault. I can see why you lost your balance." I scoot behind her. The twin leather handles of her oversized silver handbag are splayed like the jaws of a bear trap.

"I thought I felt my heel catch on something," she says as she bends to collect the spilled contents of her bag. "How stupid of me. I never leave my bag on this side of my desk. It's either behind my desk or in my desk drawer, out of the way."

I gather a package of facial tissues, a Cross pen and pencil set in a trim leather case, a checkbook, and a tortoise shell hairbrush and hand them to her. Seated in the wing chair, handbag on her lap, she looks dazed. "Are you all right, Mrs. Perducci? Did you get hurt? Your ankle maybe? Your wrists?"

She shakes her head. "Nothing like that. But look what happened when I tripped." She opens her hand: her mother's narrow silver lipstick mirror has been crushed.

I edge closer, take the shattered mirror, bent hopelessly out of shape, and inspect it. "Maybe, if you brought it to a good jeweler…"

"Wouldn't you know it? Of all the things I could have landed on, it had to be this." Mrs. Perducci massages her temple. "My kids tell me I sound silly when I talk like this, but maybe this is a sign from my mother, telling me it's time to stop grieving and move on." She glances at me, then at the bulky gray clouds outside her window. "I'm not sure I'm ready." She leans forward, her gaudy bag pressed to her chest, and rubs her ankle.

"You are hurt. I'll get an ice pack for you."

Mrs. Perducci's hand flies up. "Please don't. If my staff hears about this, they'll want to pamper me to death. They're very sweet," she adds, "but I don't think I can tolerate any more fussing today." She smiles weakly. "Don't forget, I'm the mother hen around here, not the other way around."

My lips fold into my mouth, forming a doubtful scowl. I've seen plenty of sprained ankles during gymnastics practice and I become insistent. "What if your ankle swells? Then everyone will ask what happened." I pick up the glass at the foot of her chair and drop crescent-shaped ice into it. Standing, I take the linen napkin from the tray, arrange the ice on it, and knot the napkin around it. "Try this," I say, handing her a neat sack with floppy rabbit-like ears.

"You're going to make a very caring doctor," she says, stretching out her leg, jutting her toes toward the ceiling so I can balance the pack over her ankle. "I'm sure I'll be fine." She looks at her watch. "Let's get back to work. We were reviewing the procedures we follow when we receive an allegation of abuse. Once we collect everyone's input, a panel will review it. They'll bring their findings to me, along with their recommendations, and I'll review them with the chairman of our Board of Directors." She absentmindedly massages her palms, still crimson from catching herself on her desk. "Then it's up to me to implement the panel's recommendations. In the meantime, the aides will be on administrative leave for as long as the investigation takes. That means they'll be paid to stay home."

"It sounds complicated."

"Anything that deals with people's lives—and that includes your grandmother's—is complex. That's why we take the time to gather all the information we need in order to make the right decisions. I know this may be asking a lot, but I don't want you worrying about this process or about your grandmother. Okay?" She glances at her watch. "I'm afraid I'm late for a meeting. Why don't you take this can of soda with you? One left standing out of two isn't bad."

I leave the office, warm soda can in hand. Mrs. Perducci's last quip was intended to make me feel better but it doesn't. One out of two standing? The count could refer to Mrs. Perducci's near accident, to the investigation, or to Sukie, I'm not sure which. The snow may have stopped, but the storm that rips Dorothy out of Kansas is just taking shape.

I dump the ginger ale in a trashcan far from Mrs. Perducci's office and key myself into the stairwell. Inside, it smells of wet wool coats. I trudge up the first of three flights of stairs, backpack over my shoulders, ski jacket limp on my arm. Walking wouldn't be so bad if I didn't have the most miserable cramps I've ever experienced—correction: the *only* cramps I've ever experienced—and if I weren't trying to avoid Elliot.

I know what my father was so hyped up about when he warned me about Elliot, but don't agree with his theory that the "apples that fall from the same tree wind up bruised, one way or the other." I don't believe that having a brother with a record automatically gives Elliot one. If that were true, my brother Timothy would have a record because he spent time with me when I was involved with the Blingers. For all I know, Elliot might find the fact that I come equipped with my very own parole officer repulsive. Then he would be avoiding me.

Until I figure this out, I impose a three-mile limit on Elliot. I hope he turns out to be the honest gear head he seems to be and that his affinity for tinkering with broken stuff applies only to engines, not people. Most importantly, if he's as clean as I suspect, I hope he won't hate me when I get around to telling him about my criminal debut.

On the Anne Fitzgerald Unit, Sukie is in the TV room slumped in a chair, head on her knees. I rush past several patients seated around the television, watching *General Hospital* and past the baby grand. As I get closer, I slow my pace. I don't want to wake Sukie if she's napping, something she does only if she's very sick. I look back toward the hallway hoping to see a nurse who can tell what has happened to Sukie. But no one is around.

Sukie's snowy white hair, matted from sleep, smells musty. Her clothes are mismatched, her feet bare, and she isn't wearing her hearing aids.

"Sukie?" I whisper, hoping she'll sit up and greet me. Tears puddle in the corners of my eyes. I blink hard. What if Sukie is...?

I put my hand on Sukie's; it's still warm. "Sukie?" I repeat louder than before. I bend close to her ear. "Sukie?

You'll hurt your back if you stay like this. Let's go to your room where you can lie down." But Sukie doesn't answer.

I feel her pulse, then gently rub her wrist. "Come on, Sukie. Wake up. Please." I plant a raspberry on her sticky cheek. That always got her to smile, even in her sleep. When she doesn't budge, I know something is terribly wrong.

Just then an aide with royal blue hair wheels a patient into the room. "Excuse me," I say after she settles her patient. "Something's happened to my grandmother. She won't wake up." The urgency in my voice is hard to miss.

The aide hovers by her patient's wheelchair.

Why isn't this woman upset about Sukie? Why doesn't she offer to help? Now, I'm getting upset. "Is Iris here today?"

"Lucky Iris has the day off," the aide whines like a kid being kept after school. "The weather has left everyone feeling crusty, patients included." Finally, she dawdles toward us. "I don't know what happened to your grandmother. She was sitting up the last time I checked." She puts her wide hand on Sukie's arm and shakes so hard Sukie's entire body rocks.

I'm horrified at the aide's roughness and at Sukie's not budging. "Stop that. What do you think you're doing?"

She shrugs. "I'll see if I can find the nurse."

Kneeling in front of Sukie, I slip my fingertips under her chin and gently lift her head. "Time to wake up." But her eyes don't open.

The aide returns. "Come, Cynthia, time for ice cream. Wake up so you can have a dish of chocolate, your favorite." When Cynthia doesn't stir, the aide muckles on to her arm, about to shake her again.

"That's not working. I've tried it twice." *But not as roughly as you.* "Would you mind getting a washcloth and soaking it in warm water? Maybe if I wash her face…"

The aide shuffles into the wide empty corridor by the nurses' station. No doubt, the nurses are with their patients, pumping them with medications. I check Sukie's pulse again: steady but slow, almost lethargic. Like someone who has been given an overdose! The afternoon of the concert after Sukie shoved another patient, Dr. Len, the geriatric psychiatrist, was contacted by phone. Without seeing her or understanding that she was upset because her hearing aid was whistling, he ordered new meds that were all given at the same time. She'd fallen into a zombielike state then, too.

A shrill whistle signals the opening of the locked doors. Seconds later, Corki enters the room and heads straight towards me. Gone is her winning grin; instead, her mouth is tensed, which probably means she wants to interview me about my allegations. Important as that is, it'll have to wait. "Corki, do you know when Dr. Len last saw my grandmother?"

Her bouncy steps have flattened and her eyes no longer sparkle. Corki stands, official manila folder crushed to her chest. "Your grandmother wasn't like this earlier. What's happened? Have you called a nurse?"

I point to the empty nurses' station. "I would have looked for one, but I was afraid to leave Sukie alone. What time did you last see her?"

"About 9:00. She was wandering the hall, very confused. She talked non-stop about feeling like 'a nobody.' I tried to distract her by showing her the snow, but she wasn't interested. She pretty much looked right through me, which isn't like her."

"Has Dr. Len seen her?"

Corki raises her eyebrows and sighs. "How can he? He's busy transitioning out of Highfield."

Confused, I scowl.

"Sorry, that's rehab-speak for 'he's leaving.' Between Highfield and his private practice, Doctor Len has more patients than he knows what to do with. When the doctor who was supposed to join his practice accepted another offer, Len resigned."

"Where does that leave Sukie?" Not that Dr. Len was helping her. He just kept her quiet. That, according to Iris, makes the staff happy.

Corki doesn't answer and doesn't offer to help. Which means I need to push. "Would you mind helping me with a couple of things?"

She shakes her head as though to say no, then quickly apologizes. "Sorry, I came here to see if you had time for our interview, but...."

"Corki, would you find Sukie's nurse and ask her to come here, right away? And would you check my grandmother's med chart to see when she had her last meds and how much she was given?" I sound bossy, but I'm beyond caring.

The aide shuffles in. I'm tempted to tell her to move as though the washcloth is for someone she cares about. I meet her halfway across the room, take the damp washcloth, murmur a quick "Thanks," and leave her with her jaw hanging open.

Kneeling beside Sukie, I lift her chin and dab the warm cloth against her puffy cheeks, her breakfast-crusted mouth, and her forehead, imprinted with the weave of her slacks. I hold the cloth against each eyelid for a few seconds, then wash the gooey sleep from the innermost corner of her eyes.

Marion told me even if you think a person in Sukie's condition looks like she can't hear you, you should say something soothing to them; you never know, they may be listening and better yet, they might respond. The aide stares, which makes me feel stupidly self-conscious. "Sukie, it's me, Birdie. I've sent for your nurse. You don't feel so well now, but you're going to be all right. Sukie, I hope you can hear me. Can you?"

Seconds pass. Sukie's head weighs heavy against my fingertips. I open the washcloth and finish washing the rest of her face, around her ears and the back of her sweaty neck. "Now you're fresh and clean. Does that feel better? Sukie?" But Sukie doesn't say.

Chapter 20:

"Are you coming down with something, Birdie? You look absolutely etiolated." My father hits upon the College Board word that occurred to me, too, when I peeked at the bathroom mirror, at my usually rosy complexion drained to a poisoned pallor. The acne dotting my forehead—this is my first bout of raging red pimples—didn't help. The healthy "hint-of-Tomboy look" described in last year's Granville High yearbook as "glowing with a sunny guilelessness" has vanished. In its place, is a shade of nursing-home pale that leaves me looking as rinsed out as day-old pasta.

In answer to my father's question, I shrug.

Squinting, he takes stock of my lukewarm response, highly unusual for his outspoken daughter, then pours himself a bourbon and water. "What's all this I've been hearing about your grandmother?" he asks, stirring his drink with his little finger.

I follow him into the living room, where he lights the gas fire in the fireplace. One press of a button and bright orange and royal blue flames *whoosh* into view, enveloping the far end of the ballroom-sized living room within a warm halo. Had circumstances been different, we would be the picture of father-daughter tranquility, seated side by side in matching club chairs, me blowing on the steamy peppermint tea that promises to soothe my cramps, he savoring the afternoon cocktail that will dispel his headache.

"Marion maintains Sukie is being over-medicated." The disgruntled thought lines between his eyebrows mean he's dissatisfied with my sister's diagnosis. "Of course, she's getting her information from you—not that your observations are unreliable—if there's one thing I taught you, it's the value of detailed observations—but she hasn't reviewed Sukie's chart."

"That's exactly what Marion said. She wants you to have Sukie's medical records faxed to her."

Earlier this afternoon, after Corki checked Sukie's med administration chart, something must have struck her as odd, because she beeped Robin out of an important meeting. I wasn't sure what that had to do with finding Sukie's nurse and said as much. "Sorry, I meant to tell you, the nurse is on her way," Corki said. She wouldn't look me in the eye. When I asked again about which meds Sukie had been given and how many, Corki clammed up. Then it hit me—Corki had let Robin know that I was asking too many questions. That's when I called Marion.

"You know your sister—typical doctor—asks for something and expects everyone to drop what they're doing pronto. She called me right after she spoke with you. That's when I called Robin, who assured me she would fax Sukie's records to Marion." He looks at his watch. "That was over forty-five minutes ago."

Relieved he's taking charge for a change, I sip my tea, scalding the roof of my mouth. Okay, so it wasn't the kindest of thoughts. Sukie warned me that every unpleasant thought or deed reaps its own punishment. I run my tongue over the roof of my mouth; the welt that is forming is mine.

"I had another call, too..." his voice trails off. He swirls his glass, clinking the chunks of ice against one another. This mindless activity appears to absorb him, but I know better; he's working up to something I won't like.

"Was it Phineas?"

My father releases his eyes from his depleted drink so slowly you'd think his eyelids were lined with lead. "No,

Phineas usually emails unless there is something unusual to report."

I sigh with relief.

"I heard from Mrs. Perducci." He looks troubled. "She doesn't call me often, but when she does I always expect the worst possible news. And while listening to a rundown of the process that started when you launched an institutional abuse investigation wasn't the most uplifting news, I appreciated her thoughtfulness."

I nod. "She described it to me, too. As a matter of fact, if Sukie hadn't been in such bad shape, Corki was going to interview me today. But she postponed it until tomorrow."

The worry lines on his forehead reappear. "An interview like that can be…" his pause means he's searching for the right word, "…trying. I wonder if you should have someone with you."

He doesn't offer to protect me very often and when he does, I warm to his fatherliness and find it annoying at the same time. "Someone like my lawyer?"

He squelches a smile. "That would be rather heavy-handed, don't you think? No, I was thinking that Solange might join you."

"I'd like that." And I mean it. Along with Elliot, whom I can count on to be his outrageously candid self, Solange has become the type of friend I once believed I'd never find. "Thanks, Dad."

"There's something else." He crosses and uncrosses his legs, never a good sign. "I thanked Mrs. Perducci for supporting you, given your situation."

He's referring, of course, to my juvenile-offender status. I roll my eyes and sigh. "Dad," I chant in a two-note whine, "why'd you mention that? I don't go out of my way to discuss that with her, or anyone else for that matter."

"Because she took a chance when she agreed to fold your Service Learning Project and your Community Service hours into one, and I want her to know how much I appreciate her taking that risk."

"Dad, you know darn well Mrs. Perducci had two reasons for being so agreeable." My sudden burst of energy causes him to blink in surprise. "Sukie is the first. Mrs. Perducci said having me on the unit would help Sukie adapt to life at Highfield." He mouths, *True enough.* I go on, "And you're the second reason." I shake my head disapprovingly. "Don't pretend you're shocked. When you were on Highfield's Board of Directors, you raised more money than any other trustee. That bought you favors that will be good until the end of the next millennium, you said so yourself."

It's his turn to sigh. "You're right in the sense that Mrs. Perducci and I grew to trust one another. Which is why she felt comfortable asking me about Harry Miller."

"Why was she interested in him?" Dumb question that it is, I ask it anyway, hoping to sound only mildly curious about Elliot's brother. Innocently so.

He upends his glass and swallows the last of the melted ice water. "Because of your friendship with Elliot."

The glass lands like a gavel on the coaster and I jump. "I'm sorry, you lost me there. What's one thing got to do with the other?"

"Let me put it this way: Mrs. Perducci doesn't want anything to compromise your efforts to erase your current status."

"More apologies from your obtuse daughter. I don't get it. What's that got to do with anything?"

My father leans forward and plants his elbows on his knees. It's his mega-serious pose. Afraid of what I'm about to hear, I grip the arms of the chair. "Mrs. Perducci said you were with her in her office this morning when she tripped over her handbag." I nod as slowly as I dare without breaking eye contact with my father. "Later, when she needed her wallet, it was missing. She figured that you and she had entered her office seconds after the thief had left. That he had heard you coming down the hall and, in his hurry to leave, knocked her handbag to the floor and left it there."

"Mrs. Perducci thinks a man lifted her wallet? Why?"

"She's not sure, but before you and she entered her office, the receptionist sent your friend, Elliot, to deliver a bouquet of flowers to her office."

Breathless, I drop back against the chair. I'm so incredulous I can't speak. I think of the beautiful flowers the staff sent Mrs. Perducci. After a few whirling seconds, I find my voice. "She thinks Elliot stole her wallet?"

"His brother has a record as long as my arm."

I raise my arms in disbelief and drop them, letting my hands bounce on my thighs. "The courts have a record on me, too." My father winces. "Does that mean that *you* steal tires? Come on, Dad, that's ridiculous. Elliot could have delivered the flowers after someone else swiped Mrs. Perducci's wallet." He watches me intently, admiration seeping into his eyes. "Does Mrs. Perducci know for sure that she had her wallet with her when she left for work this morning? Did she stop at the grocery store last night before the storm? In her hurry to get home, did she leave her wallet there? Here's another possibility: what if one of her kids—she has five you know—took her wallet out to get his lunch money and forgot to put it back. Do I need to go on?"

"No, counselor, you've done a brilliant job of shedding reasonable doubt on the current premise. I taught you to question, and question you did." A shiver travels from his head to his neck and shoulders as though he swallowed

170

something sour. "Little did I know that I would create a fire-breathing inquisition monster."

It's my turn to lean forward and plant my elbows on my knees. "Then until Mrs. Perducci proves that Elliot is guilty, there's no reason for me to stop my friendship with him, is there? I purposely avoided him today because of you and it made me feel like a fraud. A huge honking phony."

"Have you forgotten the terms of your Informal Adjustment Agreement? No associating with fellow offenders?"

"Of course not. But so far, neither you or Phineas have said for sure that Elliot has a record." My voice cracks with emotion—something I wasn't expecting. I promised myself I would never ever again under any circumstances let myself break down over a boy, no matter what. The last boy to bring me to tears was Bruce, when he'd pinned me against the wall in the girls' bathroom. Now I'm pinned against another wall, this time by Jake.

"Birdie..." Jake's conciliatory tone startles me.

"What?" I say a little too sharply. My heart is racing and so are my thoughts. I'd not told Jake that I'd joined Maggie's Blingers because Bruce was bullying me; I'd let him think it was the act of an airheaded adolescent bahoozle.

"You're not going to like what I'm about to tell you. I get no pleasure in delivering this news, but you need to know. As decent a fellow as you may think Elliot is, he idolized his older brother, Harry. Unfortunately, Harry wasn't the best role model. Chances are he sucked Elliot into a number of schemes, probably shoplifting tools he needed in his workshop. You remember I told you that Harry has a number of patents in his name?"

I let him think his news is making me shiver. "Yes," I sigh, feeling sicker by the minute.

"I suspect Elliot was Harry's gofer. To make a long story short, Elliot may be in the same situation as you. Neither of you should be associating with the other. If you really care about him—and I think you do—you'll stay away from him. And if he really cares about you…"

"Of course he does." My goofy girl exclamation surprises me more than it does Jake, whose eyebrows skyrocket up his forehead. I used to ridicule other girls for their declarations of undying love. Now, I sound just as lame.

"Does he know about your juvenile-offender status?" He hasn't come right out and said it, but he's accusing me of wrongdoing, which is totally unfair. *If* Elliot has his own probation officer, *he* never mentioned it. So why am I being cross-examined like this?

"Hey, Dad?" I swallow in an unsuccessful attempt to squelch the tears that well along my lower eyelids. "Have you ever done something you weren't proud of?"

His eyes dart to the mantle, across the photos of him and Solange squinting contentedly in the Bermuda sunshine, in the Grand Caymans, atop the ruins in Sicily, on the deck of a friend's forty-foot sloop, back into their meticulously restored home, and finally, to me. "Unfortunately, yes."

"How often do you broadcast whatever it is that you're ashamed of?"

He glances back at the mantle. "Almost never." I can barely hear his voice.

"That's how I feel. Elliot's lost his legs; that's all the trouble I know about him. And if he's got problems with the law, I don't want to make those worse. But it's not right for me to have to sneak up the stairwells at Highfield just to avoid him. I think he deserves to know why we can't see one another."

"How do you propose to do that if you're not supposed to be in contact with other juvenile offenders?"

I pick at a hangnail on my thumb. "How about writing him a letter?" I ask without looking up.

"What form of communication would you call that?"

"Well, what would you do?"

"I'd do what I'm told. There's too much at risk. Especially if Phineas finds out."

I roll my eyes. Phineas hasn't said a thing, hasn't run the proverbial red flag up the ship's mast to warn that Elliot might be dangerous cargo. So, now what? The one person who can clear up this mess is the same person I'm not supposed to see. How else will I find out if he's in trouble, too?

Chapter 21:

Last fall, at the beginning of my junior year, the kids in my classes at Granville High knew. The boys were too embarrassed to say a thing, thank goodness. Leave it to the girls to scream, "retarded ovaries" when they saw me, the only junior who had yet to get her period. To hear them, you'd think I'd committed a capital offense. Maggie Forester and her "Blingers," the full-breasted devotees of Victoria's Secret Wonder Bras and every known brand of tampon, harassed me about being "overly developed in the brains department and stunted where it counts." As though Mother Nature had offered me a choice: stay little or grow up; she loves me, she loves me not.

I'd have gladly exchanged my 4'9", eighty-five pound body with its mighty gymnast's shoulders, nubby boobs, and boyish muscular butt for ta-tas and hips, so round that working out on the balance beam would have been a gravitational impossibility. Confronted with the options of vaulting through the air or becoming a real girl, I quit the gymnastics team. A couch potato lifestyle in combination with a diet of high-fructose corn syrup, hormone-laced fast foods, and jumbo-sized carbonated drinks would land me on the doorstep of menstruation heaven. Then I'd be like the girls I admired: moody, mysterious, and inexplicably attractive to the guys.

I plugged my backpack and the gym locker I shared with Maggie Forester with half-empty bottles of Midol and travel-size boxes of easy glide Tampax. Every twenty-eight days, I'd mark my assignment calendar with a red X to denote the day IT arrived. Ten days before, I complained of cramps and acted as testy as the girls I described in my diary as "femme fatale role models."

Despite my carefully scripted performance, I discovered on one of Maggie's FaceBook posts that she considered me a fraud. An anorexic. A dwarf cretin. A girl who needed to be taught a lesson. I wanted to shrivel up and disappear.

In the weeks between Thanksgiving and Christmas, I became desperate; I needed Maggie; she kept Bruce away and I did whatever she wanted. That was our deal. But she turned on me. Again. Told the bling-jacking clique I couldn't be trusted. They disagreed. So far, they insisted, I'd proven myself an agile little thief, capable of crawling through the smallest window of whichever home they chose to break into, then opening the back door, all in record time. Maggie went along with them that winter, but by spring—her "hot pickings season"—she insisted the Blingers put my trust to the test. "Let's see if she cries for her mommy when she's faced with a simulated rape," was the plan her boyfriend, Avery, later reported to the police. A cruel plan I didn't know about at the time.

Following Maggie's orders, Avery pinned my arms behind my naked body, and let her snap the most humiliating photo I'd ever been forced to pose for. Seconds after I bit his arm, he e-blasted my pic to the kids in our class. Which is when a horrified parent—Mrs. Forester of all people—caught Maggie's younger brother giggling over my photo and called the police. At the same time, Avery's bird-watching neighbor focused her high-powered binoculars on a "gang of teenagers" gathered at the back of his parents' house and, knowing the Fitzsimmons were away, dialed 911.

With the whine of approaching sirens, something in me snapped. I went ballistic. Crazy screaming crying out of my mind. By the time the police arrived, I was hiding behind the bushes that lined the loneliest corner of the Fitzsimmons' property, yiffing non-stop.

"Someone tried to rape me, I don't know who," I told the officer through hysterical sobs. What I didn't understand as I wrapped myself in the blanket he tossed me was that he knew I was flat-out lying. The bird-watching neighbor had reported that all four of the kids had been partying together "until things got awfully strange."

"Until things got painful," was how I described the scene to my worried furious parents at the police station. And when Jake asked what on earth I was thinking of when I got involved with Maggie Forester, I didn't tell him about Bruce's bullying. I was too afraid.

Now, seven months later, safe within the second floor bathroom of Jake's home, soft light reflects from the peachy walls, and warm water splashes into the luxurious square bathtub. Seared into my memory, my very own Hester Prynne brand of shame, complicated by my realization of how much Maggie hated me. Call me naïve, conceited, or just plain ignorant, I'd never thought of myself as that unlikable. And dumb enough to still cry about it. Was I really that bad?

Sometimes, I hate other teenagers. Other times, I hate being one. More often than not, I hate myself.

I peel off my sweater and slowly unbutton my blouse. It's been a long day and I'm more tired than usual. All I want is a good long soak. I drop a couple of lavender-scented bath beads into the water and watch the glycerin coatings melt. Within seconds, a relaxing aroma floats on glistening mounds of bubbles. Along with bath beads, Solange gave me a clear plastic bath pillow with a blue angel fish in it. I unfold it from its tidy plastic case, pry out the nozzle, tuck it between my lips and release one, two, three deep breaths into the pillow. I forgot how readily deep breathing relaxes me. I drizzle warm water into the tiny suction cups on the back of the pillow and press them into the corner farthest from the swan-neck faucet.

I shut the faucet; the tub is like me—as full as it can be without overflowing.

I finish undressing, drop my clothing in a heap around my ankles. Stepping out of my underpants I notice a reddish brown smear, one that, had it come earlier, would have saved me the pain of learning what Maggie was really like. So that's what my body has been trying to tell me these past few days: it was saying good-bye to my girlhood.

I step into the tub, brush the bubbles aside and sink slowly and deliciously into the steamy water. In the confusing days after my arrest, I dreamed of telling Maggie that her brand of cruelty made the Wicked Witch of the West look like Mother Teresa. Now that my body is finally doing what it's supposed to, I'm no longer worried about pleasing Maggie. The angelfish in its see-though-plastic casing bobs agreeably, content with its new freedom.

Chapter 22:

Next morning, the rogue snowstorm is old news. Traffic has sprayed the mounded snow with dots of brown sand and slush, making the day before Thanksgiving look like early March. Still wearing my jacket, I pry tacks from the notice on the staff bulletin board that canceled last night's Thanksgiving celebration. "Blame the storm, sorry" is scrawled in red marker. I rearrange the sign-up sheet for the Annual Highfield Christmas/Holiday Party—one guest allowed per staff—to make room for the latest in my series of vignettes about Sukie's life before Arlene Alzheimer moved in.

In keeping with the storm, today's story describes Sukie shoveling snow in her backyard, packing it solid around a hockey rink-sized rectangle, and flooding it, one layer at a time until smooth thick ice had formed. At the other end of her yard, in the stone fireplace Pop-Pop had built, Sukie made a fire to warm my brothers and me as we sipped the hot cocoa she ferried to us, mug by steaming mug. In the second to last line, Sukie says she missed "the good days of being with my family," but notes that she is fortunate to have found "another, different kind of family." Those are Sukie's exact words, words she'd spoken clearly and fluently in the days before Dr. Len increased her meds.

Robin stops by and seems to take pleasure in interrupting my work. "Corki called and left a message for you. She wants you to meet her downstairs in the Conference Room, right away." She's as icy as anyone whose staff is under investigation.

Solange warned that I'd be demoted from "the best volunteer the unit has ever had" to a pariah. "Investigations are delicate business. Look at it from the employees' perspectives: two of their friends might get fired, and they're worried that could happen to them. Until this is resolved, they're unsure of everything they once took for granted. Call it paranoia, but they're afraid you might report them, too."

But I hadn't reported everything I'd seen. Timtiere and Sandis let a patient collapse instead of taking her to the bathroom and I never reported that. I know why I reported one incident and not the other; I feel ashamed and relieved at the same time. Imagine the "simulated raping" the staff would give me if I'd started not one, but two investigations.

I peek at Sukie, asleep in the TV room. Dr. Len never adjusted her medications; of that I'm sure. To make matters worse, as of this morning, my sister Marion hadn't called back. My father promised to call Robin to make sure she'd faxed Sukie's med records. Why is everything so complicated? If everyone did what they were supposed to do, questions wouldn't hammer the backs of my eye sockets. I kiss the top of Sukie's head and hurry downstairs.

Instead of the zingy-clingy low-cut blouse she usually wears, today Corki dresses in a tailored navy-blue suit jacket buttoned from top to bottom. Her impossibly big, curly hair has lost its volume and henna shine. Her buttoned-down expression matches her clothing. "Hummingbird," she says, glancing over the tops of the red and white striped half-glasses, a remnant from her former candy-cane image, "have a seat."

I sit on the edge of the chair opposite her, set my backpack on the seat beside me, and place my hands on the faded black jeans that match my turtleneck. Interviews like this bring out the worst in women's color choices.

"Sorry to take you from your work but..." she taps a manila folder marked *To: Corki, From: Mrs. Perducci.*

I think about Mrs. Perducci's missing wallet and wonder if Corki has heard that Elliot, the friend I introduced her to, is in trouble. Being a social worker—my father maintains they're trained to ferret out every last secret from your personal arsenal—Corki must know whether Elliot is an active member of the juvenile justice system. If that's true, it'll work against Elliot whom the Highfield judicial system has already labeled "guilty." To hope Corki will keep an open mind while this delinquent describes what she witnessed is an enormous assumption. One I intend to test.

"Mrs. Perducci said you would interview me."

"Good. That's helpful." I'm so accustomed to seeing Corki grin that I'm shocked when her mouth sinks into a zippered smile. "This is your chance to tell me your perception of what happened. I'm going to take notes, just as I've done during the other interviews, so don't let my writing distract you, okay?"

I nod. My *perception*? Does Corki think I've made all this up?

The shiny mahogany conference table is sandwiched into a long narrow space. Heavy draperies on the room's one window and a dusty silk dogwood tree squished into the corner give the room a congested feeling that makes it hard to breathe. From the overhead loudspeaker, a woman asks Mrs. Perducci to please phone the receptionist's desk. The heat clicks on and a fan whirls.

Corki picks up her pen and clicks. From within its cold stainless steel collar, a leaky blue ball point appears, eager to blur every unfocused word I utter. I'm not sure what to do. So far, refusing Solange's offer to reschedule her meeting so she could join me falls smack under the category of choices I've made and regretted.

"How about starting at the beginning? What were you and Sukie doing when you noticed something amiss?"

Corki's questions break with a patronizing rumble. *What if I report events inaccurately, or leave something out,* I worry until I remember my backpack.

I open it and, using both hands, pull out my three-ring notebook. Corki's eyes widen, two full moons rising over the crest of her glasses. I cock my head, run my forefinger down the brightly colored index tabs. When I land on the green tab marked *Observations,* I flick to the section and turn page after page of handwritten notes until I come to the page with *Abuse Allegations* written at the top.

"Aren't you professional," Corki says, craning her neck in an effort to see the notes I prepared for this interview.

I tip the edge of my notebook toward me, forming a polite little barrier. I lean back, turn the pages, and review earlier notes, jottings from the afternoon of the incident, a combination of the elements of scientific inquiry I learned in junior high and those of investigation I learned from Jake:

Date/time:

Circumstances:

Persons Involved:

Witnesses:

Observations:

Interpretations:

Questions:

Hypothesis:

Persons notified/date/time:

Follow-through/date/time:

"Is that where you keep the lovely stories you've been writing about Sukie?" Corki's shoulders relax. She sets her elbow on the table and rests her chin on her loosely balled fist.

The navy tones in her jacket soften to complement her complexion's reddish glow.

"Not exactly. They're at home on my computer. I write them after I talk with Sukie. I keep our conversations and the vignettes the same so Sukie has a chance of recognizing them when the aides and nurses mention them to her. See, here are some of my notes." I flip to the back of the notebook and tilt the pages toward Corki.

"You're amazing. The most I wrote when I was your age was a diary and those entries were frivolous at best: Whose birthday party I went to. Who had a crush on whom. Who got their first kiss and when." Delighted by her own memories, Corki laughs as she speaks. This is the Corki I like best.

"I keep a diary, too, but it's separate from this. Part of my Community Service assignment includes writing a paper about my experiences here. When I started, I had no idea that I'd be involved in an investigation, but I'm going to include it."

Oops. Corki stiffens. Her face takes on the drabness of her clothing. I don't want her to feel threatened by a kid who takes notes about everything she hears and sees behind locked doors, so I try my hand at damage control: "One of the points I'll include in my paper is how lucky patients are to live in a facility that goes out of its way to make sure their rights are being protected. That's important."

I slip my hand over my queasy stomach. What I'm learning about having my period is that the cramps don't merely announce the arrival of "that time of month," they hang around and make a nuisance of themselves.

Corki slips her glasses on. Her pen poised on her lined legal notepad says, *See? I can take notes, too.* "Okay, go ahead. Take your time and tell me everything."

I describe the circumstances surrounding Sukie's outburst, her retreat into her room, and the way she calmed down for a bit until she saw the aide, Sandis Doyle, and how that set Sukie off.

"I'm afraid Sukie said some pretty nasty things, which isn't like her."

"You don't have to apologize, that's her Alzheimer's talking. Go on." Corki waits. As soon as I speak, her pen rolls along the paper.

As I review the ugly details, I do my best to keep my temper under control, especially during the part about Sandis openly making fun of Sukie. Mocking her.

Recalling Sukie's confusion makes me want to cry, that and the fact that Sandis seemed pleased when she informed me my grandmother had bragged about entertaining men other than Pop-Pop. I tell this to Corki. My eyes lock on hers. "Sandis wasn't talking about them watching the ball game, either."

Corki nods knowingly. "Then what happened?"

"Sandis asked Sukie if she was going to have a 'hissy fit' like the one she had the night before."

"Oh dear…" Corki murmurs. "She actually said that?"

"I could hardly believe it myself—Sandis goading my grandmother." I shake my head in disgust. I remember being one against Maggie, Avery, and the Blingers; terrified doesn't begin to describe how I felt. Though Sukie and I were evenly matched, numbers wise, against the two aides, we may as well have been facing a crowd. "I managed to distract Sukie, who would have done fine if Sandis hadn't started in on her again."

"Again? You mean she wouldn't leave your grandmother alone?"

"That's right. That's when things got really strange. Sandis called Sukie a fake, claimed that she didn't have Alzheimer's. That she was a very rich woman, taking a bed that some really demented, really poor person needed."

"Then what happened?"

"Sandis told me Sukie had bragged to her about her sexual history..." Corki gasps.

I run my finger down my notes, then read aloud word for word: "'...she's known her share of guys.'" Corki's jaw drops open.

Slipping her glasses to the tip of her nose, she leans forward, her eyes fierce with indignation and curiosity. "And how did Sukie respond?"

"She just stood there, absorbing every word that came out of Sandis' mouth. I'm not sure what she was thinking because she didn't say a thing. And I didn't ask because I was hoping she'd forget. But I could see it in her eyes; she was fuming. Whatever happened between Sukie and Sandis the night before left an emotional impression on Sukie. A mean one." I purposely toss an "adult phrase" at Corki, the type that leaves kids groaning but grabs the attention of the over-twenty-one crowd. It works.

"'Emotional impression?' What does that mean to you?"

"My sister, Marion, said to think of it this way: you're driving to work and someone rear-ends you, causes a ton of expensive damage. Your car is towed to a garage. You get a lift to your office, then go directly to the staff lounge for a cup of coffee. On your way out, someone bumps you and your coffee spills on your new slacks. Back in your office, you close the door, kick your desk and break down in tears. You weren't thinking about the car accident when that person bumped into you, but the memory was festering, waiting for someone to jar it awake. And when you saw the stain on your slacks, your memory roared."

Later, as I come onto the unit, the nurses stop talking and disappear into the closest patient's room. Usually, they ask me about my weekly vignette or tell me how helpful it was to have something specific to chat with Sukie about. Not today. When I turn the corner the Somalian cleaning lady, who always smiles at me, starts rearranging her supplies. Robin takes one look at me and pages through a patient file as though it were a best-selling novel.

"How did my grandmother sleep last night?" I ask Iris once I'm in Sukie's room, where Sukie is dozing in the chair.

The compassion I usually see in Iris' clear green eyes empties faster than a plastic wading pool with a puncture wound. "I've been told to direct all your questions to the supervisor," she says, tugging a wrinkled pillowcase over Sukie's pillow.

I understand. Corki has already let everyone know that I keep notes on events that happen on the unit. No one will talk with me. Not the nurses, the cleaning lady, not the aide. Not even my grandmother, who is still sleeping. In the time it took me to use the rest room and climb three levels of stairs, Corki sounded the alarm. So much for an impartial investigation.

Chapter 23:

Gauzy light edges in around the room-darkening shades on my bedroom window. I woke at 4:30 this morning and haven't shut my eyes since; haven't fulfilled Jake's plea, issued late last night as I headed for my room: "Tomorrow is Thanksgiving. No one is scheduled to go anywhere. I'd be grateful if we all slept in."

Staring at the ceiling, I try counting everything I'm grateful for. *That I'm safe* is first on my list. It's been weeks since the spiny tingle of fear sliced through me whenever I turned a corner, wondering if Bruce was waiting. His routine was simple-minded and scary like him: back me to a wall, plunging his forefinger and thumb close to my eyes, pulsing one digit against the other, warming them for another painful titty twister. I ran whenever I could, but the lumbering giant always outran me. The last time he pinched and twisted my small breast, he left black and blue marks that stayed all week. By the time his marks faded, my fear was in full blossom. Without that bully in my life, my ability to focus on the important things has returned.

That I've come to know Solange is second. Other than Sukie, Solange is the only other adult who happily shares time with me, doing things like taking me to her dressmaker to sew my dress for the Highfield Halloween Dance. If I hadn't been so angry with Solange for stealing Jake, I'd have given her a chance early on to show me why Jake loves her. I would have loved her a lot sooner, too.

That Jake agreed to let me stay here should have been next on my list. But I'm not sure whether he opened his doors because he truly missed his "enduring mistake" or because having me under his roof was his way of protecting himself from further public humiliation. And that bothers me. *You're supposed to be listing what you're grateful for, not judging Jake's ulterior motives,* I remind myself.

I think a while longer. Red highlights stream like a halo around my window shades. What's the saying? Red sky in the morning, sailors take warning? I stretch my arms high above my head and try to decide what else I feel grateful for. Sukie's Alzheimer's is worse, and Corki didn't show a flicker of empathy when I described how the aides taunted her. Elliot, my only friend at Highfield, is off-limits according to my father. As far as he's concerned, I've probably already compromised my IAA, Informal Adjustment Agreement. My sister, Marion—my favorite person on the planet—didn't call with her take on Dr. Len's "med madness." With a measly two things to be grateful for, my list is anemic at best. If I'd ticked off five, I'd be satisfied. I promise myself by the end of the day, I'll fill in those three glaring blanks.

The closet in Jake and Solange's bedroom creaks open. His direction to "sleep in" reminds me of Christmases past, before our family had disintegrated. The kids—those of us still living at home—listened dutifully for the first sounds of our parents' excruciatingly slow rituals: the bed squeaking as Jake got up; the flattened heel of his slippers flip-flopping towards the bathroom; Mom whispering a little too loudly, asking if he'd heard the children stirring. Thinking about the "good" holidays makes me sad, so I stop.

I get up and slip my sweatpants and a hooded sweatshirt over my pjs. On the way downstairs, I overhear Jake complaining that someone—I can't tell whom—didn't call, most likely Marion.

I'm about to open the back door, where the newspaper boy has hurled the plastic bag holding the paper, when Jake and Solange appear in their cinched bathrobes. Jake greets me with a scowl. Solange rolls her eyes. "Your father is looking for a reason to be miserable." She takes a cup from the cabinet and fills it with freshly brewed coffee. "It's a holiday, Jake. Forget about Mrs. Perducci."

"What about Mrs. Perducci?" I look from Solange to Jake and back. "Did she call you with the results of the investigation?"

Purposely avoiding Solange's offer to give him her cup, Jake reaches over her head into the open cabinet for another. "No, but close." He fills his cup. The carafe clanks dangerously as he fumbles to fit it on the coffee maker's heating unit.

Except for the digital stove clock clicking off the Thanksgiving seconds, the kitchen floods with a restless silence. Solange glances at Jake and rolls her eyes for the second time. "Your father is angry with me for not going with you to your interview." She shakes her head in disbelief. "I was telling him about my day yesterday when he realized I wasn't with you." Her sigh marks this as the umpteenth time she's tried to explain.

"Birdie and I discussed it. I would have cancelled my meeting if I'd felt she was in any way uncomfortable." As she looks at me, her eyes brim with pride. "Birdie was composed and self-confident. There was no need to tag along." The coffeepot releases a leftover cloudburst of steam, hisses, then sputters into silence. "Call me the wicked stepmother if you will, but I think we both made the right decision."

"It's the ramifications I'm concerned about." Jake dons the I'm-the-professional-I-know-better-than-you smirk that sets Solange off faster than a lit match in a puddle of gasoline. "Should this allegation require legal action, we won't have a witness to corroborate Hummingbird's testimony—"

"Let's not get ahead of ourselves, shall we? This continues to be an internal investigation and until circumstances change, we all need to do our best to deal with the loads that have landed on our plates."

I admire Solange; she gives as good as she gets. "Before this gets too involved, I suggest we call a truce, sit down together, and have breakfast. What do you say?" She tilts her head and looks up at Jake. "Truce?" she asks, eyebrows raised in perky arcs.

"Truce," he nods. "But I'm not hungry. You and Birdie go ahead and eat. I'll be on the sun porch, reading the daily rag."

"What about catching the Macy's Day Parade on TV, Dad?"

The vehemence has drained from his tired face. He nods again. "Why, yes, that's a possibility, too."

After he disappears down the hallway to the sun porch, I climb onto a stool by the island and wrap my feet around its rungs. I need something to hang on to, something that grounds me. Something I can count on to always be there without becoming moody. I hoped I would find that sturdiness in Jake. I settle for the wooden stool with a concave rush seat that holds me securely in place. That's more than a lot of daughters have.

"Cereal?" Solange asks as she spins the lazy Susan in the corner cupboard.

"Sure." I rest my elbow on the cool dark granite, plant my head in my palm, and close my eyes. I didn't sleep well enough to ward off Jake's moodiness and now I feel exhausted. His disapproval bothers me more than I like to admit. It always has.

Two round bowls click against the counter. Solange and I are muesli fans: hazelnuts, dates, and organic oats spill into the bowls. The refrigerator door remains open while Solange scoops a dollop of plain Greek yogurt—one per bowl—then returns the yogurt container to the top shelf. Why can't everything be as predictable as preparing a bowl of cereal?

Solange seats herself beside me and plunges her spoon into the firm white yogurt and mixes. At first, the muesli refuses to mix with the yogurt. But as she stirs in a patient clockwise motion, grains of oats get caught in the smooth white coolness, followed by a few more and more. Soon Solange is folding the final holdouts into the mix. Two different entities: a colloid of living bacteria and a mixture of dried fruits and grains have united to form a textured whole.

"I wonder if that will ever happen to our family?" I ask softly as I begin the same process. Solange knows exactly what I'm referring to.

"Give it time," she says. "You've only been here a little over a month."

I slip a spoonful of cereal into my mouth and chew thoughtfully. Has it been that long? Time has gone by so quickly. Soon, I'll be back at Granville High, where the bullies will have me for lunch.

"All this business about you-know-who being angry with me," she tilts her head in the direction of the sunroom, where the toe-tapping rhythms of a high school brass band shield us from being overheard, "is nothing but a cover-up."

I've never associated Jake with anything as intriguing as a cover-up. Nothing as daring as the activities of the dashing attorneys on television who get themselves in and out of stacks of legal trouble. I scratch the side of my head. "My father? You're kidding."

"Aren't you the one who gets frustrated when the staff at Highfield refuses to understand that Sukie communicates through her behavior? What's the saying you like to quote?"

"Behavior is a kind of sign language."

"That's it. Now apply that to your father."

190

I scowl. Sleeplessness has left my brain thick as this bowl of muesli.

"Think about it. He claimed he was angry with me for not going with you to your interview, right?"

I nod.

"That wasn't it at all. He was angry with himself. *He* should have accompanied you, not me. Deep down inside he knows that but can't bring himself to say so. I can't tell you how badly he feels about your getting caught up in the goings-on at Highfield when he hasn't even visited Sukie once. Not once."

"Is that why he told me I was 'overly involved' at Highfield? That I ought to cultivate friends my own age? Get involved in normal activities? Just where did he think I was going to find those? Did he forget what landed me here in the first place? That I'm on a short leash until I've outgrown my juvenile-offender status?"

Solange puts her arm around me and leans her forehead against my cheek. "Yes," she says softly. "That's it exactly. He's lucky you're at Highfield and he knows it. He's terrified of what might have happened to Sukie if you hadn't been there. Unfortunately, in the process of being such a good advocate, you've reminded him of the many ways in which he's failed her and you."

Her breath feels warm against my neck. I love Solange for helping me understand what's going on with Jake. She's sweet and I appreciate that. But Jake hasn't yet introduced her to the Windsor family gremlin, one of many attached to our family. This particular gnome appears on special days, like birthdays and holidays, whenever one of us dares inject joy into a celebration.

Solange swallows her last spoonful of breakfast and looks at the clock. "Oh my gosh, it's getting late," she mumbles words pasted with yogurt-muesli. She glides off the stool and drops to her hands and knees so fast you'd have thought she mistook the rat-a-tat-tat of the parade's televised snare drums for sniper fire.

Beneath the island, the panicked rooting noises of a woman struck by the realization that she'd forgotten about the guests Jake invited to dinner. She murmurs about the off-handed invitation he extended to his colleagues, Sarah and Bill Burns, who, in an equally off-handed way, delivered their acceptance yesterday at 5:00.

Solange heard about this via her phone as she was pulling into the driveway. She jammed the car into reverse and headed for Thompson's Best Market, where she joined the frazzled legions of last-minute shoppers, wearily pushing their brimming shopping carts from Aisle 4B to 4C. "I wish you'd told me yesterday, Jake. I purposely did the grocery shopping before the Thanksgiving locusts hit." By then, Jake was apologizing profusely, admitting the entire deal was very last minute and asking would she ever forgive him. At least that's what I piece together amidst trumpets blaring their way down Fifth Avenue and the clash-bang of Solange's pots and pans.

Chapter 24:

This isn't the first time I've seen Solange function at her overly focused best. Nothing—not man, android, or emotionally attached stepdaughter—can stand in her way. Yet, the abrupt change from the warm mom-like companion helping me navigate Jake's emotional rapids into a kitchen diva, leaves me wondering if I'd missed something. I peek around the corner at Jake, dozing, newspaper collapsed on his lap, legs splayed on his elevated recliner. Between snoozing and planning to socialize with his colleagues later today, he has conveniently organized his day to avoid being alone with Solange or me. That's what the language of his behavior tells me.

"The turkey will be ready just before Sarah and Bill get here." Solange checks her calculations, talking herself through an arithmetic exercise as she taps a bright pink calculator with oversized numbers. She scribbles 5:00 PM in the margin of her stained copy of *Joy of Cooking,* splayed like my father's legs.

The simmering aroma of organizational wonder settles in around her. "By the time we remove the biscuits from the warming oven, your father will have finished carving the bird." She pauses, listening to the silence that replaces the brass bands on television. "Speaking of your father, what's he doing?"

"Last time I checked, he was trading stock options." My lips buckle into a half-smile.

Solange giggles. "It's Thanksgiving, Birdie. The stock market is closed. What's he really doing?"

"Sleeping."

She sighs. "I thought so. I can't blame him for grabbing some time for himself."

Solange's generosity makes me cringe. Not that I doubt her sincerity; its hard-wrought tone is what bothers me. Had this been my mother offering excuses for Jake, this brand of sincerity would coil up surer than a rattlesnake posed to strike. When my parents were still married, the rattling started as soon as Jake dumped yet another last-minute holiday dinner party in my mother's lap. While he snoozed, my mother quoted from the Book of Tolerant Wife Excuses Solange has adopted. As the day wore on and exhaustion gnawed at Mom's generosity, the snake rippled into a spring-loaded coil.

In the early hours of any given holiday, I've learned to judge the type of day the family would endure by the level of generosity my mother offered my father. Though this ancient brick house is a different home and this is a different holiday, it's the same father with the same snare tactic. To my disappointment, Solange allows herself to be swept along in Jake's tired game. Thanksgiving promises to be a repeat performance of the B movie I hoped never to see again. Jake's bullying is less Neanderthal than Bruce's, but by the time the movie credits roll, he'll have taken advantage of Solange just the same.

I'm tempted to tell her how making excuses for Bruce got me in trouble. How, when he first followed me at school, I convinced myself that bumping into him outside the girls' room door was a coincidence. That his presence every time I came out of the bathroom didn't equal stalking; he was just being friendly. I ignored the frightened inner voice, warning me his wasn't a case of puppy-dog loneliness, but of wild-dog meanness.

But when I glance at her, basking in the afterglow of having orchestrated a last-minute holiday feast, her gift to her hard-working husband, I back off. Sukie would say what goes on between a husband and wife is none of my business. In that department, she would have explained, I'm out of their league. If I didn't care so much for Solange, she would have been right.

Solange breezes by me into the pantry and emerges with a wooden silverware chest. Scratched and faded, it smells as though it had baked in a musty attic. She's so focused on finishing her preparations, she pays no attention to the chest's surprisingly poor condition.

Fine sawdust trails to the floor as she proceeds to the dining room. She shifts the box from her forearms toward her elbows and looks around for a free space on which to unload it. The sideboard, occupied by twin candelabra and a silver tea service, leaves no room. The breakfront, with its gleaming bowed glass doors, offers no relief. The only other furniture in the room is the dining table, covered with a freshly ironed tablecloth. Not a candidate for the stains the chest is sure to leave behind.

"Solange? Can I give you a hand?"

"Get an old dish towel from the kitchen."

"Are you sure you don't want me to take that chest...."

"I'm fine." There's a restrained, yet testy, quality to her. Fatigue, the precursor to holiday disruption, is raising its ugly head.

"If you say so. But I'm afraid—"

"Birdie, if you don't hurry..." The weight of the chest catches Solange as she turns her upper body in a Yoga twist that pulls her off-balance. The brash sound of jangled silverware, bouncing from a wooden box whose bottom crumbles on impact, adds a scorched earth quality to her cry of "Jake."

Jake barefoots it across the kitchen floor. "What is it? What's happened?" Dining paraphernalia lay scattered on the pale peach oriental rug.

"You told me you'd reglued this chest. Now look what's happened. Bring the vacuum cleaner, quick," she barks, and he whirs into a cleaning frenzy.

It's getting late. Exhaustion has set in. Solange has graduated from a substitute mom/kitchen diva to capturing top billing on Jake's list of what matters most, for now anyway. It's a start. I give her a silent cheer.

Chapter 25:

Jake buttons his long-sleeved plaid shirt without removing his eyes from the television. Seated in his recliner, he jerks left, right, then back to center in an unconscious imitation of Brett Favre, dancing through the Detroit Lions defense toward the goal post. At the first down, he grumbles, "You're the most nearsighted ref in the NFL." He rakes his hair, still damp from his shower, from his forehead and begrudgingly taps his BlackBerry.

Leaning against the doorjamb between the living room and the sunroom, Solange threads a thin gold spiral earring into one pierced ear, then the other. "How about muting the television while you're on the phone?"

"You got it, babe," he says in his most conciliatory tone. He turns on his speakerphone, waits for the recorded message on Bill's cell to finish apologizing for "being unavailable," then says, "Bill, Sarah. Jake here. Since you two are the most punctual couple we know, Solange is frantic that you're late. Worried that something untoward has happened to your appetites. Hope you're okay. Your Thanksgiving meal awaits your arrival. See you soon."

Having completed his duty, he tosses his BlackBerry on the sofa and, with his eyes riveted to the game, reports that "Bill's phone is turned off. I'll try again in fifteen minutes."

Solange moves into the sunroom by Jake's chair. "They're forty-five minutes late. By the time we have our drinks, dinner will be stone cold. I can't believe this, Jake. Something's happened. Something awful."

I tuck the crossword section of the New York Times under my arm and tiptoe past Solange into the living room. The last thing I want to be party to is an authentic Windsor holiday spat, the time-honored trademark my father stamps on every holiday. Bruising as my parents' divorce was, it resulted in a series of subdued but peaceful holidays, where my brothers and a stray friend or three gathered with my mother in what became her home.

"You know the saying, 'Hurry up and wait?' That's making you antsy," Jake quips. I'm familiar with the routine that is painfully unfolding. Within minutes, his humor will chafe like sand in a wet bathing suit, and Solange will walk off in a huff. After all these years, you'd think he'd know better, but he can't stop himself. "Because you hurried to get everything ready—by the way, dinner smells fabulous and the table looks perfect—you expect Sarah and Bill to do the same."

"No, Jake, that's not it. I know this is going to sound weird but I have the feeling that something terrible has happened..."

"You're letting your childhood experience color this..."

"As if that doesn't count for anything?"

The back and forth of their polite yet increasingly strained voices grows more and more distant, finally fading completely as I take the stairs two by two up to the third floor attic where, far from the distractions of misbehaving adults, I can relax.

The desk is stacked with photos and the pink scrapbook I'm assembling for Sukie. I've carefully arranged old scrapbooks, photo lab envelopes overflowing with strips of negatives, and photos on the floor by the desk. I sorted through half of them, chose remembrances of important family events, then mounted a dozen pages of photos. Beneath each photo, I added a self-adhering tab on which I identified the people in the picture, what they were doing, and the event. The first one reads, *Sukie and her granddaughter, Marion, eating cake at Sukie's 70th birthday party. Hummingbird, in the background, doing her best handstand.* How I loved entertaining Sukie! Making her laugh was the best gift I could give her. That's what she told me that day as she wrapped me in her arms and kissed the top of my head over and over, until I squirmed myself free. Now, Sukie forgets to touch me.

So, I touch her, as much as I can. A kiss, an arm looped in hers, a quick hug. Maybe this album will help her remember those "little touches." Still, when I showed her this picture, she dismissed it with, "That's when I was young." The wistfulness in her eyes betrayed her loss and tugged at my heart. Sukie's behavior was telling me something important: that stimulation like this photo album would help keep her memories alive.

In piecing together a scrapbook, I imagined myself as a "brain trainer," feeding Sukie's memory with raw proof that she'd had a life. Each memory formed another link in the lifeline that connected her to the people she loved and who loved her in return. More than anything, I hoped Sukie's excited memories would drive Arlene Alzheimer farther into her cage. And that Sukie would become the first to recover from this disease, a medical miracle Marion would discuss at conferences that take place in extraordinary places. *Places like Oz.*

The sky turns grayer by the minute, pitching the little room into near darkness. After several twists of the lamp switch—the ornery old thing teases me with flashes of light— it clicks into place and stays on. Lamplight flows over the worn floors and ginger walls, filling the room with a glow that offsets the chill and the fate that awaits Sukie. I close the door to keep the warmth in. With one leg tucked beneath me, I sit in the armchair, propped up and away from the broken spring. A few minutes later, after filling in the clues Will Short always tosses out to get the puzzler started, my leg falls asleep.

I rub my leg until the circulation returns, then wander into the next room. It's hard to concentrate with sirens screaming somewhere in the city. The sky looks especially ominous as a charred cloud roils past the house and sirens wail. The doorbell rings and excited voices spiral up the stairwell. I rush into the front room. From the window overlooking Bellesport's center, roofs that were identifiable by the shapes of their chimneys, wind-bent antennae, or satellite dishes are now blotted with black.

Downstairs in the foyer, Sarah's blunt-cut hair spills in golden strands as she rakes her fingers from her eyebrow to the crown of her head and describes the chaos: "We were trapped in the most hellish scene. Police were out in force, trying to reroute traffic that had just let out from the football game at Bellesport High. With all the noise from the sirens, we could barely hear them shouting into their bullhorns. Still, people were getting out of their cars, gawking, and snapping pictures. The woman in the car next to us started screaming that her mother was inside the building. Fire engines from Granville, Wilton, and Tipborough clogged the driveway."

Bill flops onto the bench at the foot of the stairs and puts his head in his hands. "It was awful. Some of the firemen formed a bucket brigade only they weren't relaying water, they were passing old people on stretchers from one to the other, wheeling them outside, where ambulances were waiting. Those poor people were sound asleep, their bodies jiggling on the stretchers. Until today, I'd not thought about what would happen if an old folks' home caught fire. By the way, how about something to drink? Something strong."

I head for the sunroom and click the remote control on. The crowd roars as the Green Bay Packers score a touchdown. I click past the frenzied fans to a tinted version of *It's a Wonderful Life*—the first of many runs it would make this holiday season—past a panel of talking heads until I get to WWGN, the local news station.

Tim Williams, the announcer, holds the mike in one hand and gestures with the other toward the smoky building behind him as he speaks in a warbly voice. "Thanks to the rigorous disaster training Chief Riftley is known for, things are as orderly as we could hope for. As soon as the fire was discovered, patients on the third floor, where the fire has been contained, were moved to a safe gathering place on the same floor. I repeat: the fire has been contained. But, as you can see—" the camera pans to a doorway from which elderly people on stretchers were being evacuated "—firemen are still working to ferry injured patients down the stairs as elevator access has been temporarily stopped. Sadly, a few casualties have been reported and names are being withheld pending notification of next-of-kin. One employee, speaking off-the-record, speculated that two recently suspended employees might be involved. Officials at Highfield—"

I drop the remote and tear through the butler's pantry into the kitchen, where the phone has just rung. Solange says to my aunt, "We just heard, Elizabeth. We're terrified, too."

"Dad," I yell as I enter the foyer, "That fire is on Sukie's unit."

Jake outruns me to the sunroom. His hand trembles as he paws his BlackBerry. "Damn," he tosses the phone onto the sofa. "It's busy."

"Of course it's busy," Solange says, her forced control camouflaging the hysteria that threatens to seize us all. "Everybody with a loved one on the Fitzgerald Unit is trying to get through to Highfield."

"Shh, quiet," I snap, wiping the tears that blur my vision, then turning up the volume on the remote control. Tim Williams' voice thunders into the room. I adjust the volume and sit on the arm of the chair beside my father.

"Here we go, folks. I've got four phone numbers that you'll want to write down." Tim Williams looks down at the paper someone handed him. "I'll repeat these numbers throughout our broadcast." Before he can swallow, the numbers appear on the screen, along with an ominous message: CALL FOR INFORMATION REGARDING THE STATUS OF PATIENTS ON THE ANNE FITZGERALD UNIT AT HIGHFIELD HEALTH CENTER.

I grab a notepad and scribble furiously as Tim Williams reads the phone numbers. He pauses, then adds: "Since this is an emergency, officials at Highfield ask that only members of the immediate families place calls."

Jake grabs his BlackBerry. "I'll start with the first number," he says to Solange, who is pressing numbers into her phone.

"I'm calling the last number," she says.

Sarah fishes her phone from her purse. "I've got the second-to-last number." And Bill takes the second.

I sit beside the television, watching cameras pan the firefighters, grim-faced men and women. Chief Riftley tilts his head back, points to the third floor, and sends two of his men running into the building. I squint, straining to see past the smoke for a sign of Sukie. Was she up there, looking down at the Chief? Did she understand what the commotion was about? Being unable to remember things that had just happened has never stopped her from sensing that something was wrong. No one had to tell her when her friend Hazel had died, Sukie merely refused to go near her room. That was before Dr. Len overloaded Sukie with medications. I pray she wasn't alone in a corner.

"I got through, I'm on hold," Solange whispers, a combination of triumph and terror etched in the newly formed creases around her eyes.

Unwilling to give up their assigned phone numbers, Bill and Sarah keep redialing, "In case they cut us off," Sarah says. Jake takes the iPhone Solange offers him. He looks as though she handed off a grenade and puts it to his ear. With Solange on one side and me on the other, he spells Sukie's full name, gives her date-of-birth and room number at Highfield. He tells the stranger cross-examining him that he is Cynthia's son, Jacob Windsor. "Yes, yes I'm the attorney," he says wearily. Then he waits as they put him on hold.

I grip his hand, something I haven't done in years. More than ever, I want to be a little girl again. I want to crawl into his arms and bury my face in his strong, unerring shoulder. I want Sukie to come out of her farmhouse and coax away my fears with the "magic ingredients" she promises to mix into one of her homemade ice-cream sandwiches. I glance at the television at patients on gurneys being taken to the hospital and pray that Sukie's name is listed among the living. Without thinking, I lift my father's hand and wipe my tears on the sleeve of his plaid shirt.

My father is incredulous. "Her name is listed among the deceased? This is a hell of a way to be informed—are you sure?" He imitates the hollowed-out voice my mother used moments before he drove out of her life. I press my eyes hard against his arm and refuse to open them while he stands for the longest time quietly listening to what I imagine is double-talk—empty explanations meant to console, what my father often refers to as "damage control." He listens again, then interrupts with, "Of course there'll be an investigation," and clicks off. He spends most of his days with judges, lawyers, county clerks, punk clients and their weepy wives; with dry cleaners, waitresses, and bankers; but to those who really know him, he is a private man, the kind who hates to get bad news from strangers.

I don't need to open my eyes to know he slips from me into Solange's outstretched arms. I stand, my diaphragm pumping up and down, driving saltwater out of the eyes I refuse to open, because if I do, then it will all be true; Sukie will be gone. All because of me. No wonder my father moved away. If I hadn't tangled with those stupid aides, none of this would have happened. The aides would still be working, their reputations intact; they'd have had no a reason to get back at Highfield and they wouldn't have started that fire. I put my hands over my head and sink to the floor. "It's all my fault," I wail. "I killed her."

In one gracefully united movement, Solange and Jake swoop down and scoop me into their arms. "What on earth are you talking about?" my father sobs.

"Baby, you had nothing to do with that fire," Solange says.

"Yes, it was me..." I suck globs of clotted air into my lungs, "I got the aides in trouble..." I gag and through a cloud of coughs say, "Tim Williams...said it...himself...the aides set the fire."

Solange and Jake ease me to standing, their arms crisscrossed around my back. I slip one arm around my father's behind and the other around Solange's, locking in their comfortable closeness.

"Tim Williams has no business sanctifying gossip that isn't substantiated. He has no idea what he's talking about." Bill's outburst startles me into a sniffling silence. "No one knows how the fire started and no one will until Chief Riftley conducts his investigation." Bill scrubs his chin and runs his fingers down the side of his mouth. "Believe me, if there's a man who can figure this out, it's the Chief."

"Besides, I got the feeling that whomever you spoke to, Jake, wasn't entirely—" Sarah's barrage of well-meaning, ill-timed words is cut short.

"Oh, so now you think I have trouble understanding the English language, is that it, Sarah?"

Our sorrowing web dissolves. Instinctively, I step away, distancing myself, just as I did when I was a small child.

"Hang on, Jake, let's not say anything we'll be sorry for. We're all upset—"

"Upset? Aren't you minimizing the situation, Solange? Am I supposed to do likewise, is that what you expect?"

But Solange refuses to let Jake rattle her. She settles into her this-is-all-business demeanor and with a soft but tough voice says, "Pull it together, Jake, the phone's ringing. Someone at Highfield is probably trying to contact you."

Chapter 26:

Sure enough, the landline is ringing. Four birds on a wire gawk as Solange crosses the sunroom to answer the phone. "Hello?" she says cautiously. As she listens, her hardness melts. Her eyes rush past Sarah and Bill, ignore Jake, and lock on me. "I'm afraid this isn't a good time. She's not feeling well, Elliot—"

"Elliot!" Jake yells. "He's got no business calling Hummingbird. What's he trying to do, ruin her? Give me that phone..."

Ignoring the killer look in Solange's eyes, he thunders across the room.

"Daddy, don't—" but he brushes me aside and grabs the phone.

"Listen, you little..."

When I peek out from behind my fingers, my father's eyes are glistening. "Are you sure about that? Absolutely sure?" His words have been milked of their poison.

"I don't get it, Dad. One minute you're going to rip Elliot apart and the next..."

"Say that again, Elliot, this time to Hummingbird."

My father presses the phone into my hand. "Elliot?" I ask incredulously.

"Sukie's okay. She's here with me at the Vietnamese restaurant."

"When I stopped to visit earlier this afternoon, she begged me to get her out of Highfield. After Mrs. Perducci laid that crap on me about stealing her wallet, I felt the same way. Sukie and I agree, Highfield sucks. So I gave her my jacket and took her for a walk. Actually, she pushed me down the street. Next thing I know, we're a block from home-sucky-home and we're hearing sirens. At first I thought nothing of it—figured someone had done a job on their Thanksgiving bird—until the sirens started coming at us from all directions. I remembered how upset Sukie got that time her hearing aids started whistling, so I brought her into the restaurant. We sat here, sipped tea, munched fried noodles, and watched the fire trucks. Sukie thought the firemen were a kick, said she liked watching "circus clowns." It wasn't until she pointed out that "some old people, too old for the circus" were leaving Highfield that I thought I should call your dad. Hope he's not too pissed at me…"

I glance up at my father. "Pissed? Are you kidding? He couldn't be happier. So happy, he won't mind if I tell you I love you." There's no response. Only silence. "Elliot? Are you still there?"

"Yeah. And Sukie is here beside me. She wants to say hello."

I'm so excited to hear Sukie's voice, I almost forget about how foolish I feel for telling Elliot I love him. "Sukie? I'm so glad you're okay," I say, relieved and amazed that Sukie, who'd been locked in, is now locked out.

"Me? I'm fine, dear, just fine," Sukie says, baffled at my teary concern. "I forget this young man's name, but you know him; he's the one who watches TV with me in the evening— he and I are having a wonderful time. It's so good to get out once in a while. I hate being cooped up." An angry edge creeps into her voice. "You have no idea how much I hate it."

"Sukie, someone here wants to say hello. Hold on one second, okay?"

"Hurry, Dad, she's waiting. Please, please, please, keep the conversation upbeat, okay, Dad? I'll explain later." I foist the phone into my father's shocked hands and let the moment work its magic.

In the meantime, as he and Sukie lob tidbits back and forth about everyone sniffling and sneezing now that cold and flu season is here, I fill in the details for Solange, Sarah, and Bill. They smile with relief, unlike Aunt Elizabeth, who, when I call her with the news, sobs, saying she's "crazy relieved."

"We won't be able to contact Highfield directly, but we do need to let them know Sukie is all right. Maybe through the police department?" More hyper than ever, Solange spins toward Jake. "What about bringing Sukie here?" Her suggestion explodes, and his eyes roll in his head.

Turning his back on Solange, Jake passes the phone to me with instructions to get the restaurant's phone number from Elliot.

Bad move, Jake-o, you're in trouble now.

But Solange isn't one to be dismissed. Face-to-face with him, she's repeating her suggestion when Bill interrupts. "What about going through the fire department? Chief Riftley's number is right here." He digs his phone out from his pocket and, miraculously, after a couple tries, gets through to the chief, who promises to tell Mrs. Perducci that Mrs. Windsor is alive and well.

Jake pours himself another Scotch. Then, in a quick-patch apology, he murmurs into Solange's ear. Her shoulders relax somewhat and she accepts his offer to refresh her glass of wine, so things are okay, for now.

"Of all days to forget my cell phone," Elliot frets after giving me the phone number for the restaurant.

"Don't worry about the small stuff," I tell him. "You're a hero as far as we're concerned. I can't tell you how relieved we are that Sukie...and you are safe."

I say good-bye and, not wanting to give anyone the chance to speak, turn up the volume on Tim Williams' live report:

"Here's one of those extraordinary occurrences, call it a Thanksgiving Day gift if you will. A reliable source has told WWGN that one of the patients who'd been reported missing has been located nearby. An ambulance is on its way to the site. Highfield personnel are said to be coming out of the building to meet the ambulance. And here they are...No, here she is, one person, I'm told this is the aide who knows the patient best, being escorted by two firefighters. Let's see if she has a moment to talk with us..."

The camera pans to Sukie's aide, Iris, walking chin down, eyes glued to the sidewalk as she tucks her short blond hair behind her ears. Tim Williams stops her by sticking the microphone in her face. "Excuse me, miss, I understand you're on your way to help a patient who wandered away just before the fire started. Would you mind telling our WWGN viewers what happened?"

Iris pulls back. "Sorry," she waves as she inches away, "You'll have to speak to the administrator."

"The patient's family must be relieved. How does it feel to be the one who will give them a day to remember?"

Iris looks Tim Williams in the eye. A surgical mask hangs around her neck. The camera zooms in close to capture the strain and joy this unexpected errand has put on an unidentified employee, presumably the face of Highfield. "As much as I'd like to spend time with you, Mr. Williams, I have work to do."

I dial the restaurant, ask for Elliot, "Yes, that's right, the boy in the wheelchair," then wait. "Elliot? Iris was just on television. She's on her way along with an ambulance."

He groans. "I was hoping to sneak Sukie back before they found us. Now I'm going to hear about taking her off grounds without permission. They'll call it "eldernapping," and if that doesn't stick, they'll tattoo AWOL on my forehead. I'll never hear the end of this from what's-her-name? Your buddy, Mrs. Perducci. Oh, god, the ambulance is out front. Got to go."

"Elliot? Are you going to be in trouble with a fellow named Walt?" I ask hesitantly, purposely not explaining that Walt is the other juvenile probation officer who works with Phineas.

"Who's he? Mrs. Perducci's husband?"

"No, you moron, you wonderful moron." I hang up and everyone, including Jake, laughs when I kiss the phone.

That night, after Sarah and Bill leave and the dinner dishes are done, Mrs. Perducci calls to tell Jake that Sukie has returned with the other residents to a "clear unit," one that's safe. Thankfully, the fire affected only a small area, which specially trained crews are cleaning.

Solange pesters him to ask Mrs. Perducci if they should bring Sukie here for a couple of days.

Jake mouths, *The nurse said NO!*

Solange presses him, "Ask. See what she says."

I consider exiting to the third floor when to my surprise Jake acquiesces: "Would it help if we were to bring Sukie here for a couple of days?"

He jabs the speakerphone on his BlackBerry, so Solange can hear Mrs. Perducci repeat the advice the charge nurse had given him earlier: "Bringing your mother to your home would only add to the changes she's gone through today. We're working to reestablish her routines. Don't forget, she isn't familiar with your home, and that in itself could upset her. I don't think you want to take that chance, for her sake or for yours. I understand your concern, but I was just with her and she showed minimal signs of stress, so let's not press it. If you'd like to see her for yourself, Jake, you're welcome to visit this evening."

"What about Elliot, the boy she was with?" he asks.

"He's back on his unit. As soon as we finish our investigation of this incident, I'll get back to you."

"Yes, I expect a detailed report." His stern words are upstaged by the radiant glow of his relief.

Upstairs in my room, I reread the list of things I am grateful for. This morning I came up with two: being safe and getting to know Solange. Now, I add *that Sukie wasn't hurt in the fire.* I think for a minute, then write. *That Elliot doesn't have a probation officer.* Last, but as important as the rest of my thank-yous, I write: *THAT JAKE BUMBLED HIS WAY THROUGH A PHONE REUNION WITH SUKIE.*

Even though he refused Mrs. Perducci's offer to give him an emergency pass that would allow him onto the unit that evening, he increased his standing on my *Dad Designation Chart.* Within weeks, he's gone from a 0% rating to 70%, to 85% and back down to 50%. Today, the 20 points I add increases his standing to 70%. Okay, so he should have gone to check on Sukie; I'm feeling generous: he's going to need the extra points. From what I gleaned from his conversation with Mrs. Perducci, he doesn't give an owl's hoot that Elliot has never been the subject of a juvenile court proceeding. By the time he's done with him, I'm afraid Elliot will.

Chapter 27:

Dressed in black jeans and merino wool sweater, hair damp from his shower, Jake paces up and down the length of the kitchen past Solange and me. Each time he waves his arm in exasperation, coffee sloshes from his cup onto to floor. "When did the all-knowing trinity of wisdom—you, Sukie, and Elliot—determine that you were exempt from the rules?" His eyebrows pucker with sarcasm. "Was it at an annual board meeting? Is that when you decided that associating with this guy would enhance your already compromised future?" I watch for him to scoop up his car keys and head for the office as he always used to do the day after Thanksgiving. I'm not that lucky.

"I can understand Sukie, she can't help herself," he continues, "but what about you and this Elliot fella? Since when does my daughter hitch her brilliant star to a guy from a family of reprobates like his?" Odors from the Thanksgiving meal linger along with the roasting pan soaking in the sink. "Is he your replacement for the Blinger Bunch?" I cringe; coming from Jake my old group always sounds hopelessly idiotic. Had this been an everyday tongue-lashing, I'd have distracted Jake with a humorous rebuttal. But it's not and I'm not. I have no choice but to suck up his sarcasm.

"What happened to the little girl born with more common sense than your mother and me put together?" he says. Solange rolls her lips into her mouth as though she's about to cry. Lately, any kind of family story—sad, happy, or in-between—leaves her looking like she found her winning mega-bucks ticket the week after it expired.

"When you were a peanut of a kid, you said things that sounded so sophisticated, so wise that your mother and I were sure you were going to skip adolescence and go right into

212

adulthood—did I ever tell you that?" I wish he had; knowing he thought that highly of me would have changed the way I felt about myself for the better. I'd like to tell him as much; instead, I shake my head, no. "Apparently, we were wrong. Which is why I agreed to meet with Mrs. Perducci today."

"But it's only twenty-four hours after the fire. Doesn't she have more important things to do?" I twist the top button of the cute but childish pajamas Solange bought me, until the fob of thread holding the emerald green hummingbird is tight enough to pop.

"You're obviously one of those things. If I were you, I'd prepare a list of talking points for this afternoon. As you said, Mrs. Perducci squeezed us into her schedule, which is no small feat. Therefore Hummingbird, you'd best be ready." Given the circumstances, all I can do is meet his glower with one of my own.

Whatever the Highfield cleaning crews used to mask the smell of smoke lingers in the air like the deodorizing Christmas tree our neighbor hangs in her mini van to tame the odor of her four dogs. Putting her iPhone aside, Mrs. Perducci mutters, "She thinks *she's* frazzled," and waits by the door for Solange and me to file into the conference room, the same suffocating space in which Corki recorded each item I spilled from Pandora's box.

No sooner does Mrs. Perducci plop down beside Corki than her assistant thunders in, slips her a note and leaves. I wonder if it's from Jake, sending his standard regrets for opting out of her meeting. Mrs. Perducci, who has already accepted Solange's apologies for Jake's absence, is too gracious to say more.

"Nothing on my agenda today is simple, and if it were, I, for one, am so tired I wouldn't recognize it. So, excuse me if I seem a little out of sorts," Mrs. Perducci says, to which we nod in appreciation. "Let's start with an item that is about to resolve itself."

She sits back in her chair and checks her phone as Corki reports that Mrs. Windsor's vitals are within normal range, that she has settled into the temporary unit, "...without seeming to realize she's in a different bedroom," and that the Psychotropic Medication Specialists Team from Dr. Brewster's geriatric research group at Tufts University are scheduled next Monday to evaluate her medication needs.

"Would that be *the* Dr. Brewster?" Solange asks, admiration seeping into her voice.

"Why, yes, we've contracted Dr. Brewster's group to oversee the administration of psychotropic meds to all our elderly residents," Mrs. Perducci answers.

"He's the best in the field. He leads a group of researchers interested in putting limits on pharmaceutical companies that sell meds that haven't been tested for use with the elderly." Solange surges with new energy. One that believes the best way to support Sukie is to combine careful medication therapy with activities she enjoys.

Still, I'm confused. Is this my stepmother, the top pharmaceutical sales person in her district? I double check to make sure she's not being sarcastic: she's not, she's more intense than ever: "As we've seen, it's difficult to predict whether Cynthia will have an adverse reaction to the meds she's given until she's actually in trouble."

Hands folded on the table, Solange is poised, confident, professional, the picture-perfect advocate for Sukie. It's exciting to hear her say things she once considered blasphemous. From conversations I've overheard between her and Jake, she's horrified to have been working for a company that has hurt Sukie and others like her. She won't be with

Healthbens for long. When this is over, I'm going to give her an enormous hug.

Mrs. Perducci faces Solange. Her seriousness taps into subtext, something more than is being discussed. "It sounds as though you'd like Dr. Brewster's group to contact you every step of the way."

"Exactly. And that applies to any plans for med changes, small or large."

"Absolutely," Corki interrupts. "Besides, we're required by law to contact the family if as much as an aspirin or a band aid is administered—" Mrs. Perducci shoots Corki a look that silences her.

But Solange isn't through. "I appreciate your candor, Corki. If there's one thing we'd like to make clear, it's that we expect to be kept in the communication loop. Because we know Sukie and her habits so well, we feel we have valuable information to share, information that will prove helpful when it comes to deciding which meds and therapies Sukie may need. We are, after all, her family." Solange speaks with the fierceness of a woman who, having lost one family, isn't about to let anything happen to her new one. I grow prouder of her by the second.

"I've just texted my assistant with your requests," Mrs. Perducci is quick to say. "Anything else on that issue?" Looking around, she pauses at me. I know she wants to move on, but I peel my fingertips from the table and wave.

"Yes, Hummingbird."

Ignoring her impatience, I fix my eyes on Mrs. Perducci who knows what it's like to love a person with Alzheimer's, to ache every time she smacks of bewilderment, especially when others make her feel insignificant. I speak slowly and deliberately: "We should never ever underestimate a person with Alzheimer's, particularly when it's convenient to rush that person along because she's interrupting our work, saying things that sound daft. But suppose that person is using her odd language and strange behavior to tell us something? Something important. We need to remember to slow down, to pay attention to what she wants us to know."

"Thank you, Hummingbird, that's a helpful reminder. I'll include it on my agenda for our next staff meeting." The edgy quality disappears from her voice, but the fatigue is stronger than ever. "Although important, the next item will be quick." Fingering the note her assistant gave her, Mrs. Perducci goes to the door and motions whoever is in the hallway to join us.

Smooth as Red Sox outfielder Dave Roberts stealing a base at the bottom of the ninth, Elliot glides into the space at the head of the table. I gasp. I didn't expect to see him. Not here. Not looking as though he'd just struck out.

Mrs. Perducci sits. "Early this morning, my staff found my wallet." The atmosphere lightens. I close my eyes and, for a quick second, am less tense. "We found it buried under the cushion on the wheelchair of one of our elderly wanderers." She leans toward Elliot. "The same morning you delivered flowers to my office, another visitor had also stopped by. Unfortunately, my staff confused that person's departure from my office with your delivery of flowers. You weren't the one who lifted my wallet in hopes of buying a soda or two. I apologize, Elliot. You were wrongly accused."

Elliot's head drops back in relief. Grinning, he turns toward me as if to say, *See? You had nothing to worry about.* I ball my fist into a fierce thumbs-up. I'm happy he's been acquitted and fuming at the injustice he was forced to swallow.

"I'm afraid I have to dampen this sweet victory with my next item: your decision to invite Cynthia to dine somewhere other than Highfield." His smile evaporates.

"Do you understand that Highfield is responsible for both you and Cynthia?"

He nods.

"And given yesterday's emergency, it was critical that we knew the whereabouts of you both?"

Another wide-eyed nod.

"And because we were unable to locate Cynthia, we were forced to report to Mr. Windsor that his mother was among the missing? You *do* understand what the euphemism 'among the missing,' says to a family?"

Elliot glances down at his stumps. His face contorts, making it all too clear that he recalls being told how painful it was for his mother to receive the call about his accident. He murmurs, "I'm afraid I do." He looks like he's going to cry.

"Then you can appreciate how heartsick the Windsors were when they got our call. What you may not appreciate is that we at Highfield also felt heartsick and utterly frantic. The fire was hideous, but being unable to account for you and Cynthia was far worse." She leans closer to him. "Do you get my drift?"

"I'm sorry. Very sorry." He lowers his gaze to the table.

"Thank you, Elliot. This must be our day for trading apologies." Mrs. Perducci sits back. She looks more exhausted than ever. "The good news is that you and Cynthia were out of danger. Unfortunately, a couple of the others weren't as lucky."

She pauses as the gravity of her words filters through the room. "For the time being, I'm restricting your evening visits with Cynthia. You're not to go on her unit. Got that?" Mrs. Perducci sounds as though she's speaking to one of her own unruly boys.

Nodding, Elliot stares at his hands. A couple of seconds pass. Finally, Mrs. Perducci says, "Elliot? Would you mind excusing us? The next matter is confidential." He looks confused, and he hesitates, which isn't like him.

Mrs. Perducci shifts as though she's about to get up and push him into the hallway when he raises the camera I thought I'd lost. "This is for Hummingbird. It needed a few adjustments when I got it back from the bus company, so I fixed it. Then, I tested it by taking a movie of Cynthia that Hummingbird will want to see."

Unamused by Elliot's prowess with camera repairs, Mrs. Perducci stands. All eyes cut to her. "Is that all right with you, Mrs. Windsor?"

Taken off guard, Solange glances at me, then at the camera. "If Hummingbird would like to have her camera and a movie of her grandmother, that's fine with me."

I don't understand why Elliot is making a big deal of this in front of everyone, but I nod. I'd love to have my camera back. But not now.

"The thing is, Hummingbird, you should look at the movie *right away.*" Elliot pushes his last two words out into the room as he passes my camera case to me.

I'm glancing frantically at my talking points, trying not to let him distract me. "Thanks," I mumble and, blushing from my neck to my eyebrows, whisk the camera bag onto my lap.

Elliot rolls his wheelchair toward the doorway, stops halfway into the hallway, and gestures for me to view the movie. *Doesn't he get that this isn't the time or the place? Why is he being such a pain?*

Chapter 28:

This Nikon Coolpix—the brand Sukie and I decided on after comparing features offered by other camera manufacturers—weights my lap, solid as river rock, smoothed to perfection by countless currents. That Elliot went to the trouble first to retrieve it from the bus where I'd left it, and then fix it doesn't surprise me—he's that kind of person, big-hearted and generous. I wish I could throw my arms around his neck and kiss him like I did the night of the Halloween dance, but there's a problem with our timing—his is ridiculous and mine, non-existent.

Still, I want Elliot to know I love his thoughtfulness. Looking up, I'm about to say a quick, more sincere thank you when Mrs. Perducci passes a file to her assistant, standing in the doorway. Elliot is no longer there.

"Let's move closer together, shall we?" We pull our chairs in and close the gap around the conference table. The Grand Inquisition is about to begin.

"All yours," Mrs. Perducci says, and Corki begins rattling gobbledy gook about Sandis and Timtiere, praising their twenty-four combined years of exemplary employment.

Whatever Corki is getting at makes me uneasy. I squirm. The room has become awfully stuffy. *Why doesn't Corki just skip to the outcomes?* Mrs. Perducci must feel the same way because she's scrolling through messages on her iPhone. Solange, meanwhile, removes and replaces the cap on her Mont Blanc pen.

Like Lucy Malloy, the deadpan commentator on the 6:00 news, Corki drones on. She stops to swallow and when she starts speaking, glances at everyone but me. "During separate interviews, Sandis and Timtiere reported they were polite and appropriate with Cynthia, and that they spent very little time with her because they wanted to go on their break."

WHAT? I'm completely blown out of the water. *They're lying. How incredibly stupid of me to think they wouldn't.*

Brows furrowed in disbelief, Solange leans forward, ready to pounce.

"As of this weekend, the aides will resume their shifts on the Fitzgerald Unit. Next week, as part of her annual re-training, Sandis will attend a sensitivity workshop. However," Corki looks up from her report, "Sandis' retraining is not an indication that this investigation finds her guilty of verbal abuse. Given the circumstances, the board suggested that it would be helpful if she started her annual re-training earlier than usual." She glances at Mrs. Perducci, nodding in agreement. "Timtiere will follow her normal training schedule." Corki slides the report into the file and closes it. Relief brightens her serious face. "That's it. I'll turn the meeting over to you, Mrs. Perducci," she says collapsing against the back of her chair.

"That's it? What happened to my interview? Wasn't it good enough? Didn't it count?" Corki sucks in a mouthful of air as though I just punched her.

"I understand how you feel, Hummingbird." Mrs. Perducci is speaking softly. "The summary doesn't begin to represent the hours we put into interviewing you or the staff. However, those details are confidential. If you were the focus of this type of situation, you'd expect us to treat you the same way. I'm sure you understand."

"I understand the need to maintain confidentiality. But the outcomes are not what we expected." Solange's hand balls into a fist. "According to Hummingbird, an interaction between the aides and Sukie occurred on the night shift. Innuendoes were made that simply can't be discounted. Quite frankly—and I believe I can speak for both of us—Hummingbird and I are disappointed."

I tap my heels one against the other, imitating Dorothy, clicking one ruby red slipper against the other, and silently chant, *I want this to be right. This has got to be right.* I'm so nervous, the tapping turns into jiggling, feet first, then legs. Solange leans forward, settles her arms on the table; she's positioned for a lengthy discussion that's sure to make everyone uncomfortable.

I fiddle with the camera bag on my lap while I brood. Corki's bullshit lies are as bizarre as Elliot's 'oh-by-the-way-I-found-your-camera' routine, and his insistence that I view his movie, *"...right away."* But, what if he was trying to tell me something? His boy-fixes-camera-for-girl-act could be a front for a message.

While Solange lectures Mrs. Perducci and Corki, I work my fingers beneath the Velcro flap and pry my camera bag open. The camera sits on my lap now. Slowly, so as to not draw attention, I turn it on, select the movie option, and quickly adjust the volume indicator to zero.

"...perhaps it's different from the investigation process I'm accustomed to at my company," Solange continues, and Mrs. Perducci counters.

But Solange is not to be deterred. "This investigation isn't complete. *Someone* is withholding information. The question is why? The answer relates to a second major issue. And that is, what is the relationship between this allegation, the investigation that followed, and the fire that broke out on my mother-in-law's unit? Has anyone asked that question, Mrs. Perducci?"

"Solange?" I tap her arm. "Solange?" I'm shaking her hand now, but she's too steamed to notice. I've never seen her this angry. I rock her hand so hard her arm jiggles. At last, she turns to me, eyes blinking, as though startled out of a bad dream.

"There's something I need to show everyone." I position the camera in the center of the table.

Frowning, Mrs. Perducci mouths to Corki, '*What's this?*' Corki sloughs off her glasses and shrugs. I extend the monitor, increase the volume, and start Elliot's movie.

Necks crane toward the monitor. Small though it is, there's no mistaking Sandis standing inches from nightgown-clad Sukie, quizzing her about the number of men she'd known in her lifetime. "Don't tell me Pop-Pop was your one and only," she sneers. "You know how I know? Because your son told me. I bet you thought I never met your son, the lawyer, but I have, believe me I have."

Too many words saddled with too much emotion confuse and overwhelm Sukie. Eyes narrowed with suspicion, she jerks her head back and forth between Sandis and Timtiere. "What's she talking about? What does she mean?" she asks Timtiere, her voice growing louder by the second.

"Your son said you're a fancy lady. And that fancy ladies talk one story and live another," Sandis says.

I hold my breath to keep from crying. Mrs. Perducci drops her forehead into her palm. Corki shifts to the edge of her chair. "Oh my God," murmurs Solange.

Whether or not Sukie understood what Sandis was getting at, she fights back like a fifth grader in an after-school brawl. "You've got a big mouth and a fat ass." I cringe; before Arlene Alzheimer and these bullies showed up, my Sukie never whispered an unladylike word.

"Come on, Cindy, tell me more about this Pop-Pop man. Does he go pop-pop?" Sandis continues while the other workers laugh and laugh and laugh. Sukie's face knots with rage. She shakes her balled fists at Sandis and, taking a few hurried steps backward, loses her balance. Timtiere grabs her by the elbows and steadies her, but Sukie shoves Timtiere out of her way.

"Leave me alone, both of you," Sukie yells, shuffling past the camera, jarring the fully stocked med supply cart Elliot later confesses to having hidden behind. The aides' shrill laughter ends the movie and blasts Corki's recommendations into the stratosphere.

My tears puddle on the conference table. Solange draws me close and hands me a tissue but in my memory's eye, the police are tossing me a blanket to wrap my nakedness in. I'm humiliated all over again, except now my heart aches for Sukie. I want to yiff: Sukie and I have both been bullied.

Chapter 29:

Hunched over the oversized desk in his study, arms encircling my camera, Jake glares at the monitor. His chest expands and contracts in short indignant breaths. The movie ends. His fingertips mush his eyebrows in quick-pressured circles. He's either about to pound the camera with his fists or weep; I'm not sure which. I've never seen him cry, and the thought of him breaking down adds to the upset of watching that video again. Between not knowing what to do if he cries and the fear that something weird is about to happen, I'm caught off-guard. *Say something*, I silently beg. *Anything.* I glance at Solange, standing behind his chair; she's not much help.

So I do what I want Jake to do; I talk: "Mrs. Perducci actually begged me to leave my camera with her. She wanted to show the movie to her Board of Directors and the team that conducted the investigation. I told her once you saw the movie, we'd make a copy for her. She was incredibly upset, said she felt betrayed. She shot dirty looks at Corki like Corki should have cracked everyone's lies, but Corki ignored her. Besides, it wasn't Corki's fault."

Jake throws his hands up in surrender. "Okay, Birdie, okay. I get the picture. Give me a couple of seconds..." He cuts me off before I can ask if Sandis really does know him. He lowers his head into his hands. "I can't believe this happened to my mother...."

"What if—" I'm about to suggest we go to Highfield, but Solange shakes her head. *Wait*, she mouths, then quietly closes the door behind her.

Jake and I are alone.

He massages the side of his head and, for the first time since seeing the movie, looks at me. "I know you had a lot on your mind what with your meeting, but you *did* see your grandmother today, didn't you?" He's downright pushy.

"I stopped in before the meeting. You know I visit her every day." My indignant meter soars into the danger zone. Does he really think I'd dump a visit with Sukie because of a stupid meeting?

Solange would label this a "distraction," the smoke bomb Jake explodes whenever he can't fulfill demands at home. "We're nowhere near as demanding as his clients," I once complained. She agreed. "But, he's good at filling their demands. He doesn't know what to do about ours."

I get that Jake is more comfortable at the office; that's where he shines. But I want him to focus on more important stuff—patch the leak in the Windsor family's emotional dike for one.

Solange claims my living here has made it harder for him to play ignorant about my needs, which leaves him more off-balance than ever. So he developed his Opt-Out Provision, also known as the Send-Special-Envoy-Solange provision. He calls on her whenever his prickly meter rises to a dangerously high emotional level like it did the night of the Halloween Dance when I'd hoped to introduce him to the boy who did more to protect Sukie than he ever has.

And yeah, Solange told me he got all choked up when he saw me on Halloween, wearing the dress Sukie had designed. I'm being a hard-ass here, but that doesn't buy him a get-out-of-jail ticket; his opting out goes back too far for that.

With Sukie, it started when Alzheimer's crippled her ability to live up to his ridiculously high standards and morphed her into our heartbreak. Her wandering away from home really got to him. Seeing her in the back seat of a police cruiser fogged his vision of a lofty life. Seeing me at the police station blew the remainder of that illusion out to sea.

Still, he failed to link my problems with his standards. He never understood the connection: by getting into trouble, I was trying to tell him it wasn't his money or prestige that interested me. I wanted him. Just him.

"How was Sukie when you stopped in to see her?" Head tilted, Jake waits for me to give him what he longs for—sweet words that will relieve him of his guilt.

"You don't have any idea do you, Dad?" I'm speaking more gently now. "Sukie is amazing. Every time the beast knocks her down, Sukie gets up, brushes off her knees, and keeps on going. She insists she's going to make the best of whatever life throws her way. Isn't that what you wanted—for everyone in our family to do his and her best? To live up to our gifts?

Well, that's what Sukie's doing. All by herself. But she'd love your support. Not the kind that Toni keeps for you in your logbook, although that helps." His eyes open wide at the mention of his logbook, but he doesn't ask. "But by going to see Sukie, by spending time with her…" my throat tightens, "before Alzheimer's wins the battle, just as it did with Hazel and the lady with the doe-like eyes."

"Who?" he asks, his face a version of Sukie's when her brain grinds with effort.

"You see, Dad? This is exactly what mean. You keep a notebook on Sukie, but you don't know those women were her friends, friends she loved because they loved her just as she is." *Without any judgments.* I pause. A new realization grabs me—I've done to him what he's done to Sukie and me: judged him against impossibly high standards.

"It's like the day I won the gymnastics competition and instead of giving me a hug and telling me how proud you were, you aimed your telephoto at me, snapped a picture, then disappeared."

"You know about that?" he whispers.

"I visited your office. Got to see the piece of you I'd always hoped for. And Dad?"

Shamefaced, he looks expectantly at me.

"I liked that you enlarged my picture and had it framed. I liked it because it told me you cared. But if I'd known for sure that you loved me, I might have headed straight to the principal's office when Bruce Talibert started bullying me. Instead, I asked the school troublemakers for help. It wasn't my smartest calculation, but since you spent so much time with their kind, I decided you liked them. And I figured if I became one of them, you'd spend time with me, too."

"You were being bullied and you never told anyone?" he asks incredulously, then pops me with one of his vintage moves: "Did your brand of illogic work?" He gets up from his chair. He's still pretty shaken from seeing Elliot's movie. I feel badly about hitting him with everything at once, but can't stop.

I force a grin. "You're hopeless, Dad, you really are. Of course not. Not in the short run. Instead…" I signal him not to interrupt, "it landed me in a heap of trouble. And *that* brought you to me. In that sense, I hit a home run." He looks so perplexed, so vulnerable, and so hurt that I can't help myself—I move closer.

He opens his arms and folds me in them. "I have four other children who could have tipped me off about all this. But no, I had to hear it from the smallest and fiercest of my brood."

I step out of my father's arms and back, where I can get a good look at him. As much as I rehearsed this line, it still feels odd to say, "So, you'll come with me to visit Sukie?"

He smiles a sad smile—the kind Sukie wears these days—and sighs, "I'll tell you what—"

Solange knocks on the door and pokes her head in. "Sorry to interrupt, but Mrs. Perducci is on the phone. She'd like to speak with you, Jake." He hesitates. "She says it's important."

Taking her phone, he answers, "Jake Windsor here."

My chin drops to my chest. We just had the conversation I'd been dreaming of. Okay, so it was brief, so what? I said things I wanted to say and connected with the father behind the man. Showed him how enduring a mistake I've really become. And then an electronic device draws my dad out of my arms and chases Jake Windsor back in.

Before I know it, Solange is pressing me to her chest. "Sorry for the awful timing," she whispers. "He'll make it up to you, I know he will."

"I feel cheated."

"I'm afraid this isn't about my mother, it's about me," Jake says to Mrs. Perducci. His quiet tone means something's very wrong. Solange and I exchange frightened looks. "That woman, Sandis? I represented her husband. He refused the DA's offer of a plea bargain. I warned if his case went to trial, F. Lee Bailey couldn't get him off. When the prosecutor wiped the courtroom clean with his case, my client blamed me. Apparently, so does his wife."

Jake listens to Mrs. Perducci for what seems like an awfully long time, then says, "I'm sorry it came to this, for my mother's sake, for the residents and staff at Highfield, and for you. I appreciate your letting me know."

He puts the phone aside. "That's it—the aides have been dismissed."

"Fired, Dad, really? What happened?"

"Fired as in told to empty their lockers and not come back."

"No, she means the business about Sandis and you," says Solange.

He slumps into his chair. "There's not much to tell. Her husband was being tried for murder, and I lost his case. I haven't seen his wife since the trial, over ten years ago. I'd forgotten about her."

"But she didn't forget about you, Dad."

"Oh, Jake, how awful for you." Solange wraps her arms around him. "Sandis hated you for doing your job...."

"Dad? Both of them, Sandis *and* Timtiere, are gone? I wanted Mrs. Perducci to can Sandis, but Timtiere didn't go half as far—"

"I'm afraid she did. The night they were suspended, Timtiere called Mrs. Perducci and told her Sandis intended to get back at everyone, but refused to give details. Who would have imagined that Sandis would set a fire? Chief Riftley is talking to the District Attorney about arson and manslaughter charges. And since Timtiere admitted that Sandis kept her informed of her plans right up to the minute she started the fire, Timtiere will likely be charged as an accessory. Stupid move on her part, not letting the authorities know—as serious as lighting the match."

"What a mess. What started as a little nastiness turned into devastation for the residents, the staff, those two aides, and for you." Solange shakes her head in disbelief.

My father corrects her. "There's no such thing as a little nastiness when you're talking abuse."

I love that he's taken up Sukie's cause. "What happens next?" I blurt.

"Mrs. Perducci wants a copy of this movie." He checks his watch. Sad as this business is, it puts him back in his element, where he's in charge. "Toni is on her way to Madrid, so she won't be able to duplicate it for me."

"Bring it to Elliot. He'll copy it, right there in his room."

His face eases into a sly little grin. "We can stop in to see your Elliot, leave the camera with him, then visit Sukie. Is that where you're headed with this, Birdie?"

"I wasn't talking about seeing *my* Elliot..." then it dawns on me. I study Jake for a long second. Just long enough for him to go sheepish, waiting for me to hit him with my special brand of father-daughter cross-examination. I've got plenty to say about not judging before the facts are in, about being presumed innocent until proven guilty, but the look on his face says he knows all that but couldn't help himself; he was just being a father. *My* father. I let out a little squeal and throw my arms around him. "I think that might work, Dad."

Chapter 30:

Phineas' call makes it official; Elliot is "clean." Not so much as a speeding ticket or citation for the boating accident that wasn't his fault.

"Sorry to disappoint you, Phineas, but my Dad already told me. Turns out Elliot had just sold one of the boats he'd built to a friend and they were taking it for a run on Sebago Lake when a drunken boater collided with them. You know the rest." I try to dredge up a drop of enthusiasm for this good news, but can't muster the energy. "You have to admit, if Elliot did have a record, and if he and I decided to stay together, we would have made Romeo and Juliet look like..."

"Hummingbird!"

I giggle at Phineas'shock. "Just kidding. But I do have a surprise for you."

"Does it have anything to do with Romeo and Juliet?" he groans.

"No, but it means I've completed the requirements of my Informal Adjustment program. I finally finished my report for school! Stayed up until 4:00 this morning writing it. You'll never believe the title. Can you guess?"

"I'm thinking," he says, then lets the phone go silent.

"*Manifesto of an Alzheimer's Granddaughter,*" I say softly.

"Very Hummingbird-like, powerful," he says thoughtfully. "Birdie, you've had one of the more complicated Community Service experiences I've been involved in. Lots of kids would use what they'd seen and heard as their chance to peck the system apart. You know, to get even. I'll be interested to see how you portray it. I imagine you'll do it justice. When can I read it?"

"As soon as I email you a copy."

"By the way, have you told Elliot about *your* status? We were so worried about him having a history, we didn't think about how he'd feel about yours."

"I feel awful about that. My dad and I are going to see him as soon as I get off the phone."

"Your father has graduated to 'Dad?' Since when?"

"Since he stopped being Jake."

When I call Elliot to tell him my dad and I are coming to see him, he sounds weirder than usual, preoccupied, like he's hiding something. Has he found out about me? I wish I'd told him my story earlier. At first, I was too embarrassed but deep down inside, I didn't want to give him a reason to hate me. Didn't want to chance losing such a strange and wonderful friend. Now, I've spoiled everything. Will I ever learn?

Elliot is exactly where he said he'd meet us—in the lobby, front and center, looking incredibly nervous and gorgeous in his royal blue T-shirt with the gold logo, *Catch Me If You Can.* He drums his fingers on the top of the four-foot high receptionist's station, real casual-like, as if this is how he greets me every day.

"Santa came early," I say, admiring the mechanical knees and flesh-toned legs protruding beneath his bright red gym shorts.

His physical therapist is by his side. A tall, athletic woman, I imagined her to be taller than Elliot, but she's not; he's taller by a head. She hovers with her hand on the purple canvas "gotcha belt" wrapped around his middle. If Elliot's strength gives out, she'll grab the loops on this snappy device and hold him upright while she maneuvers him into his nearby wheelchair.

I'm so proud of him, I could explode. I want to say something he'll never forget, but the best I can come up with is: "Now that you're equipped with those, you're not just another pretty face. You're an honest-to-goodness 'fall risk.'"

I expect him to lob me a funny remark, but Elliot isn't his usual cocky self. I raise my camera and center him in the middle of my viewfinder. I capture his expression, a special mix of triumph and pain as he stands on his two new legs. My eyes puddle and my vision goes blurry. Click! Thank goodness for automatic exposure.

I want to be the first to hug Elliot while he's standing, but his PT is helping him into his wheelchair. "This is Elliot's first time standing on his own, and he's tired," she explains as I rush over.

"Why didn't you tell me?" I ask, but he's busy reaching under his knees and lifting them, so his PT can situate his new sneakers on his new feet on the wheelchair's new foot rests.

"You did exactly what you said you were going to do today," his PT assures him. "Soon, you'll do this part, too," she continues as if getting his stumpy thighs to control the steel and plastic strapped onto the lower half of his body is no biggie.

Elliot looks up at me and asks, "Were you surprised?" His head, no longer shaved, is covered in soft brown curls that shadow his tattoo. I like his weary-boy-overcomes glow better than his angel-from-hell attitude. Besides, it leaves less to explain to my father.

"You were amazing—" I start to say, until Elliot glances sheepishly up at my father. I reach behind me and take my father's hand.

"Dad, this is my friend, Elliot." When that special word, "friend," hits the air it brims with a we're-in-this-togetherness.

Saying it aloud without flinching is the test, and my flinch-meter's "zero" reading proves *I've found a real friend.*

Elliot extends his hand and my father reaches out and shakes it, hard and firm. Man-to-man. "Good to meet you, son. Congratulations."

Son? I'm shocked that my dad called Elliot son. Elliot and I shoot my dad a double take, which he ignores.

"This is quite the accomplishment. I don't know that I'd have had the courage to do what you've done. Quite frankly, I'm impressed."

Tongue-tied for the second time today, Elliot bumbles, "Thank you, um, sir."

"I'm the one who owes you thanks."

"Excuse me, um, sir?"

"If you hadn't taken Hummingbird's grandmother off-grounds for a walk, she would have been in the middle of that fire. She might have been hurt." His voice cracks just a little, which makes me love him all the more. He excuses himself, saying he's on his way upstairs for a visit that's long overdue. Thanks to Solange, I now understand—running away is his cover-up for when he doesn't know what else to do with his feelings.

He heads toward the elevators, the code to unlock the doors on the Anne Fitzgerald Unit on the slip of paper I tucked into his pocket. Suddenly, I feel protective. What if the patients horrify him? What if he won't join Sukie in her world of memories, wherever they take her? What if Arlene Alzheimer is behaving poorly today? Will he understand what Sukie is trying to tell him with her behavior?

I call out to him, "Dad, opening the doors to Sukie's unit can be tricky. Do you want me to come with you?"

He turns and scratches his head, as if his answer would have earth-shaking consequences. "I tell you what, Birdie. Give me about fifteen minutes, then come up. I want you to show me the alarm mats you worked so hard to get. How would that be?" I like that he sounds a little scared and that he's wearing an awkward little smile. "Thanks for being here when I need you."

This little sentence wouldn't hold much weight in the annals of the now-defunct Bling Society; it's not as prestigious as a new car, or a gift certificate to a designer jean store. Off-handed as it is, it's the kind of gift I've always longed for. The kind I'll cherish.

"I heard your father is an imposing kind of guy," Elliot says when his physical therapist leaves to answer a page. He lowers his voice, "But I didn't expect him to be so gentlemanly. He reminds me of a statesman. You know, like John Adams or Thomas Jefferson."

"It's not how I describe my father, but it gives me a new way to think about him."

"Before things get too complicated, I think I should tell you about my genius brother, who can't keep himself out of trouble."

"I think I should tell you about me," I whisper in his ear as I wheel him from the reception area into a more private corner. He listens quietly as I tell him about Bruce, the Blingers, and my introduction to the juvenile justice system. "The funny thing is, all that seems so far away, like someone else's nightmare. That's a claim I wouldn't be able to make without Solange and my father, and Sukie and you."

For a moment, neither of us says a word. "So, have I shocked you onto the next planet? Are you disgusted? Disillusioned? Disappointed?"

"You realize if news of this gets out, you'll be excommunicated from the Wizard Loves Dorothy Fan Club." Elliot is trying not to smile. "Your attempt at living a life of Bling was—let's see if I can put this delicately—not one of your more brilliant moves. But then, going out on a speed boat and being nabbed by a boater who'd downed multiple six-packs wasn't one of mine."

"My stepmother would say that we've both learned a ton."

"Enough for a matching pair of PhD's." He pauses. "I wish you'd met me before, you know, my accident," he says, glancing down at his new equipment.

"I do, too. But if you hadn't made a mess of your life, and I hadn't screwed mine up, you'd never have run away with a woman six times your age."

"I'd never have witnessed you looking out for your dad."

"You'd never have given this cowardly lion the courage to start an investigation into bullying at Granville High." *Plus scoring my most important accomplishment, bringing Sukie and my father together.*

"I'm that bad, huh?" Elliot studies me, just as he did when he'd first seen me seven weeks ago, hollering for the bus driver to stop. "When are you leaving?"

With one more week to go, it's the question I've been hoping to avoid. "I've talked with my father and Phineas about starting an investigation at my high school. They warned me this kind of project can get ugly, but both agreed to help me. I wouldn't have had the guts to say this when I was hanging with the Blingers, but now I know I can help kids and old folks understand there's no room in our world for bullies."

"So, you've already started waging war on the bully-creep dragon types that prey on the unsuspecting, defenseless, and otherwise nerdy of this world. Too bad, because I was hoping you'd join me on my first whirl on the Bellesport City Bus."

I look at my watch; I'm due upstairs with Dad and Sukie. "I'm late," I say, walking backward toward the elevator and gesturing for Elliot to call me. "Of course I'll go with you on your victory lap, whenever you're ready. And don't go sentimental on me, I plan on being here every weekend—Sukie and my father haven't stopped needing us." I blow him a kiss, turn and head toward the elevators, content to be with the people I love.

MANIFESTO OF AN ALZHEIMER'S GRANDDAUGHTER

by: Abigail Windsor

Introduction:

For the last seven weeks, I have been working at Highfield Health and Rehab on the Anne Fitzgerald Memory Unit, where I have been privileged to share time with my grandmother, Sukie, and her constant companion, Alzheimer's disease. I am grateful to Mrs. Perducci, the Health Center administrator for allowing me to work elbow-to-elbow with her staff. She and her staff are natural teachers, generous and eager to share their time and knowledge. As a result of this extraordinary opportunity, I have written this "manifesto." In it, I share tips and techniques that will help you support your loved one with Alzheimer's disease.

During this Community Service Learning Project, I saw how difficult it is for the world of science to understand the workings of this disease and how much more perplexing it has been for my grandmother to come to terms with it. While science offers many different therapies that have helped her, none is as important as our family's involvement. Although my grandmother is the one fighting to keep her dignity, everyone in our family, each in our own way, is participating in her struggle. Therefore, I encourage any family who has a member suffering from Alzheimer's to become involved with your loved one's treatment. I hope this report will give you ideas and suggestions on how to get involved and stay involved with a loved one who lives in the complicated world of Alzheimer's.

Part One: Planning and Participating in Your Loved One's Treatment:

Let staff know that your family wants to be involved in all decisions pertaining to your loved one's treatment. This will: a) keep you informed of what is happening with your loved one and; b) give you the opportunity to share important information about your loved one's likes and dislikes.

1. Be sure that all treatments are designed to meet your loved one's needs (this is known as "individualizing"). Treatments generally include a combination of the following: a) medication therapy, b) activity therapy, c) speech and language therapy, d) physical therapy, e) occupational therapy, recreational therapy, and f) medical treatment, including care of the ears, eyes, teeth, skin, and feet.

2. To make communication between the facility and family easier, identify one person in the family as the "contact person."

3. Staff, including doctors and therapists, should get the family's input *and take it seriously* before deciding on which treatment recommendations to implement.

4. Give the staff information about your loved one's background and history. This will help staff understand what the person's life was like before they were diagnosed with Alzheimer's. Include what your loved one did for work—outside and inside the home; identify family members and important information about them; describe hobbies, special skills, interests and leisure activities, even the names of the television programs your loved one enjoys. Don't forget to share your loved one's dislikes; these are important, too.

5. If at first you don't succeed, don't be afraid to climb the information ladder. If you don't get a satisfying answer when you ask a staff member a question, call the supervisor, or the supervisor's supervisor. An unsatisfactory answer can be a sign that your loved one is getting unsatisfactory treatment. You don't want to take that chance! So, don't accept an unsatisfactory answer; go up the ladder to the supervisor. (If this is hard for you to do, think of it this way: you are the customer, you deserve complete and correct information.)

6. Report to the supervisor anything you see or hear that smacks of physical, verbal, or emotional abuse. Sometimes a staff member may become frustrated and react poorly toward the patients. This is unacceptable; the staff is trained in techniques that help them avoid taking a patient's words or actions personally. These techniques help staff control their emotions. If they have trouble being kind and patient, be sure to let their supervisor know. Thankfully, this doesn't happen often. But if it does, it's up to you to protect your loved ones. Don't forget: your loved ones can't take care of themselves; it's up to you to be sure they get the best possible treatment. Tell the supervisor!

Part Two: Communicating With Your Loved One:

Alzheimer's robs a person of the ability to use words effectively. To make up for this, our loved ones often communicate—many times unknowingly—with their behavior. Therefore, *because all behavior is a kind of sign language that has meaning*, we, the family members, must be observant. Our loved ones may be unable to tell us what is bothering them, therefore it's up to us (especially family members who know the person well) to take time to figure out what they are trying to tell us with their behavior. Be sure to share this information with the staff.

1. Never correct your loved ones. Instead, join their world, no matter how odd it may seem; look at this as an opportunity to learn more about the person. This will show your loved ones that you respect them and their experiences.

2. I know it's hard, but please, oh please, don't take it personally when your loved one gets upset with you. Persons with Alzheimer's are terribly frustrated by the loss of their memories and the skills and abilities they once had. Put yourself in that person's place; be patient and help them work through their difficulties. Sometimes saying "I love you" is the most helpful thing you can say.

3. Family members should share their ideas and suggestions with the facility Administrator regarding what might make their loved one comfortable. This will give the Administrator important information to share with staff. And who knows, the Administrator may find your idea helpful enough to use with other patients.

Part Three: Keep A Notebook:

Families will find it helpful to keep a notebook that includes observations, questions, and information about tests and therapies their loved one has undergone. While this may feel like a task the staff ought to be doing, believe me, there will be times when you'll want your own information to refer to (Note: the staff does keep its own notebook, but not in as much detail as the one you'll keep.) Here are the sections you'll need; don't be afraid to add others:

1. Family Observations: Each time a family member visits, jot down the date and time of their visit along with their impressions and observations. For example: How did your loved one respond when she first saw you? How did she look? Was she clean and dressed properly? Was her clothing in good order? What kind of mood was she in? Did she make eye contact? What changes, if any, did you observe? Did your loved one have any complaints? Ask for anything or anyone in particular? Was there anything that concerned you?

2. The Physician's Orders is a list of all the orders the doctors and therapists have given after they've examined your loved one. These are updated each month. The person with the Health Care Power of Attorney should ask to have a copy of the Physician's Orders sent to him each month. After reading it and noting any changes, insert it in the Patient Notebook, under the Physician's Orders section. Speak to the charge nurse if you have questions.

3. Medication Changes: It's important to keep track of the medications that are being prescribed for your loved one. The easiest way to do this is by using a chart that has the following headings: 1) Medication, 2) Date of Medication Change, 3) Previous Dosage/New Dosage, 4) Rationale for med change/Person who authorized the change, 5) Date on which family was notified of change, 6) Loved One's Responses to med change. It may seem tedious to keep track of this information, but it will prove useful if your loved one has an unexplained change in behavior. Many times, she may be reacting to the medication change. (Sometimes the staff neglects to consider this possibility.) Share your observations with the staff and speak directly to the doctor about them, too. FMI, see the section entitled "Medications."

4. Phone Log: One of the most important things you can do for your loved one is to stay in contact with the nursing staff. This is especially true if you are unable to visit. When calling a staff member or when one calls you, keep notes about that call. Include the 1) date, 2) time, 3) name of person you're speaking to, 4) reason(s) for the call, 5) outcomes, and 6) follow-up. For example, if the nurse on duty is going to speak to the doctor, then call you back; be sure to note this. Not only does it provide you with a record of important information and changes that may affect your loved one's treatment, it also serves as a reminder of phone calls and information you are waiting for. Put a huge red star beside any items that require a follow-up call and the date you expect that call. If you don't hear from the staff, call them yourself. Most likely, they'll appreciate your thoughtfulness.

5. Physical Therapy, Occupational Therapy, Speech and Language Therapy. Depending on the frequency of the therapy your loved one may need, you may want to have a separate section for each one of these. If your loved one receives any or all of these on an infrequent basis, it is just as easy to keep one section for these three treatments. Use the same procedures as you did for your Phone Log. This will give you a record of your loved one's progress and challenges, and of the updates you've received from the therapist regarding your loved one's progress. It's also a good place to record any questions you may have about the therapy or the lack of a particular therapy.

6. Case Conferences: Every three months, a meeting called a "Case Conference" convenes to discuss your loved one's status. The family is invited to attend along with the Nursing Supervisor, Social Worker, Dietician, Activity Therapist, Physical Therapist, Occupational Therapist, or Speech and Language Therapist as appropriate. Prepare for these meetings by writing down any questions you or your family may have. Reviewing the Physician's Orders for the last three months will help you think of questions. Also be sure to review the Medication Changes and other sections. Don't be shy; this is the perfect time to get clarification on treatments you may not understand. It's also a good time to share your observations about your loved one. By the end of the Case Conference, team members will generate a list of issues and questions they need to follow up on and a time frame in which they will get back to you. Keep track of these, so you can call the person if you don't hear from them. Don't forget: taking care of your loved one is a team effort and you're an important member of that team!

7. **Weight Chart:** Changes in your loved one's weight are very important. You want to avoid sudden weight increase or loss; in other words, you want your loved one to maintain her current weight. To check on this, staff will weigh your loved one as often as weekly to once a month. Make a point of calling at least once a month to ask for overall updates on your loved one and for her weight. Keep track of it by noting the date, weight and any special circumstances that might affect her weight, e.g., the introduction of a new medication or dietary supplement, or the addition or lack of exercise.

8. **Phone Numbers and Legal Documents:** List the phone numbers of the personnel who work with your loved one. Include phone numbers for Nursing Staff, Specialists such as APRNs (Advanced Practitioner Registered Nurses), Doctors, Physical Therapists, Occupational Therapists, Speech and Language Therapists, Dieticians, Activity Therapists, Social Workers, and Administrators along with any others you may need. Also, keep copies (never originals) of important legal documents such as Durable Powers of Attorney, Health Care Power of Attorney, and Your Loved One's Living Will.

Part Four: Medications:

There's no doubt about it; medication is an important part of treatment for persons with Alzheimer's. When administered properly, medication will help your loved one feel less anxious, less depressed, and more even-tempered. When misused, however, medications can cause many problems, including unusual behaviors.

1. **Communication is key:** Before prescribing a new medication for your loved one, staff (even geriatric psychiatrists!) should review their choice of medication, the dosage they are recommending, and the risks and benefits (i.e., the good that this medication is likely to do or the problems it may cause) with the family. If the family has questions about the medication or disagrees with the recommendation, discuss those questions and concerns with whoever is prescribing the medications. Be sure to tell the doctor or nurse if your loved one has used the medication before, the circumstances under which the medication was prescribed, and what her reaction to the medication was. Don't forget: if you disagree with the medication being prescribed, the family member with the Health Care Power of Attorney has the right to refuse to have that medication given to your loved one. Ask the doctor or nurse to recommend another, more suitable medication.

2. **Learn all you can:** Do your homework. Learn about the medications being prescribed for your loved one, including the risks and benefits. Go to the Internet and Google the name of the medication. Print out the information and keep it in your three-ring notebook, in the "Medication" section. That way, you can refer to it the next time you discuss medications with the staff.

3. **Be cautious when introducing new medication:** Although this is repetitive, it's worth saying again. Many medications, particularly psychotropic meds—those that alter the mind, emotions, and/or behavior—have not been tested for use with geriatric persons. **Psychotropic medications in particular can make a person (even you and me!) behave as though they have dementia.** Be sure your loved one's doctors use them with caution. When introducing a new

medication, make sure your loved one receives the smallest dosage possible. That way the family and staff will have an opportunity to see how the person reacts. Don't forget: it's easier to work up to a larger dosage than to work backwards.

4. **Introduce new medications slowly and with caution:** Also, if your loved one needs several medications, ask the doctor to introduce them one at a time so family and staff will have time to observe the effects of the medication. If you introduce two or more medications at the same time, and your loved one has an adverse reaction, figuring out which medication is responsible can become quite complicated. Adjusting the dosages of those medications can become even more difficult. Believe me, you don't want this to happen.

5. **Beware of overmedicating:** A note of caution: medications should **NEVER, NEVER** be used to keep your loved one quiet. (This is referred to as a "chemical restraint.") Medications that are used thoughtfully and with caution will probably decrease your loved one's anxiety; this, in itself, will help your loved one feel safe and comfortable. When she is feeling safe and comfortable, she is more likely to cooperate with and enjoy staff and others. If you find your loved one withdrawing or sleeping when she is usually involved and active, speak to the nurse immediately. This may be an indication of over-medication, which is unacceptable.

Part Five: Parting Tips:

Because your loved ones should never have to face this beastly disease alone, I continue to urge families to stay involved. Not only will your presence help your loved ones; it will help you, too. Take it from me, I know! Here are some tips that helped me in my work with my grandmother, Sukie:

1. Enter your loved one's Alzheimer world and be ready to learn something important about yourself. For my part, I saw first hand that all behavior, including mine, is a kind of sign language that communicates meaning.
2. Alzheimer's is a scary, confusing, and lonely place; be generous about sharing your time with your loved ones.
3. When your loved ones can't find their words, give them yours.
4. While your loved ones may forget what happened, the feelings surrounding the experience will linger (especially if those feelings are negative). So be sure to keep your visits warm and pleasant.
5. Tell your loved ones stories they are likely to remember and enjoy, for example, stories about picking apples from the orchard nearby.
6. When your loved ones don't have a smile, give them yours. Most importantly, when they feel unlovable, tell them you love them. Better yet, make it a habit to say, "I love you" as much as possible. It'll make you and your loved one glow.

ACKNOWLEDGEMENTS

I have been fortunate to be a member of the writing community in Greater Portland. Within that community rests the writing group to which I belong; its members have authored six novels and a collection of short stories. Together we have slogged through chapters, debated the fine points of characterization, dialogue, setting, plot points, and much more. Special thanks to fellow writers, Carol Semple and Frazier Meade, for your support, guidance, and friendship throughout these fourteen years; you were my steadfast readers from the initial drafts to the completed version of *The Quiet Roar of a Hummingbird.*

To writer, Janet Albright, for her sensitive perspectives on my final draft; to the effervescent Katy Weilert for her fresh insights; to Mit Thorton-Vogel, OTR, for guidance on rehabilitation and occupational therapy; and to Jeremiah Conway, fellow Irish set dancer and author, for his thoughtful review of my work, I send a hug to each of you. Mountains of gratitude go out to my editors, Anne Wood and Dawna Kemperer, for helping me unfold and polish Hummingbird's story.

Ironic as it may seem, a reluctant nod of gratitude to my mother's Alzheimer's for teaching me that compassion is the only sure way to penetrate your walls.

Finally and forever, my loving thanks to my husband, Michael, for recharging my spirit with his extraordinary gifts of love and laughter.

ABOUT THE AUTHOR

Catherine Gentile is the editor of *Together With Alzheimer's Ezine*, a family-friendly online publication featuring practical approaches to support those with Alzheimer's and their caregivers. Her fiction has appeared in *The Briar Cliff Review, American Fiction, The Chaffin Journal, Kaleidoscope, The Long Story*, and other journals. Her short fiction won the Dana Award, and achieved finalist status in the International Reynolds Price Short Fiction Award and the American Fiction Prize Contest. Catherine's freelance work has been published in *Maine Magazine, DownEast, The Writer's Market*, and *Garden Write Now*. She is a contributing writer for *Portland Trails Newsletter*, a non-profit dedicated to land conservation and healthy lifestyles. Catherine lives with her husband and muse in Yarmouth, Maine. Visit Catherine's website at http://www.catherinegentile.com.

Catherine welcomes selected invitations for readings and speaking engagements. To inquire about an appearance, contact her via email: ezine@catherinegentile.com.

A Reader's Group Discussion Guide and a *Curriculum Guide for Teachers* are available online at no cost: http://www.catherinegentile.com.

CPSIA information can be obtained at www.ICGtesting.com
Printed in the USA
BVOW01s1755101113

335912BV00001B/3/P